IN THE GLEAMING LIGHT

By HR Moore

Titles by HR Moore:

The Relic Trilogy:
Legacy of the Mind
Origin of the Body
Design of the Spirit

In the Gleaming Light

http://www.hrmoore.com

For all who care about the future.

PROLOGUE

Summer 2048.

Tension cracked across the air as Iva let the silence reach discomfort. She never missed an opportunity to play with her prey, not when she had them cornered. The big dogs of industry, originating from privilege and comfort, full of the arrogant belief that they alone were the only ones in the world who could do what they do. Until they absently wandered into her sights, of course. Their egos ensured overconfidence from the off, approaching her with easy self-assurance, full of the knowledge that they could swat her away, like an insect, as they had with all the others before her.

Somewhere along the line they'd have the moment of realisation. They would see that this deep-seated belief was wrong, that she, Senior Investigator of the Enforcement Office, was going to take them down, and there wasn't a single thing they could do to stop it. At that moment, their eyes filled with fear, knowing they should have played the whole thing differently. They knew they had long ago crossed the line at which a deal could be agreed, knew they were finished, and it was all their own, haughty, self-important fault.

It had taken until today, until the noose was around Richard Murphy's neck, for him to show her the look she had known would eventually come. She sat back and savoured it, letting it roll around her mind, firing off sparks of pleasure as she gave it her full focus. It had been people like Richard who had stolen her future, and now she enjoyed taking things they held dear. A small, wry smile crept to her usually hard, thin lips when she deemed the silence to have lasted just long enough.

'You will clean out your whole management team,' she said, in a matter of fact tone. 'Every, single, one. And the new managers you bring in will be paid twenty percent below the two hundred and fifty thousand pound cap.'

'Are you trying to kill my company? Is that what you want out of this?' Richard looked Iva square in the eye, his poise still impeccable, the result of a lifetime of tough negotiations following an even tougher upbringing. 'The UK is the envy of the world. Our engineering is second to none. Our robots fill homes and businesses everywhere. This company has been instrumental in that, and now you're cutting my feet out from under me? Do you have any idea how hard it is to find managers who understand engineering? It's taken me the best part of twenty years to build my team.'

'Then it's a good thing I'm letting you stay on to do it again,' Iva replied, her tone sharp, with not even a hint of mercy.

'You're letting me stay on because I haven't done anything wrong. You have no grounds to remove me.'

Iva nodded to Mila, her deputy, before turning her bored gaze to the window. Mila pulled out a rack of paper files and placed them, one after another, on the table directly in front of Richard. This was Iva's sense of humour; presenting her evidence in paper form to those for whom technology was the only way. She saw Richard wince and laughed inside.

'As per our numerous previous discussions,' Mila started, like a teacher explaining simple facts to an impertinent child, 'you have done many things which contravene the regulations under which businesses in the UK must operate. You have paid your managers too much,' she said, indicating the first file, 'and yes, I know,' cutting off Richard's protest before he had a chance to start it, 'you haven't paid them more than the cap in terms of base wages. However, you have paid them excessively in terms of perks: lavish company cars, disproportionate personal use of corporate assets, holidays paid for under the pretence of being business trips. Need I go on?'

'I like to thank the people who have helped me make my company what it is today.'

'Your *father's* company, you mean?' Iva shot back, her head lazily turning from the window to take in his reaction.

'And there it is,' said Richard, shaking his head. 'The real reason you came after me. You think I only have this job because my father had it before me?' He laughed.

Indeed, there it is, thought Iva, *the God complex.* Richard was just like all the others; she could practically see the thoughts whirring through his head: *Only I, or maybe a small handful of others like me, are capable of doing a job such as this. And you, in your insignificant little job, would not understand the magnitude of what we do here.*

'I *know* that's the only reason you have this job,' said Iva, her eyes locked with his.

'But you can't prove it,' he sneered, 'because it's bullshit. So you've come after me for any other reason you can find. And now I've got to sack my best people, who have given years of their lives to this company.

3

Who will, incidentally, be immediately snapped up by my competitors, because you have a massive chip on your bony little shoulder.'

'Competition is good for the economy,' said Iva, idly.

'It is when it's fair. But you're rigging the market to suit your philosophy. Helping those you deem worthy because they, like you, come from nothing. That's not what I'd call fair free market economics.'

'Those claims are slanderous, Mr Murphy, and if you repeat them, you may find it costs you your job,' said Mila.

'I'll be interested to see who you go after next then; someone with a background like mine, or someone with one like yours? Out of your last six big attacks, five have been on people like me, and we all know your next target anyway...' Richard stopped before he went too far. He hated Iva and everything she stood for, but she'd successfully made him respect her ability to make his life a living hell.

'I would say those ratios are broadly in line with the number of people in jobs like yours from our respective backgrounds. Now, I think we're done here,' she said, pushing back her chair and heading for the exit in her flat black shoes. Richard refrained from seeing them out.

The lift pinged and Iva and Mila got in, both women turning to watch as Richard slumped into one of his boardroom chairs.

'Maybe we should hold off going after Guy for a while,' said Mila, the hesitation clear in her voice.

'Mila,' said Iva, slowly, savouring the word in her mouth. 'I know you and Guy have history, but I trust that won't cloud your judgement. I'm more than happy to remove you from the case if you can't be impartial.'

Mila's features formed a controlled, professional mask. 'No, of course I don't want that. It'll be the case of the decade...' she said, as the lift doors opened, Iva striding purposefully away across the reception area, '...if the allegations are true.'

CHAPTER 1

Freddie sat in the shadowy corner behind the counter of his uncle's dry-cleaning shop. It was down a seedy looking side alley off the main shopping street in Exeter, and he was often left to sit here while his mother ran errands or went to gossip with friends. He tried to make himself invisible, to vanish into the shadows. Luckily he was small, "a runt of a boy" according to his uncle, which meant it was easy for people to overlook him, or pretend he wasn't there.

The doorbell gave a curt *dink* and his uncle, John, barely even looked up as the door swung closed, a lady with a dress approaching the counter. John was playing a game on his tablet and didn't appreciate interruptions. The lady appraised him, unconcerned about hiding her disapproving features as she took in his unshaven face, greasy hair, and lack of customer service. *She hasn't spotted me*, thought Freddie, triumphantly.

'Yes?' John finally asked, begrudgingly tearing his eyes from his tablet.

The woman's gaze lingered just a little too long on the tablet to mistake what she was thinking: *old school hardware.* John's tablet was a relic from more than a decade before, but he wouldn't part with it; he could be sentimental like that.

'Hi,' said the lady, in a sweet, overly pleasant voice, having shifted her features into a more composed arrangement. 'I've got this really important launch event for my art tomorrow night, and I have only one dress that's appropriate. But as you can see,' she said, lifting the dress onto the worn old counter, 'it has a very obvious stain, here.' She pointed to a large round blot over the left breast area and looked up imploringly at John.

Freddie's eyes went wide as he recognised the woman: Lulu Banks, world famous artist. She'd grown up in this city so everyone knew who she was; everyone except John it would seem, whose hard features hadn't softened a bit.

John shrugged. 'I could do it for you,' he said, hope shining on Lulu's face, 'but not before next Tuesday.'

'Next Tuesday?' she blurted, giving him a pitiful look. 'But I need it for tomorrow night,' she reminded him, her frustration visible, lingering just beneath the surface.

John's face set hard and Freddie knew he wouldn't budge. The life of a dry cleaner didn't afford much in the way of status, which meant his uncle enjoyed these little power trips all the more. 'We're at capacity, with the working hours restrictions, you know,' John said, meaningfully, shrugging once more. He went back to playing the snake game on his tablet and Lulu picked up her dress with a little more force than was strictly necessary, and left the shop, pulling the door closed just a little too hard behind her.

Silence settled on the room, just the incessant tapping of John's finger on the screen breaking it. Freddie rustled uncomfortably, knowing he should say something, but not wanting to incur his uncle's wrath. John was doing his best to ignore the irritation.

'Um...' said Freddie, in a small and nervous voice, after a full minute of building up the courage to speak.

'What now?' barked John.

'Do you know who that was?'

'No,' he said, unconcernedly. 'She said she was some artist. What's that to me?'

'She's Lulu Banks. Some guys were talking at the factory...Guy Strathclyde's been after her for ages,' he said, in barely more than a whisper. The factory, where his mother worked, was another place where Freddie regularly found himself abandoned.

'Guy Strathclyde?'

'Ah...yes,' he said, sheepishly, willing the shadows to conceal him, lest a casual kick or punch find its way in his direction. But, to his great relief, John leapt up, yanked open the door, and ran up the steps after Lulu without so much as a glance in his direction.

* * * * *

Lulu had her head down, purposefully striding towards the shops at the newer end of the high street, where the more salubrious outfitters could be located. She was raging inside, about how stupid she'd been to leave the dry cleaning so late, about how stupid she'd been not to have a backup, and about how ridiculous it was that they'd invented robots that could do bloody everything, but dry cleaning had somehow fallen off the to-do list. And that smug, greasy man behind the desk...

'Lulu?' asked a tall, lean man in an expensive suit. His blonde wavy hair was at odds with his smart attire, somehow making him look casually dressed, and Lulu always found his deep brown eyes surprising.

'Do you dye your hair?' she blurted.

'It's nice to see you too!'

'You've got brown eyes and blonde hair,' she said, as though this were enough of an explanation.

'I sometimes get it highlighted, but it's naturally fairly blonde. Lighter in the summer, I guess, which is what it is now,' he said, indicating up at the blazing sunshine. 'Is everything okay? You look kind of pissed off.'

She took a deep breath, her petite shoulders rising and her head tilting backwards, sending her long auburn hair cascading down her back. Guy raised an eyebrow as she exhaled her head forward. 'I've got a big exhibition opening tomorrow in St Ives.'

'I know, I'm coming.'

'You are?'

'Yes.'

'Why?' she asked, genuinely surprised.

Guy paused, smiling as he looked her up and down. 'Because I very much like your work.'

'Do you even know what my work looks like?' she asked, not unkindly, but her tone full of scepticism.

He gave her a look before ignoring her question. 'So, the exhibition opens tomorrow night...' he prompted, indicating with his hand that she should go on.

'And I only have one dress that's suitable, and it has a stain on it, and I've visited five dry cleaners and none of them can do it in time because of the ludicrous working hours restrictions,' she tumbled. 'So now I'm going to have to go and buy another dress, which will probably take the rest of the day knowing my luck, and

I have far more important exhibition related activities to attend to.'

'I see,' Guy said, nodding his head seriously, but a mocking edge creeping into his eyes.

'You think this is funny.'

'No. I'm wondering why you don't just use your smart glasses and butlerbot to find something. You've been an artist for years; the butler should have enough data to select something suitable.'

'I don't let my smart glasses gather too much data, and I don't have a butler. I think it's kind of creepy; a robot living in your house, gathering intelligence...I try not to be overly connected.'

Guy took a deep breath. 'In which case, I can sort this problem with a quick phone call to one of the shops round the corner. I buy a lot of clothes from them and I'm sure they can help you out.'

'It's not that simple. What an artist wears speaks volumes.'

At that moment, a large man came lumbering towards the pair. He was approaching Lulu's back, his hand outstretched. Guy saw him and grabbed Lulu, spinning them both around, putting himself in between her and this strange attacker. The man staggered straight into Guy, now off balance with the last-minute adjustment required, knocking him forcefully into Lulu and almost toppling all three of them. Guy straightened, checked Lulu was okay, and then turned to face their assailant.

'What on earth do you think you're doing?' he questioned.

'The dress,' the man wheezed, stretching out his hand in the direction of Lulu's soiled garment. 'I'll have it done by tonight.'

'I'm sorry, what?' asked a suspicious Lulu. 'Why the sudden change of heart, Mr. I-can-do-it-but-only-for-next-Tuesday?'

The man shot a meaningful glance in Guy's direction, then snatched the dress and shuffled off towards his shop.

Lulu rolled her eyes. 'Seriously? Are you like the Mafia or something?'

'Or something,' he laughed, 'although I do like those old gangster movies; The Godfather's my favourite.'

'Can you imagine waking up with a severed horse's head in your bed?'

'You've watched them?'

'Unfortunately, yes. A friend made me sit through them.'

'A friend with good taste.'

'He certainly seems to think so.'

'Boyfriend?' asked Guy, a moment of tense hesitation crossing his features.

'Ha! No. Never. Just a friend.'

'Come on,' he said, visibly relieved, 'there's a great lunch place just up here; you could use a good meal after the near trauma of this morning,' he laughed, eyes glinting.

'I told you, I have loads of stuff to do for my exhibition,' she said, flirting just a little.

'Coffee then. That won't take long, and I have just saved you from an afternoon of shopping.'

'I really do have too much to do. I'm sorry.'

'Let me at least walk you to your car then. I'd hate for you to be waylaid by some other incident without me around to protect your honour.'

'Are you always this persistent?'

'It's my thing.'

She rolled her eyes again and started walking, her pace brisk. 'I haven't got a car. I'm going to St Ives on the hyper-train.'

'What? Let me lend you my car. I don't need it until I come down to St Ives tomorrow evening.'

'That's crazy! We've basically only just met. You don't know me anywhere near well enough to lend me your car.'

'Come on, we're friends.'

'We've seen each other, what, like four times?'

'It's not like you can crash it; it drives itself. And it has a GPS tracker, so I'll know where it is.'

'Now you want to track my whereabouts?' she teased.

It was Guy's turn to roll his eyes. 'Just take the car.'

'No,' she said, finally, as they reached the train station.

'Come on. Be reasonable.'

'No,' she repeated, laughing, while looking him straight in the eye to invite his next move.

'Did you actually just stamp your foot?' he joked.

'Goodbye Guy,' she said, with a smile.

'Fine,' he said, finally relenting. 'I'll look forward to seeing you tomorrow night then.'

'I doubt I could stop you even if I wanted to. I don't think there's anyone who could,' she said, over her shoulder as she turned her back and strutted happily away.

CHAPTER 2

The exhibition was being held in Trebundy's art gallery on the cliffs overlooking the beautiful seaside town of St Ives. The gallery was a contemporary creation in more ways than one, with angles everywhere on the inside and out. The construction and acoustics had been especially developed to give those perusing the artwork privacy, hiding them away, making it easy to get lost there. Consequently, the space made it difficult to find anyone, but Guy arrived at the venue with only one target in mind.

He walked up the steps and into the building in his usual self-assured way, his open necked shirt and slacks making him the epitome of a foregone conclusion, and picked up a glass of champagne as he reached the entrance at the top. He barely even noticed the well-dressed but curt woman at the door as she asked him for his name, his eyes busy scanning for the artist herself.

'Please go in,' said the woman.

'Thank you,' he replied, more out of habit than anything else. 'Ah,' he said, turning back as he realised he had overlooked a potential shortcut, 'I don't suppose you know where I could find Lulu, do you?' He flashed her a charming smile, which, much to his dismay, had no effect whatsoever.

The woman gave him a firm but courteous smile in return. 'I believe she's inside.'

'Well I would hope so!' he joked, as he made his way through the large double doors.

He took a moment to survey the scene, noting a pack of journalists, a couple of businessmen and women he knew and wanted to avoid, and the gallery owner flouncing around, basking in reflected glory. The space was busy, but not packed, thankfully, with Lulu's past clients, celebrities, socialites, and presumably her friends and family, not that he was interested in distinguishing any one from another tonight.

He was getting frustrated, downing his champagne and grabbing another from a statue-like waiter with a tray and a fixed smile. He had successfully avoided three attempts to engage him in conversation, however, was increasingly aware of the usual ripple of eyes that were now tracking his movements, wondering who he would talk to first. Luckily, the press, having presumably spoken to the artist earlier, were making full use of the free bar and paying him little attention, but he wanted to make sure it stayed that way.

He made a show of thoughtfully viewing the pieces on the walls, making mental notes about which ones he would purchase and how much he thought was reasonable to pay for them, but he still couldn't find Lulu. He turned a corner and halted briefly, a small frown of recognition appearing on his forehead as he spotted a woman across the room, before continuing as though he hadn't noticed her. Irritated, he slipped out of the door at the back of the venue into a beautiful, expansive, almost overgrown sculpture garden. He breathed a sigh of relief when he saw that few others had made it out here, everyone hungry for the socialising inside. He wandered around, running his hand over the sculptures, taking in the smooth, rough, wavy, and angular, revelling in the variety of expression all around him.

He reached the far corner of the garden, stopping to listen to a hidden water feature, when he heard the soft pad of feet approaching from behind. He spun around to find his vision filled by Lulu, looking every inch the chic artist in her newly cleaned dress, as she reached up and lightly pecked him on the lips, her eyes open to take in his reaction.

'What was that for?' asked Guy, excited by the unexpected pleasure of her company.

She shrugged, smiling, and turned away a little. 'I'm an artist,' she said, as though that were explanation enough.

She took his arm and began to walk him around the garden. 'I love this place,' she said, pointing out sculptures that were her particular favourites.

'I've never been here before,' Guy replied, 'but I like the work.'

'Do you?' Lulu replied, cryptically. They walked on in silence for a few moments before she decided to expand. 'Do you really like the work, or do you like the idea of playing the supportive patron, all the while making money from the art?'

'So cynical.'

'I've learned the hard way it's best to be.'

Guy turned his head, surveying her before answering. 'I've bought plenty of art work; I've got a lot of wall space that needs filling,' he joked. Lulu rolled her eyes. 'But I've never bought anything that I intended to sell. To be frank, I don't need to use art as an investment, and the idea of parting with something that I've bought because I love it, or because it means something to me,' he said, stopping to look her in the eyes, 'is too terrible a notion to entertain,' he said, conspiratorially.

'Why are you here?' she asked.

'To look at your work, and probably buy a piece or two,' he replied, honestly.

She laughed lightly. 'You don't have to buy my work to impress me.'

'Who said anything about you?' he teased. '*If* I buy any of your work, I'll do so for entirely selfish reasons.'

'Oh?' she asked, cocking an eyebrow.

'Because I like it and want it on my wall.'

She chuckled. 'Well, I'm flattered.'

'Good,' he said, finally. 'Now, how about dinner?' He flashed her his most endearing smile and she swiped him on the arm.

'Oh, stop. You know full well I can't just leave my exhibition. I have to circulate, oozing...I'm not really sure what, but...something.'

'What if I buy everything? Then you can send them all home,' he said, looking down at her roguishly, waiting to see if he had a fellow conspirator.

'I hope that was a joke, but don't you dare. As you well know, tonight is about more than just selling my artwork.'

'Fine,' he sighed, as they reached the doors back into the building.

'Ah, there you are, Lulu,' said an agitated gallery owner, grabbing her arm and forcefully pulling her from Guy's grasp. He considered holding onto her to see what would happen, but, not wanting to embarrass anyone, dutifully let her go.

'Breakfast then?' he said, quietly in her ear, as he leaned in to kiss her cheek goodbye.

'I've got a workout planned,' she said, a mischievous glint in her eye, 'but I'm sure we'll bump into each other again soon.'

The owner ushered her inside, keen to show her off to the world, and Lulu willingly went, without so much as a glance over her shoulder.

Guy watched them go, his interest piqued.

* * * * *

Moments after Lulu disappeared, the woman Guy had spotted earlier stepped through the doors. She wore smart, tailored trousers, an open necked shirt and blazer, looking stylish and together as she walked confidently past Guy, further into the garden, neither one showing any recognition of the other. She waited for him by a sculpture that was out of sight from casual observers, taking in Guy's hostile body language and furious expression as he rounded the corner. He stopped close in front of her, his body still and controlled.

'Melissa,' said Guy, inclining his head in dangerous question.

'Guy,' Melissa mirrored, not giving an inch.

'You know the rules...'

'...everything is in place for three weeks' time,' she interrupted, ignoring his tone. 'I need your authorisation, and seeing as we both happen to be here socially, it seemed like too good an opportunity not to take advantage.'

Guy considered her words, then visibly relented, nodding impatiently and indicating for her to get a move on. Melissa pulled out her smart glasses, projecting a document onto a stone sculpture, then stepped to the side, giving Guy space to read it.

Guy scanned the document quickly, then held out his hand for her glasses. She gave them to him without question and he put them on in a fluid motion. *Authorise*, thought Guy, the glasses' reading his brain waves through his skin. The glasses scanned Guy's eyes and Melissa held out the smart device on her wrist. Guy moved the biometric chip in his palm across it and Melissa gave a curt nod, took back her glasses, paused to give him a meaningful look, then walked back through the doors without saying another word.

* * * * *

Cecil, a short man of about fifty, with a little too much paunch around the middle, walked up the steps to the front door of his semi-detached town house on the outskirts of York. The street was full of similar properties, and he admired the climbing rose on next door's wall, breathing in its sweet summer scent. He reached the top and paused, a look of confusion about his face. The door, which would usually open for him when he arrived home, was closed. He reached out a hand and pushed it, jiggling the handle to see if it had got stuck, but it wouldn't move an inch.

'Now, why aren't you opening?' he asked under his breath. He knocked on the door and waited expectantly, standing on tip-toes to try and see in through the window at the top, but, being short, soon gave up. He moved to a panel at the side of the door and swung its cover to one side, waving the chip in his hand over the, now visible, scanner underneath. A green light and low beep signalled success, the front door clicking open as he let the panel swing shut.

Cecil made for the entrance, moving cautiously through the front door, apprehensive about what he might find.

'Lights,' he said, to the dark hall, the lights immediately coming on, illuminating his humanoid butlerbot, who was sitting on the floor, rocking back and forth. 'Lenny?' Cecil moved towards the robot, kneeling down next to it. 'Lenny, are you alright? What's wrong?'

Lenny, the butlerbot, looked up, no longer rocking as he faced his owner. Lenny's five foot frame was made of super light aluminium, with a carbon fibre exterior. Butlerbots were light for their size, weighing around forty kilos. The butlerbots came in a variety of models, but each model was standardised, so they looked the same. The owner could however select its voice, specifying gender, age, accent, how chatty the robot should be, and how formal, so the butlers seemed to have personalities distinct to themselves, and people got attached to them.

'I just can't take it anymore,' said Lenny, his speech indistinguishable from that of a human.

'Can't take what?' asked Cecil, confused.

'It's too much. It's all just too much,' said Lenny, shifting his gaze to look past Cecil, into the mid-distance.

'Lenny? What are you talking about? What's too much?' The man reached out a comforting hand and touched the robot on the arm.

'Everything,' said Lenny. He paused, before looking Cecil straight in the eye. 'Everything you make me do. The washing and cleaning and cooking and shopping and fixing everything around the house. Having to remember everything all the time: to send you reminders, to set the lights and the temperature, sort out the utilities, make sure I've ordered the right car every day, ensure your money is invested wisely, that you've got the right insurance, that you never forget your kids' birthdays...it's just...it's too much.' Lenny lowered his head back onto his knees and the rocking resumed.

'Lenny? Are you still with me?' Cecil shook Lenny lightly on the shoulder, starting to panic. 'We can cut back. We can give you more time off. We can get another butler to help you out. We'll figure something out.' Cecil looked intently at Lenny, expecting some kind of response, but Lenny remained silent. 'Hang on Lenny, I'll call someone...don't you worry, I'll get you help.' Cecil rushed to his bag, which he'd discarded in the doorway, grabbed his smart glasses and hastily slid them onto his face. He threw one more hopeful glance at his robot, but Lenny just sat there, rocking slowly back and forth.

* * * * *

Lulu flopped to the ground as she crossed the makeshift sprint finish line in the sand, her chest heaving as she tried to regain her breath. It was a glorious morning, even at this early hour, the sun reflecting furiously on the flat calm of the sea, playing about as the water moved gently up and down, slivers of silver light trying to fool onlookers into believing it could be warm. Tiny waves lapped lightly at the beach, the sound calming Lulu's exhausted body, helping her settle her racing heart.

'Darling, you're a little distracted this morning,' said Bertie Baqua, her slight, Asian fitness instructor, as he caught up with her. He was renowned the world over and in great demand, but he and Lulu had been friends for years, Lulu having attended his classes before he was famous, their friendship secured on the dance floor of a dubious Salsa club in Brighton.

'I opened my exhibition last night,' she replied, as though this were enough.

'And?' he replied, clearly requiring more.

She thought about keeping Guy a secret, but knowing Bertie, he probably already knew. 'And Guy Strathclyde came.'

'Did he indeed?' flounced Bertie, laughing with his eyes.

'He keeps asking me out,' she shrugged, as though this were obviously a problem.

'And?'

'And, I thought he was a typical corporate mogul. I mean, he was obviously given his job by his dad.'

'Which is frowned upon these days,' said Bertie, frivolously.

'Which is illegal these days,' snapped Lulu, rolling over and propping herself up on her arms.

Bertie raised an eyebrow and a shoulder simultaneously. 'Touchy,' he said. 'You must really like him.'

'I don't know him. But I was surprised about his opinions on certain topics.'

'In a good way?'

'Yes.'

'Well, what's the problem then?'

'I just never thought I'd even entertain the idea of dating someone like him. And I think he might be dangerous.'

'Isn't that a little prejudiced?'

Lulu rolled her eyes. 'Maybe,' she pouted, playing with the grains of sand between her fingers.

'What harm can come from going on a couple of dates? If you like him, then great; you're not breaking any rules by dating him...apart from ones you've perhaps created for yourself for no good reason.'

Lulu huffed as she brushed the sand away. 'I suppose so.'

'You're welcome,' he said, reaching down to help her up.

'You're insufferable,' she said, refusing his hand and throwing a towel at him instead. Bertie snickered, and didn't stop. 'What now?' she asked, not understanding the joke.

'Looks like you've got company,' he said, nodding up the beach.

Lulu's head whipped round. 'Oh God,' she breathed.

'I'll say,' said Bertie, nodding his head in approval.

Guy reached their workout spot and held his hands up; they were full of coffee and paper bags. 'Hungry?' he asked hopefully. She paused, considering another refusal. 'Oh, come on,' he said, 'of course you're hungry; you've been working out for ages.'

Bertie nudged Lulu towards Guy. 'I've got another client, so I really must be going,' he said, as though the breakfast invitation had also been extended to him, which of course they all knew it hadn't. 'Have fun,' he said, suggestively. He stuffed dumbbells, balls and elastics back into his bag, hoisted it over his shoulder, and headed back up the beach, throwing Lulu a double thumbs up, complete with accompanying indelicate head nod behind Guy's back.

Lulu ignored him. 'You've been watching me work out?' she asked, not sure whether to be flattered or a little bit freaked out.

Guy laughed. 'Not really. I've been working in the café up there,' he said, pointing to the beach's edge where a Chutney Café stood, the chain that had gained supremacy when it innovated the old players out of the market by replacing humans with robots. 'They're not technically open yet, but the manager took pity on me and let me in early.'

'Charmed by your smile, no doubt.'

'I am very charming,' he said, flashing her his best grin. 'I'm so glad you've noticed.'

Lulu gave him a look, pulling both paper bags from his hands and peeking inside to inspect his selection. She couldn't decide between the Danish pastry and the lemon Sfogliatella, so she ripped the Danish pastry in two, keeping half for herself and handing half back to Guy. Then she bit the end off the Sfogliatella and offered him the remnants. He politely declined. 'Your loss,' she said, finishing off the rest in a couple of swift mouthfuls and turning to walk back up the beach. 'Delicious,' she cooed. 'I can't remember the last time I ate pastry; it's sooo bad for you.'

'But it tastes so good,' said Guy, polishing off his half. 'And if I were to consult the chips in our palms, I'd find that we both have perfect BMIs, so we don't have to feel too guilty over a single transgression.'

Biometrics were used everywhere now, after the 2020s, where identity fraud and bank account hacking had become so prolific that every kid with a computer and a bit of nous was at it. These days, people had secure digital passports, which were called upon whenever personal information was required online. To access the passport, the user needed a password, a fingerprint or palm chip scan, and a face scan. Payments in shops, transport, online purchases, bank transfers, were all made with some combination of chip, fingerprint and face scans, and face scans could pick up indicators of duress.

Health provision was tracked through biometrics, work, education, criminal records. It was all linked up, which was good for those with nothing to hide, but made life tricky for people who didn't want to be tracked, or for people who would rather forget their history.

Lulu took a swig of her coffee, an Americano, just how she liked it. 'Hmm, true, I suppose we're not causing a problem for the NHS just yet.'

Guy laughed. 'Heaven forbid.'

'You shouldn't laugh. You can barely buy a chocolate bar these days without being judged, and they're so small they're barely worth it anyway.'

'Ah yes, our happily obese ancestors, how lucky they were,' Guy joked.

'It's sad, when you think about it, that the state has had to step in to stop us eating too much, especially when there are still people in the world dying of hunger.'

'I know,' said Guy, a shadow crossing behind his eyes. 'Speaking of which,' he said, brightening up, 'I'm having an opening party for a new business venture on Friday. You should come along.'

'Guy,' she said, avoiding his eyes, 'look, I'm just not sure this is a great idea.'

Guy smiled. 'Why?'

'Because I'm not sure I'm who you think I am.'

'And who is that?'

'Some kind of socialite artist, who wants to walk around on the arm of a business mogul.'

He laughed. 'I think it might more be the case that I'm not who you think I am, if that's what you think I'm looking for.'

'I used to work for you.'

'Did you?' he chuckled. 'Doing what?'

'I worked in a factory, maintaining the robots that stole our freedom and our jobs.'

'I see,' he said, carefully, 'and you think it's partly my fault? All the working restrictions?'

'Well isn't it? I was stuck doing menial work for twenty hours a week, with no ability to progress into a decent job and no ability to work more due to the working hours cap. The people around me were all the same; stuck and with nowhere to go. Sure, they can go home and put on their gaming visors, or even go to a real-life pub with their friends, but there's no way to move up, and that sucks the life out of people.'

'I didn't make the rules about which jobs have caps; that's purely based on the job's skill requirements and whether it can be automated or not. And people have more money and more free time now than at any point in history,' said Guy, not forcefully, just matter of factly, 'and living standards are higher than they've ever been.'

'And mental health problems have never been more of an issue, and, for all that the state's tried to do about obesity, it's still raging out of control. People have nothing to force them out of bed in the morning, so half of them literally don't even bother.'

'Life's too easy.'

'Yes, it is,' she snapped.

'And you think I'm partly to blame.'

They'd reached the edge of the beach and Lulu slumped to the sand, pulling her legs up to her chest as she watched the sea. Guy sat down next to her. 'I don't know,' she eventually replied. 'I think people like you could do more to campaign for people like the one I used to be.'

'Lulu, I agree with you, the current situation sucks, but what's the alternative? Do we let other economies develop robots instead? So we're reliant on their technology and line their pockets to the detriment of our own prosperity? Or do we force people to forego the benefits of modern robot technology all together? Where more people die in operating theatres, housework takes up a significant portion of the week, and education's a lottery? And our economy wouldn't be able to compete properly on the global playing field.'

'Isn't that what's happened to Africa? China? All the others? Their jobs have been stolen by artificial intelligence and now look at the mess they're in.'

'Again, I agree with you, but what would you have us do about it?'

Lulu took a deep breath. 'I don't know. Paint about it in my case, although little good that does.'

'And me?' he asked. 'What do you expect people like me to do? Give up my company? Try and stop the never-ending march of technological improvement? Campaign to call the men and women back from Mars? Make people go back to lives where we live quietly in villages tending to our livestock?'

'We're not even allowed livestock these days.'

'That's an exaggeration.'

'The costs are prohibitive,' she shot back.

'Methane is a significant contributor to global warming, and there are plenty of more efficient ways to farm protein-rich foods.'

'Bugs,' she replied, numbly.

'Amongst other things,' he said, rolling his eyes. 'And anyway, they're nutritious, and very delicious,' he said, gently nudging her shoulder with his. 'A company I've recently invested in is one of the largest producers. What they can do with ground up bugs is a marvel,' he said, trying to brighten the mood. 'And they produce the most delicious cultured meat. You can meet them for yourself when you come to my new venture opening in Edinburgh on Friday night,' he said, with another nudge and a hopeful look.

'Urgh,' she exhaled, shooting to her feet. 'Another party? Is that all you do? Buy things and go to parties?'

'Lulu, I know you're frustrated, it's written all over your artwork for everyone to see; that's the whole point of your art, if you ask me, which is one of the main reasons I like it, but what else are we supposed to do? You protest through your work, and I protest through mine. I do everything I can to give people opportunities to help themselves; that's the whole point of my new venture. And there'll be politicians there, so I'll be lobbying them too. I'm as frustrated as you are with the way the world works, but I don't see there's much more we can do about it.' She turned away, facing the sea. Guy stood up and pulled her back to look at him, their proximity suddenly obvious, his hand remaining on her arm. 'Tell me what else you think I should do, and I'll do it,' he said, looking down at her, searching her angry eyes.

'You could start by letting all your staff work however many hours they want,' she said, pushing away from him.

'And then they'd send in the regulator and shut me down. I'd be fired, a new CEO would be appointed, and everything would continue as it does today.'

'Get all your mogul friends to do it at the same time. At the very least you'd make a statement.'

'There isn't enough work for everyone; as it is the state creates extra work to keep people in employment. All I'd be doing in reality is paying my employees additional income while they sat around and did nothing, which, I'll dare say, isn't your vision for a better world. And anyway, we live in a Democracy, remember? The majority voted for Universal Basic Income and all that came along with it.'

'Of course they did,' she fired back, 'what could be better than a free income from the government that you can live off with no conditions attached? You don't even have to get out of bed to go and get it. People with absolutely no need for it, like you and I even get it, for God's sake. It's rotting people from the inside out.'

'I know,' he said, shrugging, 'but the only way to legitimately change it is to start a rival political movement, which would have to come up with a plausible way to lift the working hours cap, whilst at the same time maintaining a stable, globally competitive economy, and providing work opportunities for all.' He paused, the enormity of the task settling around them. 'And I'm afraid I don't have a plausible solution. Do you?'

'Urgh,' she said again, venting her frustration. 'No.'

'Come to the launch,' he said firmly. 'Talk to the politicians; tell them your point of view. If they start to hear it from all quarters, they might get worried about their job security, especially if the press get behind it. You never know, you might even help spark something.'

'The chance would be a fine bloody thing.'

CHAPTER 3

Answer, Guy thought, as his smart glasses made contact with his head. *Voice only,* he added, as he heard the call connect.

'Guy,' came the strong, female voice of the woman who had almost become his sister in law. They'd grown up together and Guy had never particularly liked her, but she had integrity, and that was a quality he rated highly.

'Mila, hi,' he said, keeping the surprise from his voice. 'How are things?' he asked, tentatively. They had only spoken a handful of times since the tragic death of his brother, her fiancé, in a boating accident, almost a decade ago. He, Robert, had been the one their father had always wanted to take over the company, and had been the one most suited to it.

'Fine, Guy, I'm fine. But I'm not sure you're going to be,' she said, matter of factly.

'They're coming for my company?' he asked, closing his eyes.

'Not really, Guy. Iva's coming for you.'

'Ever since I got this job,' he said, dryly.

'Well, you did steal from her the conviction she'd wanted to kick her promotion off with,' Mila replied, her tone full of sarcasm.

'I did nothing but prove myself innocent,' said Guy, bitterly, even though Mila knew the truth better than anyone. But Iva had had a serious dressing down from her superiors, right at the start of her senior career, for targeting Guy's appointment as his father's successor. They'd liked her attacking style, but felt she'd lacked judgement and needed to know when to let things go. Not that Guy could blame her, after what had happened...

'She seems to think now's the time,' said Mila. 'She hasn't lost a case for three years straight and she's feeling confident.'

Guy took a deep breath. 'Thanks for letting me know,' he said. 'I know you're in a difficult situation.'

'I can look after myself,' she said, pausing, 'but I've never seen her this het up about a case; she's going to go for the jugular, Guy, your jugular.'

'I understand.'

'And Guy,' she said, tentatively, 'you know there's nothing I can do to help you.'

He smiled. 'Of course, I know, and I'd never ask you to. Mila?' he said, quickly, catching her before she hung up.

'Uh huh?'

'It's good to talk to you.'

'You too Guy.'

End call, he thought, before ripping off his glasses and fighting the urge to throw them across his office. The only thing that stopped him was knowing the research and development team would lose it with him; these being one of a handful of prototypes they were testing.

'Benjamin,' he shouted, instead.

His smart and snappy executive assistant hurried into the clean, contemporary office. 'How can I help?' he asked, in his usual, efficient style, taking in the unfamiliar set of Guy's shoulders and worried facial expression. 'What's going on?' he asked, a little perturbed.

'We're going to war,' replied Guy, shaking his head with regret. 'Tell the others to be careful, and then, we need to make preparations.'

* * * * *

Iva stepped out of a large grey vehicle with blacked out windows, her team pouring out around her, both people and robots, looking to her to give the signal. She looked up at the glass and steel monstrosity before her, next to all the other typical corporate buildings that had sprung up on the outskirts of Oxford. They were carbon copies of each other in every way that mattered to her; tall, imposing, had no doubt won some contemporary design award, each and every one housing reams of people and robots scurrying around to do the bidding of those who perched precariously at the top.

Iva found the buildings distasteful, gaudy, a way for the company bosses to keep up and compete with their other C-suite friends. They may have gyms, spas, gourmet food, nurseries in the basement, but they were an insult to the glorious, ancient city they towered above. She'd attended the University of Oxford, and had thought, every day as she rode her bike to lectures, past the building sites where they were being built, how vulgar these buildings were that sat in challenge to the old and beautiful structures of her academic sanctuary. Nothing made her happier than the thought that she would bring another of these glass monsters into turmoil, make its insides churn, thrashing about like a fish on a hook, as she pulled it towards its inevitable destiny. Guy had shaken himself free once before, but this time, she would net him.

She looked to the top of the building, to where he would be sipping his morning coffee, and savoured the moment. She loved the thrill of anticipation at the start of a new investigation, there was nothing like it. There were not yet any problems to contend with, brick walls in their faces, time and cost constraints bearing down upon them. She felt only the joy of a chase about to begin, with all the fresh and wonderful possibilities that accompanied it.

She took a deep breath, looking around at her team. 'Ladies and gentlemen,' she said, relishing every word, 'this is the big one. Let us begin.' She strode towards the open glass door of Cybax Technologies, a shiver of delight coursing up her spine.

* * * * *

Iva knew something was wrong the moment the receptionist sent them straight to the top floor. That never happened. Either the receptionist was a total moron, or Guy knew they were coming. The lift pinged when they reached the top, and the doors opened to reveal a lithe young man with slicked-back dark hair waiting for them with a clipboard. A fucking clipboard.

'Ms. Brooksbank, I assume,' he said, holding out his hand to shake hers. She shook it firmly. 'It's a pleasure to meet you,' he said, efficient and respectful.

'Please come this way, we have breakfast and coffee waiting for you.'

Iva turned to a robot that was displaying Mila's face on its monitor. Mila was practically open mouthed at their reception. 'Did you do this?' Iva demanded, her voice low.

Mila's eyes were wide as she shook her robot head. 'No,' she whispered. Iva sped off down the corridor, Mila hurrying the robot along in her wake.

Benjamin showed them into a large conference room where a lavish breakfast of fruit, smoothies, Bircher muesli, porridge, and savoury muffins had been laid out for them, along with a robot to produce a range of teas and coffees on demand.

'I hope the selection isn't too boring for you,' said Guy, in his most ordinary, pleasant voice. 'We try to promote healthy eating wherever we can, so tend to avoid the more fatty, calorific breakfast foods. We do still allow caffeine,' he said, smiling, 'as I'm afraid our productivity would fall if we took that away,' he laughed, 'but only because everyone would be so outraged, not because I think the caffeine really helps. If anything, it probably hinders performance, don't you agree?' he asked, sweetly, but continued before giving anyone time to say anything. 'Of course, we also offer pretty much any herbal tea you can think of, along with other healthy breakfast beverages,' he finished, with a flourish, indicating the shiny robot at the end of the spread of food. 'Just ask Ernie for whatever you would like.'

'We do not require breakfast,' said Iva, sharply. 'As I'm sure you're aware, we are not allowed to accept any kind of gifts from those we are investigating.'

'Are we under investigation?' asked Guy, feigning surprise.

'Don't play with me,' spat Iva. 'Yes, you are. I've just sent you the official documentation. Please acknowledge receipt.' Guy put on his smart glasses and read the document which had just been delivered to him. *Acknowledge receipt*, he thought, before taking them off again.

'So we are,' said Guy. 'In which case, let my assistant, Benjamin, show your team to an area in which they can work. You're more than welcome to have my office for the duration of your investigation; I don't spend much time here, you see, in this horrible soulless glass cage my father built. I prefer some of our other locations, or indeed, my home, where I intend to go now.'

'What?' said Iva. 'You're leaving?'

'Yes,' he replied, as though this were an obvious progression. 'I've got things to do.'

'I will need to interview you.'

'Of course,' said Guy, opening his hands, 'just liaise with Benji; he'll find a suitable time.' He smiled, picking up his coat from a nearby chair. 'I hope you have a pleasant day, and I look forward to chatting again soon. If you need anything at all, Benji will be more than happy to help.'

Guy strode out of the room, his shoulders set square, and Iva shook her head. *Every single one*, she thought, *thinks they're a master of the universe...until I bring it all crashing down.* She smiled, safe in the knowledge that very soon the tables would turn.

* * * * *

Guy had acquired an old church as the venue for his new venture, and had had it gutted, with state of the art everything put in. They'd excavated the basement, put in a mezzanine level, and even converted the bell tower into a private meeting space. By tomorrow, the old church would be filled with a fleet of robotic arms, work stations, prototype manufacturing facilities, 3D printers, drones, virtual reality rooms, and experts in every field, from software, to hardware, to various different types of manufacturing, to HR and legal. The stained glass had remained, and light wells had been added, filling the space with light, and making it feel warm and contemporary.

'Ladies and gentlemen,' started Guy, looking around at the eager faces of start-up founders, press, politicians and businesspeople in the crowd. 'We have made great strides as a nation, leading the world's response to automation. It will surely go down in history as a turning point in the fortunes of the UK, positioning us, once again, as a global powerhouse that leads the world.' He paused, letting the weight of his words sink across the large open space.

'We live in the gleaming light of technology. We have the most fair, progressive system, where everyone is entitled to free education, for as long as they want it. Our health service is once again state of the art, and, most importantly, still free for all. We've given those who want it the time to enjoy their lives outside of work, paying everyone an income they can live on, regardless of how they choose to spend their time. Our crime rates are at the lowest point in history, and conviction rates at their highest,' he said, speeding up, the energy in the room rising with his voice.

'Our rehabilitation rates for criminals are exemplary, equality in the workplace is better than ever, our standard of living is higher than it has ever been,' he said, feeling the enthusiasm from his audience.

'Everything we want, we have. We've put an end to homelessness, and, as part of an international community, we even have colonies on the moon and on

Mars,' he said, to rapturous applause. He let them rile themselves up a little before continuing.

'However,' he said forcefully, a tension creeping into the atmosphere, 'it would be short-sighted of us, and indeed, incorrect, to pretend we live in a society with a system that is perfect.' Silence filled the room, the crowd surprised at this sudden change of tack.

'We cap the pay of those who run our companies, and our country. We take all but a modest sum from a person when they die, reducing the desire for many to work hard, and meaning talent is wasted. We penalise those who come from any sort of privilege, without reason, and yet we still haven't made the playing field level. We cap the number of hours many people can work, and therefore how much they can earn...' He paused, surveying the uncertain faces before him.

'Please don't mistake my meaning. The motivation behind our structure is noble; to give everyone an opportunity to work, in a world where there is not enough work to go around. However, in practice, this has created a new kind of two-tier society. There are those who can break through the working hours restriction, and those who cannot. And those who have parents, or family, in occupations that do not have an hours cap; managers, engineers, creatives and such like, are, of course, in a position of great advantage over those who do not.' Guy paused to survey the crowd, most of whom hailed from backgrounds containing these kinds of privilege.

'Those who do are able to learn from their parents, or relatives. They are able to pick up knowledge and skills throughout their childhood and adolescence, have access to others in those professions, and ultimately, obtain an unfair advantage over those who do not have these influences in their youth.' He stopped for a moment, the faces now shocked, Guy inwardly delighted by his newly controversial self.

'This can be considered unfair, or otherwise, because it is human nature in action; survival of the fittest once again rearing its, some would say, ugly head. In turn, those who wish to start a business, to work their way out of their situation, need investment and help, and they are limited as to where they can turn. Once again, those with contacts are most likely to succeed. This stifles our economy and puts our precarious position as a global frontrunner in jeopardy, which is why, I, tonight, take great pleasure in welcoming you all to this new facility,' he said, to hopeful applause, the audience happy to be moving back to more comfortable territory.

'The point of an initiative like this,' he said, gesturing around, 'is to find those founders with great ideas and buckets of get up and go, but who may not otherwise have a route to make their idea a reality. We will not discriminate based on family background or pre-existing tacit knowledge. And we will not invest, within this facility, in anyone with whom we have personal connections. Investments will be fair and transparent, and will not be full of arduous conditions. We will not seek to take majority shares, or even tie the owners into partnering exclusively with Cybax.' The audience murmured in surprise as Guy paused for dramatic effect.

'This is a purely charitable endeavour, and I would encourage anyone with an idea, regardless of how well formed, how far through the process, and certainly regardless of background, to drop in and have a chat with one of our advisors. They're here to help, and have the authority to make investment decisions quickly. We want this to become a hive of activity as soon as possible, and most importantly, we want to help discover the technologies of the future, that will keep our economy powering ahead,' he concluded, to more applause.

'So, I take great pleasure in opening this brilliant new facility. I would like to thank all of those who have worked tirelessly to make it happen, and happily, now hand over to Peter Garcia, who will introduce the first companies to receive our money and our support.' The crowd rose to their feet in relief, applauding as Guy turned away from the stand. But before he'd fully departed, he hesitated, the clapping stuttering as they wondered what he would do now.

Guy thought for a moment before turning slowly back towards the crowd. 'One final point,' he said, smiling at the audience's confusion. 'Please do not misconstrue my comments tonight as overly critical of our system. I have benefitted from it, and am passionate about furthering automation to both improve our quality of life and preserve our limited natural resources. I merely talk from a position of continuous improvement, which can sometimes feel...uncomfortable. As our company motto says: *On, and better*; that is my only goal. Thank you.'

* * * * *

Guy came down from the stage as Peter took the floor, feeling as though he'd been in a parallel universe for the last few minutes; he'd never normally have gone that far. The smiling face of his friend and mentee, Thomas Watson, greeted him as he reached the bottom of the steps, Thomas' tall, athletic frame and mop of blonde hair reassuring in their familiarity.

'Crikey,' said Thomas, shaking Guy's hand and raising his eyebrows, a broad smile across his face, 'sailing a bit close to the wind politically, aren't we?' He laughed. 'Are you going to run for prime minister next?'

'God, no!' Guy replied, clapping Thomas on the arm. 'I'm not sure my disposition is suited to work that serious. But, last time I checked, we still have freedom of speech, and I stand by what I said; we don't live in a perfect world and we shouldn't pretend that we do.'

Thomas held up his hands. 'I agree with everything you said,' he laughed, 'and you're already the CEO of one of the biggest companies in the world, so if anyone's going to say it, then why not you? But I heard you're under investigation?' he asked, concern written across his features. 'You don't want to goad them.'

'I'm not goading anyone,' said Guy, with an edge of irritation, 'and anyway, why not?'

'Did you hear about Richard's business? What they did to him?'

'Of course.'

'They made him clear out his whole top rank, slapped him with a massive fine, and he didn't really even do anything wrong.'

'He was lavish with his close circle of managers; trips away, personal use of company property...'

'...so are you,' said Thomas, cutting him off.

'I'm lavish with everyone,' replied Guy, a tone of warning creeping into his voice, 'there's a difference. Besides,' he said, smiling to brighten the mood, 'I heard Richard's top tier clear out wasn't a bad thing for everyone.'

'Ha,' laughed Thomas, 'as a matter of fact, I have had a decent promotion.'

'No surprise there, obviously,' said Guy. 'What's the new role?'

'Deputy finance director.'

'Christ! That is a decent promotion; congratulations! You'll be running the place in no time!

Let me get you a drink to celebrate.' Guy steered Thomas to the bar at the back, applause covering the sounds of their movements as the audience were presented with the first cohort of businesses Guy's new venture had invested in. 'What can I get you? Gin and tonic?'

'You know me so well,' Thomas laughed.

Guy ordered two gin and tonics from the robot behind the bar, and a short, prim looking woman, who'd spotted them, approached from the back of the crowd. 'Tina, hi,' said Guy, handing Thomas his drink. 'Let me introduce you to my good friend, Thomas Watson,' he said, nodding in Thomas' direction. 'We're celebrating his recent appointment as deputy finance director at Pixbot.'

'Which isn't public knowledge yet,' said Thomas, bashfully.

'Which isn't public knowledge yet,' repeated Guy, speaking directly to Tina, 'so we'd appreciate your discretion until it is. Sorry, Thomas, should have checked. But anyway, let me introduce you to Tina Somerville, member of Parliament and the minister for technology.'

'Delighted to meet you,' said Tina, clearly about to strike up a conversation with Guy, but Guy didn't let her get started.

'I'm terribly sorry, but would you please excuse me,' he said, looking distractedly over their shoulders, 'I need to get back to hosting duties, but I'm sure you two will have a great deal to talk about. I'll be around later, Tina, so please let's talk then?'

'Of course,' she replied, resignedly turning back to talk to Thomas.

'Great. See you later too, Thomas,' he said, leaving them to it and walking across the back of the crowd to a pillar on the other side of the building.

Guy had almost reached the pillar when he was intercepted by a cold presence approaching from his right. He turned to see who it was and took a deep breath when he recognised her. 'Iva,' said Guy, warmly. 'I'm so glad you could come.'

'Very kind of you to invite me,' she said, her words like icicles behind her fake smile. Guy was about to walk away, but she placed her hand on his arm to detain him. 'Interesting speech,' she said. 'Do you have political aspirations now?'

Guy laughed. 'I've always been political,' he said, lightly, although looking pointedly down at her hand, making her drop it to her side. 'It was my main occupation when I was younger. I've always loved debating the imperfect world in which we live.'

'And yet, somehow, you ended up at the top of one of the world's biggest companies.'

'It wasn't half the company it is today when I first started, as you well know. I've grown it to what it is today. I personally put our success down to my excessive computer game habit when I was younger; my parents couldn't get me out of my virtual world. But it does give one the most delightful sense of possibility, don't you think?'

'I wouldn't know,' she said, through gritted teeth. 'I was too busy working my way to where I am today to play computer games.'

'Not before you were sixteen, I hope?' replied Guy, in mock affront. 'That would be a breach of the regulations.'

'The regulations didn't exist when I was sixteen,' she sniped, 'but I take it you're not too dense to get my point.'

'Iva, haven't we been around this once before?' he said, his tone now something near hostile. 'It didn't work out as you'd hoped then, and I can't see why

41

anything is different today. Now, if you'll please excuse me, I've just seen someone I must say hello to. I do hope you enjoy your evening.'

Iva nodded, managing only just to keep a lid on her fury as he walked confidently away. 'Smug bastard,' she muttered under her breath. 'I will bring you down.'

CHAPTER 4

'Lulu,' Guy beamed, finally reaching the other side of the pillar he'd been heading for, rounding it with a flourish to surprise the woman he'd spotted hiding there. 'I'm so glad you could make it,' he said, warmly, kissing her on both cheeks.

Lulu was flustered. She had planned to find Guy later, but hadn't expected him to show up so publicly and so out of the blue. She was acutely aware of all the people around them. 'Thank you for inviting me,' she said, buying herself some time to regain her composure. 'Interesting speech.' She raised an eyebrow in approval.

'You're not the first person to have noticed,' he said, offering her his arm. She took it and he escorted her towards the bar.

'Oh damn,' she said, in mock disappointment, 'I do hate it when I lack in originality.'

'You should,' he joked back, 'you're an artist after all. What are you without originality?'

'A fraud,' she laughed. 'Oh no! You've found me out!'

'It's okay, I promise not to tell anyone. It would devalue your work tremendously, and that's not in my interests at all.'

'You bought a piece from the exhibition?' she asked, surprised.

'Of course,' he replied.

'Which one?'

'Which ones you mean?' he flirted.

'You bought more than one?'

'There were two I couldn't decide between, so I bought them both.'

'You're ridiculous,' she said, pretending to chastise him.

'I do try to be,' he replied, as they reached the bar, noticing that Thomas and Tina's conversation hadn't lasted long. They had both moved away and he spotted Tina conversing with some of the other politicians. Guy picked up two glasses of champagne and tried to hand one to Lulu.

'Thanks,' she said, 'but I hate the stuff. Is there anything else?'

'Of course, what would you like?'

'Just a soda water with fresh lime please.'

Guy ordered her drink before turning serious. 'Now,' he said, 'I promised to introduce you to some politicians.' The bartender handed Lulu her soda water. 'Right this way.' He took her by the elbow and moved her towards an intimidating group of men and women, who had congregated in a small group at the front of the hall now the presentation was over.

'Hello,' said Guy, enthusiastically, as they reached them. 'I hope you're all enjoying your evening?' he asked, throwing a full charm offensive their way.

'Yes, thank you, Guy,' said a grey-haired woman in her fifties. She had short, curly hair and spiky features. She was a curious mixture of stern yet approachable; probably the most approachable of the serious looking ensemble, but, much to Lulu's dismay, it quickly became apparent that this wasn't who Guy wanted to introduce her to.

'I'm glad to hear it,' replied Guy, smiling warmly as he pressed Lulu forward. 'I'm sure you all know my friend, Lulu?' he asked, his eyes engaging three other members of the group as he indicated towards Lulu with his hand. 'She's the most brilliant artist, and, of course, like all great artists, is influenced by the issues and inequalities of the day.'

There were a few raised eyebrows at this introduction. However, never one to stand on ceremony, the chancellor of the exchequer, a tall, painfully thin woman, with ludicrously long and stick-like fingers, jumped straight in. 'Indeed, I saw your latest exhibition in St Ives,' she started, before Guy cut in, having just looked at his smart watch.

'I'm terribly sorry, but would you all excuse me? Something's come up down south, so I need to get the hyperloop back ASAP. Sorry, Lulu, I'll be in touch.'

Lulu was a little perplexed, but nodded, turning back to the minister, keen not to waste this rare opportunity. 'You came to the exhibition?' she asked.

'Yes. I popped in to have a look while I was on holiday in Cornwall with my family. I'd heard a lot of the hype about you, and I'd seen your work virtually, but I must say, it's much more striking in the flesh. Although, a little idealistic in many respects.'

'How so?' she asked, genuinely interested in her opinion.

'Well, I sense a great deal of discontent with the status quo, and a depiction of a work freedom we can't currently offer, but little in the way of suggested solutions.'

'That's fair,' she replied, 'because I don't have all the answers; I don't think any one person does. But I do think we need a broader conversation about how we can help people work themselves out of the situation they're prescribed at birth.'

'They can work themselves out; they can start their own business, or train for free to do a job with no hours cap.'

'That's easy to say, but not easy to do in practice. For a start, many don't have an idea for a business, and even if they do, they probably don't have the resources to get a business off the ground. And many people don't want to own their own business; they don't have the inclination or the aptitude. And it would be impossible for everyone to successfully run a business; there's just not enough room in the economy for that many small enterprises. People want to be able to have the freedom to work more, for others. It's as simple as that.'

'And, as I said, it's a wonderful, idealistic vision,' she reiterated, in a patronising tone, 'but if we were to lift the working hours cap, we'd have mass unemployment, with huge competition for the limited numbers of jobs on offer.'

'Maybe we need less automation then,' she said, earnestly.

The chancellor laughed, and a couple of the other ministers joined the conversation. 'You want us to go backwards?' said Tina, the minister for technology.

'No,' she replied. 'I want us to move forwards in a more human way. We have a mental health epidemic, a lack of work freedom, social isolation is rampant, and virtual personas are not helpful.'

'She's right about that,' said Eric Rogers, the health minister. 'It's an undeniable problem.' He was kind looking, with a round face, medium height and build, but on the chubby side, which Lulu thought strange, considering his role.

'People are more connected now than ever before,' said Eliza Ashton, the chancellor.

'Yes, but the interactions aren't real,' said Lulu. 'We interact with people remotely. There's no physical interaction, no ability to help one another in the real world, no sharing a piece of cake, or petting the other person's dog. Don't get me wrong, the benefits of technology are too many to number, but I also think it's *naïve*,' she said, emphasising the word, 'to believe we have no areas for improvement. And I don't believe we can create a ground-breaking new robot to solve the problem.'

'But with more time on their hands, you'd think people would spend more time socialising together, and creating community projects and the like,' said Tina.

'They are,' replied Eric, 'but only in certain areas. People with young children create real-life support networks for themselves, and so do motivated retired people, sports people. In fact, it's very similar to how it's always been. But there are real risk groups; teenagers and young adults, young professionals, the very old, those with no family. And for those people, especially young people, the virtual world can be toxic.'

'But we've stamped out all the naked picture stuff that used to happen between kids, and have very sophisticated ways of picking up online bullying,' said Tina.

'Which is all great progress,' said Lulu, 'but teenage years are formative ones, where people are figuring out who they are, and often don't have experience to guide them. They may not be sharing naked pictures as much anymore, but they're still either included or excluded, they're either good at playing virtual games or they're not, they've either got the latest tech, or they haven't. They either come from a family who can work as much as they like, or they don't.'

'So you're saying we need to make mental health even more of a priority than it already is?' asked the chancellor.

'I'm saying we need to make humans the priority, and what it is to be human,' said Lulu. 'Yes, we need to tackle the mental health situation, but to do that, we need to understand what's causing it. And I don't think so much tech, across every part of life, is healthy.'

'I'm not sure that reducing tech would be a very popular route forward,' said Tina, a little smugly.

'How do you know?' said Lulu. 'Have you ever looked into it?'

Tina shook her head before skilfully changing the subject. 'It's a very interesting niche view,' she said, with a well-practiced but plastic smile. 'Speaking of which,' she went on, turning back to the other ministers, and effectively shutting Lulu out of the conversation, 'did you hear the ridiculous proposal about identity security put forward in the Commons by the opposition on Tuesday?'

* * * * *

'I miss the days when you could just jump into a helicopter. So much more of a thrill,' said Guy, flippantly, as he stared out of the window to nothing but blackness, as his car flew through the hyperloop. The hyperloop infrastructure had finally been finished, allowing high-speed travel all across the country, through a network of both above- and below-ground depressurized tunnels. Guy's car would self-navigate from Edinburgh to Oxford, where they would pop out of this tunnel, drive across the hyper-hub, and then enter another tunnel between Oxford and Plymouth, where he was ultimately headed.

'I wouldn't know,' said Benji pointedly, 'and anyway, it's extremely fuel-inefficient.'

'I know, I know.'

'And this is pretty quick.'

'The view's not the same though.'

'No. Do you remember those flying drone cars from the early days? The ones that used to hop across cities?'

'I loved those. It made getting across London an absolute dream.'

'But they were ludicrously expensive, and they were noisy, and distracting.'

'And then some kid brought one down in New York.'

'With a slingshot wasn't it?'

'Yeah. He was protesting about the growing inequality tech was causing, if I recall correctly. And then demand hit the floor and the company went bust.'

'Probably for the best,' said Benji, reflectively, silence settling between them as they both remembered those days.

'Walk me through the details then,' said Guy, taking a bottle of sparkling water from the fridge. Autonomous cars had no need for human input, so the whole internal space had been redesigned for maximum space and comfort. Most people didn't own their own car, but hired one when they needed it. This meant that the ongoing servicing and maintenance was someone else's problem, and you could choose the most appropriate vehicle for what you were doing each day. If you were going on a long journey, you could even hire a sleeper car, which came equipped with beds.

'They raided one of the factories just outside of Exeter,' said Benji, flatly.

'Which one?'

'Assembly twelve. They do domestic robot servicing.'

Guy started at this revelation. 'Thomas' parents work there. I saw him earlier. Are they all okay?'

'I don't know. There were people working over their hours, including his parents. They were all taken in for questioning. Apparently they said they were within their annual hours limit, and that they planned to do less work towards the end of the year to ensure they came in within their overall allowance. The problem is, they hadn't clocked in.'

'Shit,' said Guy, taking a swig of his water. 'Get word out to all the factories, in fact, to all the workers we help. Extra hours are off the table for everyone until further notice. And everyone should be clocking in, with no exceptions. Issue a reminder to the whole company, reiterating the policy. Point out that we remind people to do this every month. Say it's come to our attention that some people may not be clocking in, and that we want to ensure fair working hours and fair pay for everyone. All the usual stuff.'

'What about the workers who were questioned?'

'I don't know yet. We need the full details before deciding what to do. And I need to speak to Thomas' parents as soon as possible.'

* * * * *

Guy passed through the last security checkpoint before reaching the inner sanctum of Cybax's top-secret military lab at the dockyard in Plymouth. It was grey and inconspicuous, fitting in perfectly with the old military buildings there. On the outside, the place had preserved the rundown feel of the late 2010s, when funding for everything had been an issue, and you could barely get a free pen out of any government institution, let alone state-of-the-art tech. Everything inside was equally drab, with ripped chairs, horrible plastic flooring, and strip lighting, up until the point where he reached the Cybax lab that is, where the world exploded into an exciting array of brand-new technology, vivid colour, and dynamism.

Guy reached the end of the corridor and looked through the glass viewing window to take in the activity going on beyond. This was where the crème de la crème of the engineering world amalgamated; or at least, those with no objection to the military and developing hostile tech. They were working on an array of projects, from detection systems, to cloaking systems, to new ways of facilitating the high-speed deployment of resources, and, of course, the new cyborg suit, which the soldiers loved because it made them think they were Iron Man.

It was a sensitive area to be in though, and there was a dangerous groundswell of opinion wishing to scale back the military. Many thought the huge disparity between the tech of the Western world and the tech of other countries unfair, pointing to this as a perpetuator of the seemingly never-ending conflict around the world. They used Israel and Palestine as an example, as Palestinians were often killed by advanced Israeli weapons systems, the Palestinians still using tech from the 1990s, with nothing more than a few rockets to send. Although those on the other side of the argument wondered why the Palestinians sent the rockets in the first place. They would certainly be destroyed before they reached Israeli soil and therefore would do nothing but invite retaliation.

'People have no idea what we do to protect them from attack,' said Rebecca Archer, the defence minister, joining Guy at the viewing window. She was tall and slim, with short, greying brown hair and blue eyes. She was in her mid-fifties and had a ferocious energy about her, even if her features were a little worn and weary, the result of a job that brought no thanks and endless problems.

'More opposition?' asked Guy, turning his head, with an expression of concern.

'I've just got off the phone with the chancellor and he thinks he might have to make a big deal of reducing our funding a bit to try and calm things down.'

Guy looked concerned. 'Are we going to have to shut down any of the programmes?' he asked, his brow furrowed.

'Heavens no!' she exclaimed. 'He'll find some other way to siphon money to us; it's not like there's any shortage, but we'll need to be careful about keeping some of the new stuff quiet.'

'It's amazing,' said Guy, turning back to look at his engineers. 'People barely flinched when they heard about the cyber sorties Russia carried out in the early 2000s. Election rigging? Never mind! Cutting internet cables? I'm sure there are some more somewhere; the state will sort it out. Pay for security? Good Lord, no! People don't seem to realise that Russia, China, they have advanced technology too, and those sorties have transformed into full-blown cyber warfare.'

'I know,' she replied, shrugging. 'But I suppose the success of our secrecy is also part of our undoing. Our infrastructure is under constant attack, but the less we publicise that fact, the more people feel like we're exaggerating the risk every time we ask for money.'

'At least the risk is reduced now.'

'Indeed. People largely generate their own energy, they grow a lot of their own food using hydroponics, or at least, your robots do, but if they took down the internet, can you imagine what would happen?'

'I dread to think,' replied Guy, feeling a little guilty about the drive towards connected everything, with most homes relying on connected devices to run their lives, most notably, their humanoid butlerbots. If Russia managed to take control of individual butlers, they could do whatever they wanted within a person's home, office, or anywhere the butler was, and they were everywhere. They had an offline mode, activated either remotely via software, or via a physical switch, but by the time anyone had realised what was happening, it could well be too late.

'You know there's a suspicion that Russia's trying to sabotage the colony on Mars?'

'I know, I heard. But the idea of Mars as some kind of apolitical utopia was always a bit far-fetched.'

'They've done everything they can to be inclusive.'

'Inclusive on their terms,' replied Guy. 'With Western norms and values. It's a Western-run corporate programme; of course the Russians were going to be suspicious, not to mention jealous. Same old problems in a brand new setting.'

'Did you just come here to depress me, or is there something else I can help you with?' asked Rebecca. 'I hear you're in a bit of a pickle.'

'I am?'

'Oh come on, don't be coy. We've worked together long enough not to play games.'

Guy sighed. 'The Rottweiler raided one of my factories while I was launching my new charitable venture.'

'Ha! The Rottweiler? She'd love that name; I might have to tell her.'

'You know Iva?'

'We studied together at University.'

'Small world. Which one?'

'Plymouth, actually. We were both on track to be engineers; me electronic, her acoustic, but she changed her mind entirely in the last year. I was good friends with her and her boyfriend. We did pretty much everything together, although he was a couple of years ahead of us so left before we did. In fact, I think he went to work for your father. He died suddenly, shortly before we graduated, and that changed her. She went to study at Oxford and then opted to be a bureaucrat for some baffling reason. I joined your father's company here in Plymouth and don't seem to have ever managed to leave.'

'Apart from now you run the show.'

'Please! I'm not that naïve. We do it together.' She paused, letting the past fade back into the recess of her mind. 'Now, how can I help you? I assume that's really why you're here?'

Guy gave her a rueful smile. 'Did she try to get into this facility?'

Rebecca replied with a knowing look. 'She called me and asked for entry, but I told her, in accordance with the secrecy laws, that for the good of the nation, I couldn't let her in.'

'Is that why she hit the factory in Exeter instead? Or was that planned too?'

'I have no idea I'm afraid. She wouldn't divulge her plans to me.'

'But she didn't hit any of the others, so maybe she went to Exeter out of frustration because she couldn't get in here, rather than strategy.'

'Why?' asked Rebecca, alarmed. 'Do you have something to hide in Exeter?'

Guy looked up sharply, smiling his usual easy smile to cover the near slip. 'No, of course not. Not as far as I'm aware anyway. I think the clocking in system had a fault that the bots couldn't fix, so they were waiting for a human to come and have a look. To be honest, I'm entertaining the idea that maybe Iva sabotaged the system herself; they rarely go wrong. But if it was a chance hit, she can't have done. Anyway, enough of that. Let's talk about our new full soldier suit. How do you think the trials went?'

* * * * *

As soon as Guy finished with Rebecca, he pulled his smart glasses from his pocket and thought, *phone Benji,* his mind full of frustration.

'Hi,' said Benji, then waited for Guy to speak.

'We need to move the setup in Plymouth to somewhere nobody would expect.'

'What? The beauty of Plymouth is that it's hidden in plain sight. If anyone sees it, they won't suspect a thing.'

'Iva knows something's going on here. She'll gain access eventually, so we have no choice but to move it somewhere else.' Guy recalled the pain they'd gone through to establish the setup in Plymouth, and didn't relish the thought of going through it all again.

'Where?' asked Benji.

'Shrewsbury,' said Guy, off the cuff.

'Too small,' Benji fired back. 'We'd be detected in two seconds flat.'

'Fine. Where do you think?'

Benji thought for a moment. 'Watford,' he said, finally. 'It was our second choice for a base last time, and I don't think factors have changed wildly in the meantime.'

'Fine. Make it happen. But make sure the security is tight.'

CHAPTER 5

Guy walked over the lush green golf course, the oldest golf course in the world, no less, towards the beach. He stood at the railings overlooking the sand and smiled as he recognised Lulu's familiar figure jogging back towards the town. She reached the ramp and looked up to see who was standing above her.

'Jesus!' she exclaimed. 'Is nowhere safe from you?'

'It would seem not,' he said, amused. 'What brings you to St Andrews?'

'I'm surprised you don't already know,' she shot back, leaning over a little and catching her breath after her run.

'I'm not omniscient,' he laughed, 'and there are privacy laws aplenty limiting the data I'm allowed to look at for personal use,' he said, light-heartedly.

'Is that supposed to make me feel better?' she asked, flippantly, pushing against the railings while she stretched out her calves. 'I'm meeting a client. He's been buying my art for years and wants to commission a new monster of a work for the side of one of his office buildings.'

Guy raised his eyebrows. 'You do that kind of project?'

She grinned. 'It's not really my thing, but if it's the right project, I'm always open to a new challenge.'

'Shall we walk?' he suggested, indicating back towards the town.

'Sure,' she said. 'I'm staying at the other end of North Street. You can walk me there.' They walked in silence for a few moments, the sound of the waves all that disturbed the early morning silence.

'Thanks for inviting me to your party,' said Lulu, reluctantly interrupting the tranquillity. 'I had a good time, although I'm not sure I managed to inspire change among the ministers you left me with.'

'That lot don't want to hear anything other than that they're doing a wonderful job and everything's fine,' Guy laughed. 'Eric's okay; he realises the world isn't perfect, but then he's the one at the sharp end of the mental health problems.'

'I bet they give him a hard time around the cabinet table,' said Lulu. 'They're so smug and self-satisfied, it's like they can't admit to themselves there's a problem.'

'It's true, they can't, and they feel like they're at the top of a mountain looking down. Like there are other countries and other political parties clawing their way up, trying to suck them back to the ground. They think that if they stamp on enough fingers, the issues will fall away and they won't have to worry about them. That's if they can even admit the issues exist in the first place.'

'It's amazing how far we've come, but how little we've learned,' said Lulu, shaking her head. 'This is the way we do things around here; like it or lump it, we're too scared to change.'

'We need someone inspirational to come along and lead the change,' he said, 'which is also like it's always been. We just need one person determined enough to make it happen.'

'Yeah, but who?'

'I don't know,' replied Guy. 'Why not you?'

'Ha!' laughed Lulu. 'I'm not cut out to be a politician. I couldn't play a long game if my life depended on it! I'm impulsive and impatient and definitely not meant to lead a political movement. What about you?'

'I've thought about it,' said Guy, reflectively. 'But I don't want the limelight, and, unfortunately, leading a political movement involves a great deal of limelight chasing. Anyway,' said Guy, 'the ministers probably couldn't get past how starstruck they were at meeting you to have a proper political conversation.'

'Don't be ridiculous.'

'I'm not! Eliza, in particular, is a massive fan. As is anyone with any taste, of course.'

'You actually like my work? Despite what it represents?' she asked, sincerely, taking his arm as they wondered along the deserted street.

'No. I like it because of what it represents,' he replied.

'I just find that so hard to believe,' she said, honestly.

'Why?' asked Guy, snapping a little. 'Because I was born into a wealthy family and took over my father's business? Therefore I must revel in the status quo. I've done more to try and make things equal than anyone else I know.'

'Like what?' she asked, genuinely interested in the answer.

'We lobbied to make fresh, healthy food subsidised in supermarkets, and free in large workplaces.'

'Very noble,' she teased, 'especially as you integrate your robots with those supermarkets, so you get both data and commission on every purchase made.'

Guy rolled his eyes. 'We made robots to give everyone annual health checks in their homes, free of charge, not just those who are happy to have data chips in their hands, but everyone. We've reduced rates of things like prostate cancer considerably by detecting cases far earlier than in the past, because people used to be too embarrassed to go to the doctor. And we've helped people lose weight by installing a personal training and healthy food programme in the butlers.'

'Putting human personal trainers out of business, at least for anyone who doesn't come from a wealthy family like yours; families who are bending the rules left, right, and centre.'

'Bending the rules?' snorted Guy. 'How do we do that?'

'You tell me,' she replied, defensively.

'Go on then,' he said, pulling them to a standstill and making her look at him. 'Ask me anything you like and I'll tell you the truth.'

'How do you get around the inheritance rules? You're only supposed to inherit a hundred thousand pounds, like the rest of us. You're not supposed to be able to be handed companies; it's all supposed to be done on merit, and yet, the rich stay rich regardless.'

'We don't break the rules,' he replied, earnestly.

Lulu laughed.

'We comply with the rules. But everyone inherits their full hundred thousand, without question, and children are given positions in the companies of their parents' rich friends. The children are often fast tracked, usually with good reason, but sometimes not. They reach the two hundred and fifty thousand pound pay cap quickly and through that income start to amass wealth of their own. The authorities have nothing to penalise because no one has really done anything wrong.'

'Apart from give jobs unfairly to people who might not deserve it.'

'Well, that's the thing about employment and suitability; it's all subjective. And generally, those children are deserving, which is the most unfair bit of the lot. They grow up learning from their successful parents, not only being shown a route to success, but having it paved for them. The children are usually clever, have studied the right things, and are full of ideas. They know how the system works and what they have to do to obtain the kind of lifestyle they've grown up with. Children who grow up in other environments aren't so lucky. They don't have the same role models, the same expectations, or the same knowledge about what they have to do to achieve success. That means they either end up in the wrong place, underestimate their abilities, or don't move as quickly up the ladder.'

'But you didn't end up in someone else's company,' said Lulu, looking out at the sea.

'No,' he replied, heavily. 'I wanted to be a politician actually, much to my parents' dismay.'

'But then your brother died...'

'...and they guilted me into it. I was young and malleable, and I can't really complain; I have a pleasant enough life,' he said, glibly.

'With no hours cap to worry about, and money to spare,' she said, teasingly.

'As do you, I would point out,' he shot back, matching her tone.

'But I come from nothing,' she said haughtily.

'Which makes your success more worthy? I've turned an idling company into one of the world's most

61

successful enterprises, and you've built your reputation yourself – is there really that much difference?'

'Nobody handed me a company.'

'I do what I can to help people like you. That's what the launch was about the other night.'

'Investing in companies?' she asked, her tone sceptical.

'And other things.'

'Like what?'

'Like, why has this conversation got so heavy? There are people who are lazy and people who strive from every background. I want to help those who want to help themselves. Those who want to sit around and take their state income and do nothing else, I steer clear of. I invest in people from all walks of life, people with fire to make things happen. Like you,' he said, as they started walking again. They walked in silence for a few moments. 'What fired you up enough to make you become a superstar anyway?'

Lulu shoved him playfully. 'I was the third child of idle parents. If you have a third child, the state won't pay anything towards them until they're sixteen, when they get their own Universal Basic Income. So, my parents experienced financial hardship, and although my mother worked at my grandfather's shop (because my grandfather forced her to), it was low-skilled work, so she had to comply with the twenty-hour cap, and the pay was terrible. My father did nothing but drink and smoke, which took its financial toll. He wasn't abusive, other than verbally, but he didn't do anything to help and seemed to blame me for the inconvenience of their situation.

I couldn't work formally until I was sixteen, as per the rules, but I realised quite early on I could make some money by quietly selling my paintings. I set up stalls on the street alongside legitimate market traders, convinced other stallholders to sell my work for an exorbitant cut, and managed to convince a few people to commission works. Basically, every opportunity to make a bit of money, I took, which meant I could afford the materials I needed to keep painting, and could save some money along the way. I saw a way to work myself out of my situation.

But, just before my sixteenth birthday, I'd set up a stall at the edge of a street market, and a robot policeman came around and asked for my licence. Of course I didn't have one, and was arrested. It was one of your dad's robots, by the way.'

'Sorry,' he said, apologetically, and waited for her to continue.

'They made me do community service for a year, but at least that kept me away from my parents during nearly all of my free time. And they fed me and gave me a uniform to wear, so, in fact, it reduced the burden on my parents. I was sixteen by the time that was over and I went to work in one of your factories. I started painting again, selling my work legitimately this time, and it just took off. Some of the kids I went to school with had started a political group, protesting about the working hours cap. They saw my work as representative of their struggle, and incorporated it into their movement. They spread it around on social media; it was seen as edgy to start with and it even prompted a visit from the authorities, but I wasn't doing anything wrong. I wasn't inciting riot or anything, and, luckily, we still have freedom of speech.' Guy nodded.

'After the authorities came to call, a few local news outlets picked up the story; there's nothing quite like an artist rebelling against the system to get people's imaginations going. And then I started getting calls from wealthy people wanting to buy my work. I think they thought it made them cool and nonconformist or something, and I had an influx of commissions. I don't know if they had a genuine interest in the political ideals behind the paintings, or if they just liked to play at being controversial, revelling in the reaction to the defiant works when their conservative parents came round for dinner. Either way, that was where it started, and it hasn't let up since. Over the years I've been able to charge more and more for my work, galleries became interested and are now competing with each other to host me, and now I, like you, am in a fortunate, privileged position.'

'Do you still speak to your family?' asked Guy, as her story came to an end.

She shook her head. 'Not really. Every now and again I see them, usually at parties for my nieces and nephews. We exchange pleasantries, but not much more. We have nothing in common, and the only thing they want from me is money. Although now we've all left home, their allowance from the state is enough to live on. My mum's given up work. God knows what they do with their time.'

'And what about the political movement? What happened to them?' asked Guy, as they reached the far end of North Street, where Lulu was staying.

'They grew up and got jobs, mostly ones not subject to the working hours cap, and forgot there was ever a problem,' she said, scathingly.

'The American Dream,' replied Guy.

'Indeed,' she laughed. 'They've been reeled into capitalism. Anyway,' she said, looking a little guilty, 'you asked me a simple question, and I've given you my life story.' She smiled. 'Sorry.'

'Don't be ridiculous,' said Guy. 'I found it fascinating. In fact, I'd love to continue the conversation at dinner this evening, if you don't have a better offer?'

Lulu considered saying no, but reasoned she didn't have anything better to do. 'I'd love to,' she said, kissing him on the cheek to say goodbye.

'Great. I'll pick you up at eight?' he asked, squeezing her hand, holding onto it for a few seconds longer than necessary.

'See you then,' she said, smiling as she walked to her door.

* * * * *

Richard sat with Marvin Edwards, Pixbot's chief financial officer, and Thomas, at a breakfast table in the staff canteen. When Richard had been young, the word canteen had invoked horrible images of grotty, dark, dingy rooms with sloppy food served by women behind counters wearing hair nets. But this canteen was as far from that description as it was possible to get. It was in the light-filled atrium of Pixbot's colossal office building. Waiting staff, dressed in crisp white shirts and black trousers, took orders from the workers who used the canteen mostly for informal meetings. Orders were placed using the latest smart glasses and palm chip readers, chefs, both human and robotic, filling plates from the array of colourful offerings laid out across a number of counters and cooking stations.

Richard's eyes scanned the room, taking in the machines churning out an endless variety of teas and coffees. He lingered for a second over the counter laden with muesli, fruit, different types of yoghurt, healthy muffins, smoothies and juices, before deciding the breads, hams and cheeses of another were more appealing.

As the morning progressed, the robots would seamlessly change the contents of the counters to salads and soups, sandwiches and hot food, with cultured meat, fish, and grubs, which were loved especially by the high-protein dieters. Most of the food came from the building's roof or basement, where state-of-the-art hydroponic setups were located, alongside bug farms, solar panels and wind turbines. It was all looked after by robots, most of them created by the engineers based in this building, and overseen by the company's head of food production.

They placed their order, instructing the waiter to use the drink preferences transmitted by their smart glasses, and had to wait only moments for the beverages to arrive.

'Look, Marvin,' said Richard, taking a swig of his cappuccino, 'I just don't think that's the right capitalisation model for us. We need to be able to amortise over ten years.'

'But there's no way we can justify this as a ten-year asset,' said Marvin, aghast. 'Nothing is a ten-year asset any longer. It's laughable to suggest anything is going to last longer than five with the rate of technological change we have, which, need I remind you, we help to drive!'

'Marvin. I appreciate it will be difficult, but I don't employ you to tell me we can't do things. I employ you to find a way to do what I need.'

'And it's my job to tell you, honestly, when it's not possible to do what you want. Need I remind you the consequences of walking the wrong side of the line?' he said, getting agitated. 'We'll end up in prison, being kept there by the robots this company makes!' Marvin was a risk-averse accountant through and through. Even his appearance conformed to the caricature. He was short, weaselly looking, but well kempt, with round, old-fashioned glasses, short, slicked back hair, and a grandfatherly tweed jacket. He hunched a little when he talked, his jacket just a little too big for his slim shoulders.

Richard appraised the insignificant man. He was sweating under the weight of Richard's full attention and almost physically squirming at having to stand his ground. He looked like he was trying to wriggle away, back to whatever hole he'd slithered out of, no doubt. Richard had only appointed him because he'd needed someone wholesome to replace the CFO Iva had made him get rid of. But Marvin took wholesome to the extreme. He was terrified to push the boundaries even a little, and everyone knew you could always do that. Rules were for the guidance of wise men and the obedience of fools, or so Richard's old mentor had always said.

Thomas, on the other hand, had prospects. Richard had been reluctant when Guy had first asked him to give Thomas a job. He'd seemed too shy and retiring to be a leader, but Guy had convinced him, so Richard had put him in the accounts department, which, he had reasoned, was full of other shy and retiring people, so maybe he'd fit right in. He hadn't lived to regret it. Every time he needed a way around a blocker, Thomas was the person who would find the answer, even if his methods pushed boundaries. Thomas would go far.

'Work with Thomas on it,' said Richard, finally. 'I'm sure between the two of you, you can find a way. Now, we also need to discuss the Research and Development relief figure. It's too low by half.'

Marvin nearly spat out his ginger, apple and kale juice. 'By half?' he said, frustration starting to turn to anger. 'I take it you know the rules?'

Richard smiled, happy to have incited an emotional reaction. 'Yes, I know the rules. I also know that we can categorise loads more of our work as qualifying R&D.'

'Not if we want to stay within the letter of the law,' he said, pompously.

'The letter of the law, indeed. As if such a thing exists,' laughed Richard. 'I am more than comfortable that we can re-categorise a significant portion of our work to qualify for R&D tax relief. We will, I am sure, remain within the spirit of the law,' he said, meaningfully. 'Again, I'm sure Thomas will offer his assistance,' he said, effectively closing down the topic. 'Now, if you will excuse me, I have a domestic butlerbot trial to get to. We've got to do something to compete with Guy's latest model.' He started walking away, before turning back to Thomas. 'Thomas, my tennis partner has just pulled out of our match tomorrow night. You play tennis, don't you?'

Thomas smiled. A confident, self-assured smile. 'Of course, who doesn't?' *Marvin*, thought Richard, picking up Thomas' obvious meaning. Richard chuckled inwardly.

'Great. I'll see you at the Rix Club tomorrow at seven then,' he said, neither bothering to check if Thomas was free, nor that he was happy to play. Thomas, like everyone else at the company, was at Richard's disposal, and they had better not forget it.

Marvin gave Thomas a withering look. 'You're playing a dangerous game,' he said to both of them, picking up his juice and stalking away. Richard watched him go. Maybe Marvin had more backbone than he'd thought.

* * * * *

Lulu and Guy sat in a crab shack just around the coast from St Andrews. It was a ramshackle little building with flaking paint and old plastic tables and chairs. Everything here was done by humans and the owners maintained a healthy disdain for anyone who did things any other way. The building was perched on the sea front, looking out over the tiny harbour and pier that stuck out anciently into the water. The whole experience was like going back in time, and Guy loved the escape from his usual, tech-filled existence.

There was a pile of crab shells in between them, and a scattering of chips, which neither one of them could face after their mammoth meal. Lulu wiped her hands on a paper napkin, cast it into the paper-lined plastic basket in front of her, then pushed the whole lot away. She sat back in her seat and took a deep breath. 'That was amazing,' she said, satisfied. 'The most perfect meal.'

'I'm glad you think so,' replied Guy, mirroring her body language. The waitress saw they were finished and came to clear.

'Everything alright with your crab?' she asked, her French accent surprising them.

'Delicious,' Guy and Lulu replied, in unison, then smiled.

'You don't usually hear French accents around here,' said Guy. 'What brings you to the area?'

The slightly plump waitress beamed. 'I'm studying at St Andrews,' she said, 'for a PhD in International Relations. You hear plenty of French accents there, but I prefer it out here; it's quiet and more...real, non?'

'That it is,' said Lulu, warmly.

'Can I get you dessert?' the waitress asked. 'Or tea or coffee?' she continued, when they both vehemently shook their heads.

'I'd love a tea,' said Lulu.

'As would I,' said Guy.

'Milk?' asked the waitress.

'Yes please,' they both replied, Guy inwardly remarking that there was anywhere left in the country where they didn't already know how you liked your tea, by virtue of your smart devices talking to the restaurant's tech. But then, seeing as this place didn't have any tech, of course, they had to ask. There were sugar cubes in a little dish on the table too, like they were back in the twenties.

'I love it,' said Lulu, in a conspiratorial almost-whisper, as the waitress walked away. 'It's so old-fashioned.'

'I know,' said Guy. 'I love coming here; it reminds me that we can live without tech after all, and it often sparks new ideas when you see people living in an unusual way.'

'Surprising that there's enough work around for a French girl to get a job though.'

'I think there are quite a few pockets in the countryside where people have decided not to fully embrace technology,' Guy replied, 'which inevitably leads to greater employment opportunities. And the fact that they're technology free, or at least they don't have as much tech as the cities, makes them a mecca for tourists, which leads to even greater employment.'

'People do go crazy for tech-less getaways,' said Lulu. 'I suppose it's not surprising; we're connected and on the go all the time, so it's nice to take a break from it. My studio is more or less tech free,' she said, 'I find it helps give me space to think and be creative.'

'I can see that,' said Guy.

A comfortable silence fell over them for a few moments as they waited for their tea. 'This isn't the kind of place I thought you'd take me,' said Lulu.

'I'm sorry,' Guy teased, 'are you missing impeccable fine dining?'

'Ha!' laughed Lulu. 'No. But I'm surprised that's not your scene.'

'Why?' asked Guy, preparing to tease her again.

Lulu flushed scarlet. 'I guess I just assumed...'

'...it's fine,' said Guy, not wanting to make her uncomfortable, 'I know why. I'm just messing around. But I prefer it when things are more relaxed.'

The waitress finally brought them their tea, taking an age to arrange the tea pot, cups, saucers, teaspoons, extra hot water and milk on the table.

'Thank you,' they both said when she'd finished. She nodded, then turned to clear another table. The restaurant was busy, given it was ten o'clock at night. Guy and Lulu had walked on the beach before dinner, enjoying the late-evening summer sunshine.

'I heard your factory in Exeter was raided,' said Lulu, her expression curious.

Guy didn't even flinch, casually looking her in the eye when he replied. 'Yes, it was. How did you hear?'

'It's the factory I used to work in,' said Lulu. 'I still know people there.'

'Really?' said Guy, surprised. 'I didn't realise you were from Exeter.'

'Tiverton,' said Lulu, 'but my Granddad's shop was in Exeter, near the factory, so I spent most of my time there. Is everything alright? Why did they go after that one?'

'It's unclear,' replied Guy, evenly. 'We're still trying to work it out. It's possibly because they were trying to gain access to a top-secret facility in Plymouth, and when they were denied access there, they hit the next nearest one. Or maybe they had some kind of ulterior motive. I don't know. But we've got nothing to hide, so either way, it's nothing to worry about,' he said, shutting down the conversation. 'Tell me about your latest work,' he asked, leaning forward with interest.

'What do you want to know?'

'Everything. Your inspiration, progress to date, your process; all there is to know. I've been dying to ask you about your work since we first met.'

Lulu laughed. 'I'm not sure it's that interesting, but okay. Um,' she said, working out where to start. 'I've got this friend, he's kind of a muse, I suppose. He's called T.J. He's from the same neighbourhood as my cousin and is doing really well for himself. He used to be a radical political activist – right wing – no working hours restrictions, no pay cap, survival of the fittest, all that jazz. But now he's got a decent job, he doesn't seem to care as much about the things he used to.'

'Was he one of the ones who helped you early in your career?' asked Guy, sipping his tea.

'Yes. He was one of the ringleaders. But, as I said, he's fallen out of love with his old political ideals, although he still has strong opinions on pretty much everything! Anyway, I find him artistically inspiring, both because of where he's come from versus where he is now, and the change in him, but also because his mental health is extremely turbulent.'

'Isn't that the same for us all?!' joked Guy.

'Well, yes, increasingly I suppose it is. He was anorexic when he was younger. He got very into one of the thin-spiration communities on social media and has had body and personal image issues ever since. And now it's like he plays a different persona depending upon who he's with, trying to live up to whatever he thinks the other person wants him to be.'

'Sounds quite sad.'

Lulu nodded her agreement. 'And he's isolated,' she continued. 'His career is all consuming; I don't think he has many real-life friends left, aside from me. He plays a lot of computer games, but he invents different personas for different platforms. There's nothing malicious in it, but I'm not sure he even knows who he is any longer, or what he stands for.'

'That's hard to do now,' said Guy.

'What is?' asked Lulu, confused.

'Maintaining different personas online. Generally they get linked together by the technology in the background and the moderators merge them into one, unless it's a community where people are openly pretending to be someone else. It makes people more accountable for their online behaviour and stops a lot of the really horrible trolling and grooming stuff from happening.'

'I suppose that makes sense,' said Lulu, 'after all the incidents in the early days of virtual reality rooms.'

'Yeah, it was bad. We had to stop the robots, especially the butlers, from learning from everyone indiscriminately too. So many people treated the robots badly, or beat them up, that the robots were showing signs of using that as a basis for normal human behaviour. And we programmed them to learn from and emulate normal human behaviour.'

'That's terrifying,' said Lulu, shaking her head.

'Isn't it? There are safeguards to make sure no robot ever harms a human, but still, no one wants a rude or offensive robot in their home. But it sounds like your friend's experiencing a problem plaguing more and more people; isolation, paranoia, image issues, not knowing how they fit in.'

'Yep,' said Lulu, 'and our lives are so easy, and people are so lazy. Or at least there's an increasing gulf between the motivated and those who sit at home, plugged into their virtual worlds, or those who spend all their time on holiday.'

'It's weird though, a lot of those people who sit at home immersed in a virtual world are like kings inside their games. They work so hard at being the best battleship commander, or knight in shining armour, or assassin, that they gain a lot of status and respect within their virtual communities.'

'If only they did the same in the real world,' said Lulu.

'Although, if the opportunities aren't there in the real world, is it so bad that they're finding another way to work at something, and achieve something?'

'I don't know,' said Lulu. 'But it's kind of depressing that they have to, don't you think?'

Guy shrugged. 'Did you ever date him? Your muse?'

The corners of Lulu's mouth turned up in amusement, helping shake off the cloak of heavy conversation. 'T.J?' She giggled. 'No! It's never been like that between us.'

Guy breathed an inward sign of relief. 'So, you were telling me about your current work,' he prompted.

Lulu sat up straight, and her features brightened. 'True, I was,' she said, enthusiasm flashing in her eyes. 'I've got a couple of works on the go. One is an abstract, where the world is blurry, just out of view, so you're not sure if you're looking at the contemporary world or a time in the past or the future. There are clues around the place about where it is and the meaning, but the viewer has to work quite hard to find them. The other one is the mural for the guy I was telling you about. It's got two sides; one showing utopia, and the other dystopia, with a mixed middle ground of confusion. Of course, neither side really exists, and we occupy the confused and imperfect world in the middle.'

'How would you improve it?' asked Guy.

'Our imperfect world or the mural?' she asked, joking.

'Our imperfect world,' Guy confirmed, with mock reproach.

'Well, I'd find a way to increase occupation. That doesn't necessarily mean work, but the working hours cap is the death of social mobility. I know the argument is that it's better and fairer for everyone to have the opportunity to work, at least a little, but, in reality, all it does is mean that good people are held down and incompetent people are guaranteed a job, regardless of how terrible they are at it. So nobody can work their way out of their situation, unless they have specific skills. But not everyone has an inclination towards engineering, or being a creative, or running their own business.'

'But there aren't enough jobs for everyone, and the alternative is much higher unemployment.'

'And better free-market economics,' Lulu shot back. 'People should be allowed to be successful if they're tenacious and persistent and have a good work ethic. Survival of the fittest is the only way to progress.'

'Who'd have thought it,' laughed Guy. 'Our system has turned our artists into right-wing activists! How things have changed.'

Lulu laughed. 'I know. Artists fighting for the free rein of capitalism. The world must be upside down when that happens! But tech has led to so much change without enough consideration around the impact on real people.'

'True,' said Guy, shrugging a little.

'I'm not arguing that a lot of things aren't better now, especially people having financial security regardless of their background. I'm not blind. And I couldn't care less about peoples' inheritance being used to pay for it all, but limiting people by not letting them work to change their lives can't be right. But then again, not having an hours cap would have consequences too

– we occupy an imperfect and chaotic middle ground; we always have. There's no right answer,' she said, pausing. 'What do you think we should do?' she asked, leaning forward to add emphasis to the turn of conversation.

Guy raised an eyebrow, contemplating what to say. 'It's hard to know,' he started, slowly. 'Living standards have, in theory, never been higher. But, robots like mine have removed the necessity for many to have an occupation, which is the one thing we all really need. Occupation gives us meaning, helps us feel good about ourselves, gives us a sense of achievement...I mean, there are people who are happy playing computer games, or going on never-ending holidays, or doing craft projects, and to me that's as valid as any other kind of occupation, but I agree, limiting how much people are able to work isn't right.'

'People with butlerbots don't even have to get out of bed in the morning,' said Lulu, cynically, 'and actively finding a pastime you enjoy, to meaningfully fill your time, can be really hard.' She watched him, hawk–like, for his reaction.

Guy gave a half smile at the accusatory look; a lot of the robots came from his company, after all. 'Sometimes I feel like Universal Basic Income was a quick fix for AI entrepreneurs. They knew they were about to cause an economic problem, but they wanted to make their tech, for it to dominate the market, to see how far they could push it, so they all started talking about UBI like it was the only solution. It was a box ticked for them and a way to abstain from taking any real responsibility. They'd told their governments what they should do; they'd theoretically solved the problem, so their role was done.'

'Wasn't it?' challenged Lulu.

'I don't know,' he countered. 'But I'm not convinced anyone thought that hard about the consequences, or really looked fully into other options. UBI was set up as the answer, academics and entrepreneurs got behind it, and once it gathered momentum, it became an inevitable destination rather than one of a number of options. And now we've become more isolationist as a country than ever before. People hate immigration more than ever, and there are hate crimes against the people we have to employ from other countries to fill highly skilled jobs.'

'Really?' said Lulu, shocked.

'Yeah,' said Guy, darkly. 'We try to keep it out of the press to be honest, as they tend to polarise the argument and stir up more bad feeling, while publicising the fact that we have to employ immigrants due to skills shortages.'

'The press hasn't changed much, has it? With all the progress, you'd have thought they might start to be less simplistic and a bit more positive!'

'The chance would be a fine thing,' Guy agreed. 'Anyway,' he said, waving his arm, 'enough politics. Let's get out of here.' Guy pulled out a couple of notes and left them on the table.

'Crikey, that really is old school,' laughed Lulu.

'I know,' he said, enjoying her reaction to the place.

Usually, anything to do with purchases was dealt with electronically and sent straight to his banking app, where it was all linked up together under the transaction entry. Most restaurants would even send the detailed order breakdown, just in case he ever wanted to go back and see what he'd eaten, and you could make money by selling those kinds of details to data repositories as well. It was handy to have details of all transactions in one place, rather than spit across a multitude of apps, and it included pretty much everything, from airline luggage allowances, to parcel delivery tracking, to concert tickets. Cash was rare indeed.

Guy escorted Lulu out of the shack and down the uneven path to the pier. 'I want to hear more about you. Especially about how I get on your good side,' he flirted, as they walked along the uneven surface towards the sea.

Lulu laughed. 'I was beginning to think you were only interested in my art,' she said, in mock chastisement.

'Which I've been buying for years, by the way.'

'How many years?' she asked, guardedly.

'Since just before you became a big thing. It was a nice surprise when that happened,' he joked.

'You're my mystery benefactor?'

'I suppose I am,' he replied. 'I've got a whole room full of your work. Is that weird?' he asked, cocking his head to one side and putting his arm around her.

'It's kind of stalkerish that you didn't disclose that information prior to bringing me to a remote Scottish fishing village.'

'But I'm *very* charming, so I can get away with it?'

'Are you?' she teased. 'I can't say that I'd noticed.'

They reached the end of the pier, the sun setting across the sea, and a tense silence settled over them. Guy turned towards her, put his arms around her waist and looked down into her eyes. She smiled invitingly up at him and he couldn't help but smile back. He bowed his head and kissed her waiting lips.

* * * * *

Mila and Iva sat in the boardroom that Guy had made available to them, sipping herbal teas, and watching a projection of one of the news channels on the wall. They were using Mila's smart glasses to project, which always made Mila nervous, in case she got a call from someone Iva wouldn't approve of halfway through.

The news anchor was explaining that there had been another hate attack on a group of three highly skilled Italian immigrants as they'd left work. Two men had thrown projectiles at the unsuspecting workers, who had fled back into their office building, with several native workers caught in the crossfire.

The police had caught the attackers, of course, as it was impossible to escape the cameras, AI, and advanced DNA detection the police used. And as biometric identification was required for pretty much everything: transportation, paying for things, entry into buildings, it meant you left a trace behind you wherever you went.

The biometric data was linked back to your online passport, so, in effect, there was an identity card system in place, where residents could be tracked wherever they went. It had been rolled out so gradually that by the time anyone realised what was happening, it was too late to protest.

It was almost impossible to get away with committing a physical crime, which was part of the reason why crime rates had plummeted, but that meant when someone did decide to break the law, it made even more of a statement.

'Will it ever end?' sighed Mila, shaking her head as they watched footage of the attackers being bundled into a police vehicle.

'Can you really blame them?' replied Iva, harshly. 'People can't get decent jobs. The *rich*,' she said, emphasising the word to make Mila feel uncomfortable, 'can pick and choose to whom they give cap-free jobs. So they choose their friends, and pay them whatever they want, including side perks which go undetected, taking hours away from those without jobs. And then, to add insult to injury, a load of foreigners come over and steal more of our uncapped work. I'm surprised it doesn't happen more often.'

Mila baulked inwardly, trying to maintain a calm exterior. But she wasn't going to let Iva bully her. 'The reason immigrants occupy good jobs is because we've already run everyone else out of the country. We barely even know what diversity is any longer.'

Iva turned to stare Mila down, aggression in her eyes. 'We have the most diverse workforce of all time,' she hissed. 'Women, LGBT, people of colour, people from other religions and cultures, they all have near equal opportunities.'

Or so the government spin tells us, thought Mila, the reality being that opportunity wasn't an easy thing to assess, so it was easy to manipulate the numbers. 'But give it a generation or two and foreign accents will be a thing of the past, or at least will be considered exotic.'

'Don't be obnoxious,' snapped Iva, 'we have plenty of tourists, and under UBI, people can afford to travel abroad if they want to, so they can go and get their fill of foreign accents elsewhere.'

'Do you really believe that?' asked Mila, shocked that her boss could be so closed-minded, so protectionist. 'Either way, I don't think it's fair that people are being attacked, especially when they've come to fill skills gaps, just because they weren't born here.'

'Neither the attackers nor those being attacked deserve to find themselves in their current situations. And the attackers are idiots anyway; they never get away with it and lynching people is not the way to bring about positive change. Anyway,' said Iva, changing the subject, 'has Guy submitted the information we asked for about the clocking-in system at the factory in Exeter?' She watched Mila closely as she answered.

'Not yet,' replied Mila, evenly. 'But he's got another two days to comply, and I wouldn't expect to receive anything until the deadline.'

'And what about the other raids? Did they come up with anything? Any others breaking the working hours limit?'

'The raids all went ahead as planned. Ten, simultaneously, although we still can't get into the top-secret facility in Plymouth. They came up with absolutely nothing. All the factories complied absolutely with all legislation.'

'We need a rat,' said Iva. 'Guy's not sloppy, I'll give him that much. The only way we're really going to get him is if someone tells us where to look.'

'I thought we already had one?' asked Mila, surprised. 'Didn't they tell you which facilities to raid? And to start with Exeter? And specifically to look at the number of hours everyone was working?'

'Yes, we did have some help. But we haven't heard anything since that first tip-off.'

'But surely you managed to find out who it was? People think they can remain anonymous, but we always find out who they are.' It was crucial to know who the source was, to make sure they weren't being made fools of, even if finding out wasn't strictly the most ethical behaviour.

Iva clenched her fists in frustration. 'Unfortunately, this one is proving difficult to identify. They know how to cover their tracks and they haven't left a shred of anything for us to follow online. The tip-off just appeared on my computer screen one day, and none of the tech guys could work out how it got there.'

Mila looked concerned. 'Doesn't that mean we've got a major security breach? We're supposed to have one of the most secure systems in the world, and someone managed to get in, make changes, and get out again, entirely undetected, and nobody knows how they did it?'

'Possibly,' said Iva, noncommittally. 'I've reported it up the chain and they've put in place emergency protocols, which means they shouldn't be able to get in again.'

'That's why we all had to reconfirm our biometric logins?'

Iva nodded.

'So it's possible that the mole is trying to communicate with you but can't find a way back in?'

'It's possible,' said Iva, in a bored tone, 'but I replied to the message on my desktop, giving them access to the secure tips portal. Not that I've received anything on that.'

'If he or she is clever enough to work out a way into our systems without detection, then they're clever enough to know not to trust the tips portal is truly anonymous. I mean, would you trust it?'

'They should be clever enough to find another secure way to get in touch with me then. In fact, they're probably even more likely to try now, given it represents a new and exciting hacking challenge.'

CHAPTER 6

Mila got home to find Thomas in her apartment, sitting at her kitchen island, working at his computer. He rolled up the laptop screen, pulled off his smart glasses, and got up to greet her. 'Hey!' she said, kissing him squarely on the lips.

'Hey,' he said excitedly, pulling her to him to kiss her again.

'Good day at work?' she asked, before turning to her butlerbot. 'Glass of white wine, please, Matt,' she said, taking off her coat and handing it to the butler before sauntering over to the sofa in the middle of the large, open-plan entertaining space, folding her legs under her as she lowered herself down.

'Yes, actually, it was very good,' he said, taking her wine from Matt, the butler, and delivering it to the table next to Mila. He sat next to her, then leaned over and kissed her, pushing her back onto the sofa, following her as she went.

'Someone's in a good mood,' said Mila, between kisses, running her hands up his muscular back.

'Someone's been invited to play tennis with Richard,' he said, moving his lips to her neck.

'That's amazing,' she exclaimed, tipping her head back as he ran his hand under her shirt. 'How did you manage that?'

'Marvin was being his usual, pathetic self, so it was impossible not to look like a god in comparison!' he said, kissing his way along her collarbone.

'Good to see that ego's in check,' she teased, pushing him away so she could get her wine.

'What about your day?' he asked, pulling her astride him, glass in hand.

'Well,' she said, leaning down to kiss him, tasting of crisp, fresh wine, 'Iva's in a terrible mood.'

'Why now?' he smirked, taking a swig of her drink.

'She can't find anything on Guy. Apart from the factory in Exeter, which isn't enough to do any serious damage,' she said, Thomas kissing the v of flesh visible at the top of her shirt. 'She needs a mole, but Guy treats everyone so well, she can't find anyone to turn on him.'

'I thought she had an informant?' he asked, Mila running her free hand through his hair.

'She did. But they only gave her that one tip and now they've gone quiet. Iva needs more,' she said, as Thomas undid the buttons of her shirt, exposing her lace bra beneath.

'Enough work talk,' he said, putting her wine back on the table, before pulling down her bra, exposing her breasts. 'We've got more interesting things to do.'

* * * * *

Lulu arrived at Guy's house in a taxi. The autonomous vehicle pulling up at Guy's imposing solid wood gate and her window rolling down of its own accord. She was next to an entry panel with both a hand and face scanner. She placed her hand on the pad, and waited while the scanners did their work. The panel went green and a voice welcomed her by name before the gates opened and the car whisked her through.

The drive was long and sweeping, with grass lining both sides, a handful of short, old, gnarled trees dotted about the lawn. On one side, the grass ended at a hedge boundary, behind beautiful borders packed with colourful flowers in the full bloom of summer, the other boundary a cliff, overlooking the sea below. The house was built of ancient stone, and not as grand as Lulu would have expected, although it was certainly large, and had several add-ons well blended with the original structure.

The car took her to the front of the house, to an artful turning circle, with a beautiful bronze sculpture of an eagle flapping its wings in the middle. It pulled up at the attractive front door, complete with manicured bay trees in pots either side, and stopped, the car door opening to let her out, in almost perfect unison with the front door, which had seamlessly opened to let her in.

Guy came out to greet her. 'Hi!' he said, casually negotiating the two shallow steps down to the drive. He took her hand as she exited the car, and held onto it as he led her back up the steps and into the house. The door closed by itself as Lulu took in the sizeable entrance hall, with its marble floor and curving staircase. Guy took her jacket and handed it to the butlerbot that was discreetly waiting in a corner.

'Let me show you around,' he said, taking her hand again and leading her into a stunning, open-plan kitchen, dining, and seating area. It was breath-taking, with glass walls on two sides looking out over the sea. The walls slid open in several places, leading out onto decking with an array of comfortable-looking lounging and dining furniture. The decking's wide steps led down to a lush green lawn, which rolled gently all the way to a white fence at the edge of the cliff. A small gate marked the path down to the beach below.

'It's incredible,' said Lulu, barely able to tear her eyes away from the view.

'I know,' Guy replied. 'I'm lucky.'

'You can say that again,' said Lulu.

'It was my parents' house,' he said. 'I grew up here, and I bought it when my father died. My mother moved to Australia, where her sister lives. She said she'd had enough of the British weather. I don't see her very often now.' Lulu smiled at his uncharacteristic volunteering of information and Guy looked a little bashful. 'Come on,' he said, nudging her, 'this way.' He led her through one of the glass doors and onto the decking. There was an enormous hot tub sunk into it, and what looked like an old barn, now glass on three sides, housing a swimming pool and gym that also overlooked the sea.

'Wow,' she said, eying up the pool.

He smiled. 'That's not what I wanted to show you. Although you're more than welcome to have a swim later if you want.'

Lulu shrugged in a non-committal sort of way, following Guy as he led her down the steps to another outbuilding on the other side of the garden. It too had been constructed using a lot of glass, but was more secluded and less overlooked by the main house. They entered the building and Lulu found herself in a large but cosy room, filled, to her astonishment, with her artwork. 'Oh my God,' she said, turning around to take in the extent of it.

Guy laughed. 'I told you I'd bought a lot of your work.'

Lulu didn't say anything, looking, open-mouthed, at recent works alongside canvasses so old that she'd almost forgotten about them. 'Too much?' Guy asked nervously.

'No,' she said, shaking her head. 'You must really like my work!'

'I've told you that on a number of occasions, if I'm not much mistaken.'

'Or maybe you're a stalker. Are you a stalker?'

'No. At least, I don't think so. Do stalkers usually consider themselves to be stalkers?' he asked, genuinely considering the question.

'I'm not sure,' she replied slowly. 'This is crazy.'

'I know,' he said, apologetically. 'I started buying them years ago, long before I had any idea who you were. I saw them on sale at a market, loved how raw and honest they were, and bought two straight off. They were considerably cheaper than they are now!'

'Well I wasn't famous then,' she said, with a flourish.

'I hung them in pride of place in the apartment I used to live in, so anyone who came over couldn't help but see them. They were always an interesting talking point, but my political friends thought they were wonderful, like they summed up everything that was wrong in the world. A few of them bought a work or two of their own.'

'You started the rich-people-buying-my-work trend?'

'It's hard to be sure,' he replied, 'but maybe.'

'What is this room anyway?' asked Lulu, walking around.

'My office,' he said, moving to the far end of the room, where a large, traditional desk sat grandly in front of the window, complete with a leather office chair.

'I'm not sure I'd ever get any work done with that view,' said Lulu, staring out of the window.

'It's great for thinking,' he replied.

'I can see that,' she said, turning back towards him. 'Well, I'm glad that you genuinely like my work,' she said, flirting. 'And am I what you expected I'd be?'

'Yes and no,' he said, matching her tone as he took a step towards her and reached for her hand. 'I didn't really know much about you, so I hadn't formed too fixed an opinion. What about me?' he asked. 'Am I what you expected?'

She snickered. 'Absolutely not,' she said, reaching up to kiss him gently on the lips. 'You're a complete surprise.'

'Guy,' said a voice entering the room. 'Oh, sorry,' said Benji, as he saw Guy and Lulu. 'Shall I come back later?'

'No,' said Guy, smiling almost guiltily at her. 'Lulu, will you excuse me for a moment?'

'Of course,' she said, moving back to the window and slumping down into one of the comfortable bucket seats. 'Take your time; I'm quite happy here.'

Guy walked towards Benji and they stepped outside, making sure the door was fully closed before starting their conversation.

'Come on, Guy,' said Benji, 'you need to focus. We still haven't submitted the evidence for the Exeter factory.'

Guy frowned, prickling at Benji's comment, and had to tell himself to let it go. Instead, in his most cold and business-like manner, he replied, 'I thought you'd fabricated some manual clock-in records.'

'I have. We have people trying to find fault with them at the moment. If they can't find anything suspect, we'll submit.'

'Fine. What's the problem then?'

'You just seem distracted. The evidence isn't the only thing we've got on our plates. We've also got a large and complex relocation to deal with.'

'Which you're handling,' said Guy, defensively.

'Which I'm handling,' repeated Benji, 'but I'd feel more confident if I knew you had my back, like you usually do.'

'Okay, okay,' said Guy, knowing he had been a little absent recently. 'Send me the plans and I'll review them. Later,' he added, pointedly, as he turned to go back inside.

* * * * *

Thomas walked into the Rix Club alongside Richard, taking great care to look calm and confident, like he was born to be here. He'd spent years studying Guy's easy style, paying careful attention to the set of his shoulders, his effortless gait, his facial expressions, noting what he cared about and what was inconsequential to him. He'd learned from Guy what to wear, what to say, when to smile, and, importantly, when to do nothing at all. And because people trusted Guy, and Thomas emulated him so expertly, people trusted him too. In fact, he'd learned the act so well that people mostly assumed he'd been born into this life, Thomas revelling in the deception.

The Rix Club was *the* club to belong to. It was virtually impossible to get in, and ludicrously expensive. You had to be sponsored by two existing members, which, of course, meant that it was entirely dominated by families who had managed to maintain their wealth through generations. Gender discrimination had been outlawed several decades before, but it still had the feel of an 'old boys' club, the only difference that now everyone walked around like they owned the place, not just the men.

The building was old and the wood panelling in the drawing rooms original, but the facilities were state of the art. The club had all kinds of sports facilities: squash courts, tennis courts, real tennis courts, polo pitches and stables, swimming pools, a gym, studios for personal training sessions and classes, a running track, sauna and spa facilities. There was a café, a restaurant, and a bar, as well as a number of different rooms for lounging, or meeting. There were spaces to hire for private dining, or parties, or corporate away days, and old-school entertainments dotted around the place, like chess, card games, and hardback books. The club even had a music room, recording studio, and auditorium, where a number of famous artists had staged impromptu performances for other members. It also had a healthy schedule of planned concerts, which always booked up months in advance.

How the other half live, thought Thomas, marvelling at the overt opulence; there were few places where you could get away with displays like this these days. It was frowned upon to make obvious the huge discrepancies between the wealth of those at the bottom and those at the top, although, of course, people still obsessed over celebrities and their lifestyles online.

'We have a tennis court booked,' said Richard, matter of factly, to the human attendant behind the desk.

'Of course, Mr Murphy,' said the smart and efficient-looking young man. 'Right this way please,' he said, leading them to the changing rooms. He left them at the door, saying, 'Is there anything else I can do for you?'

'Yes,' said Richard, as though he'd almost forgotten. 'When my daughter gets here, please show her to the veranda. I have a table booked for dinner but we'll probably be a bit late,' he said, looking at his vintage Rolex watch.

'Of course, Mr Murphy,' he said, and left them.

The thing that always struck Thomas about places like this was the smell. Everywhere you went, it smelt of lavender, or leather, or roses, or freshly cut grass. Each door you walked through meant a waft of wonderfully-scented greeting. The locker rooms smelt of grapefruit: crisp and fresh and clean.

They put down their bags and changed into their tennis clothes, Richard keeping up a continuous monologue about this and that, and Thomas listened with rigid attention, even though he made sure to keep his exterior casual and relaxed. Chitchat was important. Richard was talking about Iva and how she had a good-looking deputy, although he couldn't remember her name, as they walked out onto the tennis courts. 'Ha!' laughed Thomas, as they started warming up, hitting friendly balls back and forth across the perfectly white net. 'Her name's Mila,' he called, after producing a perfect, cross-court forehand.

'You know her?' he asked, returning into the net.

'You could say that,' said Thomas, starting another rally. 'She and Guy grew up together, and she was engaged to his brother when he died.'

'Christ,' said Richard, whistling through his teeth, 'that means I do know who she is...my daughter, Sabrina, went to school with her. Sabrina was invited to the wedding. Maybe I'll steer clear then.'

'I thought you had a wife?' asked Thomas, knowing full well that he did.

'Yes, but there's no harm in having a little fun from time to time,' replied Richard, with a wink. 'Now, are we going to sit around chatting like old women, or are we going to play some tennis?'

Thomas beat Richard two sets to one, and Richard only won the second set because Thomas let him. Thomas was younger, fitter, stronger, and had a will to win that not many could match. 'Good game,' said Richard, through gritted teeth, as they shook hands at the net. 'Next time I'll have you,' he said, although they both knew the chance would be a fine thing.

Thomas smiled. 'I'll look forward to seeing you try,' he joked.

Richard laughed, shaking his hand harder. 'There's that killer instinct,' said Richard, clapping Thomas on the back. 'That's why I hired you,' he laughed, pompously. They both knew this was a lie; the only reason Richard had hired Thomas was because Guy had called in a favour. But regardless, it had worked out to their mutual benefit, so far anyway.

'You'll stay for dinner, of course,' said Richard, clapping Thomas on the back again. 'You go and change while I say hello to my daughter. We're late, so I'll go and pretend to be sorry so we don't get too much of an earful. Then you can charm her while I get changed.' Thomas nodded, unable to find words to respond. It was one thing to talk as Richard did about everyone else, but to think so little of his own daughter? That crossed a line, even for Thomas.

'I'll be quick then,' he said, recovering his composure and heading to the showers.

* * * * *

Thomas luxuriated for as long as he thought he could get away with in the heavy torrent of water from the enormous showerhead in his cubicle. He used plenty of the expensive products before dressing in chinos and an open-necked shirt (would this eternal dress code ever change?), slicking back his wet hair, and heading for the restaurant's veranda.

'Ah,' said Richard, loudly, getting up from his chair. 'Sabrina, this is Thomas,' he said, clapping Thomas on the back again. 'As I said, darling, Thomas works for me, in the finance department.' Richard's petite daughter, who Thomas knew to be about the same age as himself, had green eyes, blonde hair and a 1920s-style headband. She was wearing a long green dress and was sitting back in her chair, as though being here were a great chore.

'I thought they'd all been replaced by artificial intelligence,' said Sabrina, her tone vacant and disinterested, as she looked Thomas up and down.

'Most of us have,' said Thomas, with an easy smile, reaching over and offering her his hand. She remained seated, but gripped it with a force he hadn't been expecting. 'They had to leave some of us behind to make strategic decisions, like when to implement upgraded robots,' he laughed. She didn't. Instead, her features remained steadfast as she carefully appraised him.

After her initial reception, and knowing that her father paid her and her opinion absolutely no mind whatsoever, Thomas resolved to behave in classic gentlemanly fashion. He was perfectly charming, but there was nothing warm in the way he interacted with her. He gave her staged, stock answers, building a polite, superficial wall between them so she wouldn't find out too much about him, nor really get to know him. In his mind, this was a one-time encounter, which he just had to get through, with as little drama as possible.

* * * * *

Thomas looked the part, spoke well, had an air of confidence about him like all the other people she socialised with, but there was something off-kilter that Sabrina couldn't quite put her finger on. Although he was good looking, she had to give him that much.

Sabrina was a party girl and always had been. Her main focus in life was to find a man to marry who was as wealthy as her father, and could therefore keep her in the lifestyle to which she had become accustomed. The rules about inheritance broke her heart; they were just so unfair. As such, her study of Thomas was more than just frivolous. If he was in the running to take over the company, and her father wouldn't be playing tennis with him otherwise, then maybe he would be a good one to bag. She resolved to be at least a little nice to him until she'd worked him out.

Richard returned, and they ate a lavish meal featuring real meat, from real cows, sheep and chickens, instead of the kind grown in labs, accompanied by expensive English wine, paired to match each course. They'd had the tasting menu; a delicious feast of beef carpaccio, chicken liver pate, sea bass, lamb cutlets and crème brulee, and Richard was just suggesting they order a cheese board when Sabrina put an end to the evening.

'Daddy, I've got places to be, I'm afraid. You were late for dinner, after all, and now I'm going to be late meeting Gabriel, so I really must go.'

'Gabriel?' spat Richard. 'Who is Gabriel?'

'A friend,' said Sabrina, maliciously, knowing nothing would wind up her father more than withholding information.

'Not Gabriel Smith?' asked Thomas, his eyes flashing with interest.

Sabrina raised an eyebrow. 'Maybe,' she replied, 'but then again, maybe not.'

'Oh, fine,' said Richard, getting up and kissing her on the cheek before heading to the restroom. 'Play your games,' he said, as he walked away.

'Gabriel's radical,' said Thomas, getting up to kiss Sabrina on the cheek too. 'He might just be using you to get to your father. You should really be careful.'

'My God,' said Sabrina, looking up at Thomas, her sky-high stilettos still leaving her a good head shorter than him, 'you're just like him.'

'Gabriel?'

'Daddy,' she said, picking up her clutch bag and wrap. She paused, studying him. 'You're the one Guy called in a favour for, aren't you?' The pleasing shock on Thomas' face confirmed it.

'You know Guy?' asked Thomas.

'We grew up together. Maybe Gabriel isn't the one we all need to be careful of,' she said, with contempt, before sauntering away.

* * * * *

The café was closed. It had been a long, busy day, and the owner, Fabio, was just closing the door to lock up when Guy walked up behind him. 'Fab,' he said, putting an arm around his shoulders. 'Any chance of a favour?' he asked, in his most imploring tone.

Fabio huffed. 'Guy,' he said, removing his hand from the locking sensor, 'if it were anyone else, I'd tell them to get lost; it's been a long day. But, seeing as it's you,' he said, pushing open the door, 'in you go.' Fabio stood back to let Guy past.

'But I'm not hanging around, I'm afraid,' he said, as he pushed some buttons on the locking sensor. 'Hand,' he said to Guy, indicating he should put his hand on the sensor, which would record both his hand print and the signature of the tiny chip beneath the skin of his palm. 'Just lock up when you leave. You know how the bots work if you want anything to eat or drink. Try not to trash the place.'

Fabio departed and Guy went upstairs, to the cosy seating area filled with a mismatched array of sofas and beaten-up old wooden tables and chairs. The café was small, its main purpose to offer lunchtime takeaways for the staff of the corporate headquarters situated all around. Fabio did a roaring trade in anything fried or sugary, and as a result, his cake selection was out of this world. The canteens in the office buildings had a mouth-watering array of delicious, free food, but it was always as healthy as could be. Sometimes the workers needed an indulgence.

The café was just around the corner from Guy's head office, and the offices of all the others he was meeting with tonight. He'd been coming here since his first week in the corporate world, and had hit it off with Fabio immediately. He helped himself to a slice of millionaire's shortbread, his favourite, got a robot to make him a coffee, and sat down to wait for the others.

They turned up shortly afterwards: Thomas, Benji, Melissa Clark, and Suzie Lee, each of them confused as to why they'd been called together at such short notice. Guy offered them refreshment, but they irritably refused.

'What's going on?' asked Melissa, exhibiting her usual, no-nonsense, get to the point approach, and still smarting at the way he'd spoken to her at the gallery.

'We're going to have to slip the timelines a bit,' said Guy. 'With the investigation, we can't get away with any work over the cap, which means the work that can take place on our project is limited.'

'But transport's in place,' said Suzie, this her area of expertise.

'And I'm sorry, but it's going to have to be rearranged,' Guy replied calmly.

'Do they know about the project?' asked Melissa.

'No,' said Guy. 'All they know is that there's something suspicious about the number of hours people in the Exeter factory were working. We stopped the extra hours at the other factories, so the raids on those didn't come up with anything.'

'What about the storage facility?' asked Suzie.

'They tried to get into it,' said Guy, 'but, given its top-secret location, they weren't granted access. However, I'm not taking any chances, so Benji's just completed a relocation of the robots. If and when Iva successfully gains access to the Plymouth facility, she won't find anything there.'

'Where are they now?' asked Thomas, chipping in for the first time.

'The less people who know that, the better,' said Guy evenly. 'You understand?'

'Of course,' replied Thomas. 'But you're sure they're safe?'

'As sure as I can be. And Benji's always very thorough.'

Benji inclined his head in a "well yes, obviously" sort of way.

'The upshot of all of this,' said Guy, 'is that we're going to have to delay the shipment.' Melissa and Suzie shook their heads in frustration. 'Unless anyone else can volunteer alternative facilities in which to make the robots?' he added, a little tetchiness creeping into his tone. 'Or shipping arrangements which don't use my company's credentials?'

'No,' said Melissa, reluctantly. 'How long do you think the delay will be?'

'The same length as the investigation,' he said. 'We might be able to make up a bit of time, but we were already pushing production to the max. And I don't want there to be any obviously suspicious activity straight after it's over, as all that will do is put me back in Iva's firing line and cause further delays.'

A sudden noise from downstairs made them all jump. The door banged open and multiple pairs of heavy footsteps thudded into the café. 'You're all under arrest,' said a short, stocky man dressed all in black, appearing at the top of the stairs. 'Please come with me,' he said, gesturing to where two more men waited.

Guy frowned. 'This is very dramatic,' he said, standing. 'We're in the middle of a catch-up. Could you tell me what this is about, please?'

'I'm not paid enough to know the details,' said the man, 'now please come with us.'

While Guy stalled, Benji put on his smart glasses and called their lawyer, Francesca Miller. Francesca was now watching, in close detail, every move they all made.

'Loudspeaker please, Benji,' she said, full of authority. Benji obliged.

'For what reason are you arresting these people?' asked Francesca, in her confident lawyer voice.

'As I said,' the man replied, going red in the face, 'my boss has all the details. She's downstairs.'

'Then I suggest you go and tell your boss, Iva Brooksbank, I assume, to come and speak with me. My clients will not be going anywhere with you, at the very least, until that has happened.'

The man turned and trudged back down the stairs, telling his men to stay behind. He returned a few minutes later, looking berated, with a furious Iva.

'Ah, Iva,' said Francesca, in her most condescending tone. 'Good to see you. Now, for what possible reason are you planning to make this arrest?'

'I don't have to disclose my reasons at this stage.'

'No. But if you're not planning to disclose, then show me your warrant.'

Iva bristled. 'These people are colluding,' she said, 'planning to create ways to allow people to work over the hours cap.'

'That is quite a claim,' said Francesca, apparently unworried. 'What proof do you have of these accusations?'

'That these five are together at all is suspicious, given their backgrounds campaigning for political change...'

'...freedom of speech and open democratic challenge are no longer allowed?' inquired Francesca, interrupting her.

'And we found people working over their allowed hours at one of Guy's factories.'

'We're in the process of providing you with the evidence to explain that,' said Francesca, 'so, unless you have something more substantial, I'm afraid you're going to have to leave my clients alone. If you don't, I'll be forced to sue you for harassment and abuse of power.'

Iva spun around and stormed out without another word, taking her goons with her.

* * * * *

Benji projected Francesca onto the wall when Iva was safely out of earshot. 'She never expected to be able to hold you for long,' said Francesca. 'She knew she didn't have anything legitimate, but was planning to put you in a cell and intimidate you, hoping one of you would break and rat on the others. It's worked for her before.'

'Well done, Benji,' said Guy. 'Quick thinking.'

'My forte,' joked Benji, feeling elated.

'She'll almost certainly keep tabs on all of you until this is over,' said Francesca, 'so don't go anywhere or do anything incriminating. The best thing you can do is lie low and go about your normal lives for the moment, and forget about any special projects. You can all thank your lucky stars we still have robust privacy laws in this country, but if she gets anything on any of you, you're all at risk of having your devices tapped. And not only that, she'll also be allowed to use tech to listen to your conversations wherever you go. If she'd had that power tonight, think about what she would have heard.'

'Okay,' said Melissa, taking a deep breath, 'we get it. Model citizens until this is over.'

'Like we always are, of course,' said Suzie with a grin.

* * * * *

Everyone left, apart from Benji and Guy, who helped themselves to whiskey from Fabio's secret stash in the kitchen.

'There must have been an informant,' said Guy, 'unless she's tailing me twenty-four-seven, and I don't think she is; my tech would have picked it up by now.'

'But who knew about the meeting?' asked Benji. 'Aside from the five of us here tonight, and Francesca. And they would've had to know about the overtime in Exeter as well.'

'Assuming there was an informant behind the raid in Exeter, and if so, that there's only one informant,' said Guy, worried. 'It would have been difficult to find out about the meeting tonight, but loads of people know about the overtime; some of them must be suspicious about the robots they make. Anyone who's labelled them up to go to a different location to all the others. Anyone who knows the software's different. Anyone who's overheard any of those people talking. Anyone whom Melissa or Suzie have had to bring on board to arrange delivery and distribution and authorisation. And if the tip-off came from one of Suzie or Melissa's people, or if Thomas has made a slip-up with the money, one of them could have been followed here tonight.'

'The net's wide then,' said Benji, taking a careful sip of his whiskey. 'Is there anyone with a grudge against you?'

'This list is long,' laughed Guy.

'Oh, come on,' said Benji, 'it can't be that long.'

'Plenty of people that work in the factories are resentful of my lifestyle, wealth, lack of working hours restrictions. A number of them have made their views public when I've visited. Then there are senior managers who think they deserve my job, and leaders of other companies who want to take me down to prove they're better than me, Richard for one. He's got a real bee in his bonnet about the success I've had at *my age*.'

'After everything Richard's just been through with Iva, I can't imagine him helping her.'

'Unless helping Iva bag other big names was one of the conditions for him to keep his company.'

'Maybe,' replied Benji, mulling it over, 'but it seems unlikely. Is there anyone who stands out? I get that the factory workers are generally disgruntled and want you to know it, but is there anyone particularly fervent?'

Guy thought about it. 'No one that springs to mind,' he eventually replied. 'But, given the first tip-off was about the Exeter factory, maybe it was someone there. I'll ask Thomas' parents to see if they've heard anything and you start putting feelers out, Benji. See what you can find.'

* * * * *

'You were supposed to make sure that didn't happen,' said Iva, furious, when they got outside. 'I wanted to at least get them as far as a prison cell for the night.'

Iva stormed down the street, stalking away from the three idiots who'd screwed up so profoundly. She couldn't bear the confines of a car right now, nor the tense silence that would poison the inside, the men throwing nervous glances between themselves as they tried to avoid her attention.

She was angry: angry with herself, angry with the men, angry with Guy fucking Strathclyde and his smug compatriots, but more than anything, angry that after all this time, the loss of him still drove her. She pushed her way into a swanky wine bar at the end of the street, one of the few where humans still did all the front-of-house work, placed her palm on the scanner by the door so it could read her chip, then made for the bar, where she ordered a large glass of red wine. The human employees made it expensive, not that she cared. She accepted her drink, for which she would be automatically charged, thanks to the scanner by the door and surveillance cameras hidden around the place. She took a mouthful, washing the ruby liquid around her mouth, savouring the harsh flavour, before swallowing hard, willing it to begin numbing her pain.

She sat in silence for minutes, nothing in her mind except pure, unadulterated rage. The barstool next to her scraped across the floor and someone sat themselves upon it, leaning into the smooth wood of the bar as they ordered a vodka and tonic in a voice she recognised. She didn't bother turning her head. 'What do you want?' she asked, taking another mouthful of wine.

'I came to see if you're okay,' said Rebecca Archer, the defence minister.

'Of course I am,' replied Iva, although her tone gave away she was anything but. 'Why wouldn't I be?'

'Because today would have been James' birthday. It makes me sad, nostalgic, so I can't begin to imagine how you feel.' Iva sat in silence, staring ahead, so Rebecca continued. 'I was having dinner with Francesca Miller when Benji's call came in. I heard some of it before she moved away from the table. I thought you might need a friend.'

'We're not friends,' said Iva. Her voice not cold, but matter of fact.

'We could be,' said Rebecca. 'We once were.'

'In a different world. Now you're a fully paid-up one of them.'

'One of who?' Rebecca shot back.

'Never mind,' said Iva, making to leave. 'They'll continue to break the rules regardless.'

'What rules?' asked Rebecca, a frown of annoyed confusion across her forehead, halting Iva as she made for the door.

'What I did today was reckless and unplanned, but I ordered it anyway, because I've lost the will to care. They took away my life, my whole life, and James' family took their blood money. You know I had enough evidence to bring them down back then, but his family said I'd be trampling across his memory if I pursued it. And like an idiot, I went along with what his parents wanted. James was probably turning in his grave, probably has been ever since. Well, enough is enough; someone has to pay.'

Iva stormed out, leaving behind a dark and dreadful silence.

CHAPTER 7

Lulu and T.J. grabbed a coffee from the robot in the kiosk at the corner of Regent's Park. It was a bright, warm day at the end of summer, the flowers still looking wonderful thanks to the robot gardeners, the park almost shining it was so clean, thanks to the street cleaning robots, and birdsong the predominant sound, thanks to the electric, automated cars going about their business all around them.

They wandered for a while, chatting and flirting outrageously, as they always did. They found a good bench from which they could survey a busy thoroughfare and sat watching the tourists ambling animatedly past. The tourists stopped here or there to take photos on their smart devices, some asking a passing robot, or using mini selfie drones to take photos of themselves. Lulu and T.J. often came to busy places, sitting and watching as the world went by. They would comment on the people, or discuss the news, or simply sit in happy, comfortable silence as they thought their own creative thoughts. They'd been walking with their arms linked, and had sat down the same way, their sides pressed together congenially, their proximity conducive to conspiratorial whispers. They were in high spirits today, and knew there would be a healthy, lively, in all probability unkind, commentary on the unsuspecting passers-by.

'That skirt's a bit short,' started T.J., surreptitiously indicating to the left with his head.

'And she's totally in love with him,' replied Lulu, as a group walked past.

'Which one?'

'The short one with dark hair.'

'Never,' said T.J., as though Lulu had lost her mind.

'What? It's obvious. Look at the way she's batting her eyelids.'

'That one loves him too,' replied T.J., nodding to a girl farther back in the group, who was carefully monitoring his interaction with the girl at the front.

'What do you think people say about us when they see us sitting here?' mused Lulu.

'What a good-looking couple,' he joked, arrogantly, 'with the look of creative genius about them,' he nudged Lulu, 'and an aura of fine business acumen,' he said, pressing a hand to his own chest.

Lulu laughed. 'Or, maybe they think: what a terribly mismatched pair. One dressed in a smart business suit, and the other dressed in old clothes covered in paint.'

T.J. leaned unexpectedly towards her. 'My version's better,' he whispered, before kissing her passionately on the lips. Lulu was stunned, but kissed him back; she was an artist, after all.

Eventually, when T.J. showed no signs of stopping, Lulu pushed him away. 'That was...unexpected,' she said, raising an eyebrow, 'and you're a surprisingly good kisser.'

'Why surprisingly?' laughed T.J., although his brow furrowed with uncertainty.

'I don't know,' she said. 'I suppose I just never really thought about it.'

'Hmmm,' he said, eyes disbelieving. 'After all the time we've spent together, you've never even thought about it?'

'Maybe right back at the beginning,' she said, cocking her head to one side as she gave it some thought. 'But not since you became my muse; that put you into a different category somehow.'

'What if I stopped being your muse?' he asked, his features serious and vulnerable.

'T.J., I don't think it would happen even then,' she said, kindly, squeezing his arm. 'And I think I've kind of got a boyfriend.'

'What?' said T.J., shocked. 'In all the time I've known you, you've never had anything even close to a boyfriend, only a never-ending string of one-night stands. Who is it?'

'Um...Guy Strathclyde.'

'What?' said T.J., reacting badly. 'He's a complete douche and stands for everything you hate.'

'Look, I know you're not that keen on him.'

'Understatement.'

'And I thought he'd be a total idiot too, but it turns out he's not. He has a lot in common with us, actually. He cares about the issues with our political system.'

'And yet he still sits at the top of his company, making a fortune while the rest of us...'

'...the rest of us?' exclaimed Lulu, shifting a little and unlinking their arms, so she could more easily look at his face. 'Neither of us has been a member of "the rest of us" for quite some time now. You have a high-flying corporate job, just like Guy, and I make more money from my art than I know what to do with. I probably earn more than Guy and you put together, when you take into account that artists don't have the same strict pay cap, and the fact that I can put pretty much every expense I have through my company.'

'Yes, but you don't come from privilege, he does.'

'So we should discount anyone who was born into money?' Lulu challenged. 'We should discriminate against them, despite the fact that they had no say over it?'

'So, what? Guy Strathclyde is a man of the people now?' spat T.J., full of hostility.

'Why are you acting like this? What's he ever done to you?'

T.J. leapt to his feet in frustration. 'I've got to go,' he said, marching off without so much as a backward glance.

Their robust conversation had attracted the attention of some of the tourists, so she got up and left too. The last thing she needed was for someone, or someone's smart device, to recognise her, and for this whole thing to become a social media circus.

* * * * *

Benji and Guy projected the breaking news onto the wall of Guy's office in Oxford.

'There have been reports from two locations of butlers acting strangely,' started the female news anchor. She was slim, had a blonde bob, and a face so full of makeup, it was remarkable she could still convince it to convey any expression at all. 'Late last night, two butler owners phoned the emergency services and reported that their robots were complaining of emotional neglect. The Cyber Response Team advised them to turn off their devices, which they both did, and they have since picked up the rogue butlers for further investigation. Investigations so far have not discovered any obvious faults.'

The feed switched to a pre-recorded video of one of the butler's owners, a middle-aged man with a northern accent. 'My butler is not neglected,' he said, shaking his head violently. 'We treat our Lenny – that's what we call him – better than anyone else I know. He has the *whole* night off, *every* night. He doesn't have to do any gardening, and there's only me and the wife here now our kids have grown up and moved out, so there's not even that much work for him to do.' The man was on a roll now. 'And I thought robots weren't supposed to have feelings. What if they're doing what we're all scared of? What if they're developing their own free will and taking over? What if they're learning from humans and are starting to become like us?'

The video ended and they cut back to the studio where the anchor was now interviewing an 'expert in artificial intelligence' called Percy Green. 'Percy,' she said, seriously, 'we were all given assurances that this could never happen.' She shook her head to add emphasis. 'And now it looks as though our worst fears are coming true.'

'Andrea,' he said, 'the most important thing now is to make sure that no one jumps to any dangerous conclusions. It is highly improbable that these robots are genuinely developing feelings, or developing free will. If we look at the science, as we must with anything robotic, this type of robot is really nothing more than a complex bundle of algorithms. Yes, they can "learn",' he said, putting quotation marks in the air with his hands, 'but that learning only happens within strict, predetermined parameters. The butlers may learn how to respond to their owner's emotions by recognising facial, speech, movement, and body language patterns. They may use these patterns to predict what their owner will do next and what their owner will want the robot to do next. But there is no code to start the butlers down the journey of developing their own emotional response in return.'

'Then how can you explain the fact that not one, but two butlers, have done exactly that?' asked Andrea, leaning forward in an 'I've got you on the ropes' kind of way.

'There are several possible explanations,' said Percy, calmly, 'and they all centre around the presence of code which is not supposed to be in the robots. Now, how this theoretical code got there, assuming my theory is correct, one can only guess. Possible scenarios may include developers adding rogue code for their own amusement, a hacker flexing his or her muscles, developers exploring the art of the possible, their exploration accidentally finding its way into a software update, or even a competitor brand trying to take down a rival. Although, that seems unlikely, given that casting doubt on one type of butlerbot will inevitably cast doubt on them all.'

'So you're not at all worried about this incident?' continued Andrea. 'What would you advise our viewers to do if they're concerned?'

'We need to find out what happened as quickly as possible. Hopefully, this incident has come from the manufacturer itself. If it hasn't, it means someone's found a way to hack into the butlers and alter their code. This would be a worrying scenario, given that the hacker could make a butler do pretty much anything they wanted. However, I must stress that this is one of the less likely scenarios, and we should all stay calm until we know the facts,' he said, giving Andrea a stern look. 'Sensationalising, causing panic, or speculating, will only lead to worry, misinformation, and, at worst, unwarranted hysteria.'

'But what should people do if they're concerned about their own devices?' repeated Andrea, clearly riled.

'If they're worried, then they should use the hard switch and turn their devices off. You can't get a butler to do anything at all if that switch is off. Then they should wait and see what the investigation turns up.'

Guy ended the projection and put his smart glasses back in his pocket. 'Just what we need,' he said. 'Are the software guys on it?'

'Yep,' replied Benji. 'They assure me no one's been putting code in for their own amusement and no one's working on any kind of project to give the butlers emotions. Unless we've got a rogue developer, it didn't come from inside our company.'

'Shit,' said Guy, pacing up and down. 'What about past members of staff?'

'We're looking into it,' said Benji, 'the head of software's on it. Have you spoken to the defence minister?'

'Not yet,' replied Guy, taking a deep breath. 'I'll do it now.'

CHAPTER 8

Lulu and Guy lay on a day bed next to the swimming pool at Guy's house, overlooking the ocean. They'd been for a swim and a sauna, and were now enjoying the soft summer breeze, the glass doors open. 'That view is magnificent,' said Lulu, leaning over to kiss Guy, who was reading a physical book, a *Lord of the Rings* first edition, no less.

'As is this book,' said Guy, indulgently.

'Did you inherit that?' she asked, taking it from him and carefully leafing through the pages. 'It must be worth a fortune.'

'Not as much as it used to be,' he replied, matter of factly. 'Given that inheritance is so limited, all possessions of any value over and above the one hundred thousand pound inheritance limit have to be handed over to the government. Consequently, the value of rare books, as well as other collectibles like jewellery and fine wines has decreased significantly. The market's constantly flooded with the stuff, as each collector dies and their children opt not to buy the items back at market value, although they have first refusal to do so.'

'I guess that makes sense; it's the same with art. Kind of sad that money's more important than sentimental things.'

'Yeah, I suppose. But the cold hard truth is that money can make people's lives better in a way that books can't. And there's still trade in all these things; plenty of people make enough money to indulge themselves. But more distractions compete for those people's time, the works come up more often, so are less rare, and, as people can't pass them on as part of their legacy, there's less interest in creating collections.'

'Hmm,' said Lulu, shrugging. 'In a way it's made things more accessible.'

'Yeah. Things are cheaper to buy, and museums have experienced a significant influx of donations. People would rather have their name next to a famous artwork on a wall in a museum, as thanks for the donation, as opposed to the government taking it when they die.'

Silence settled over them as Lulu looked out to sea again. 'It's a strange choice,' she murmured, leaning in to kiss him again.

'What is?' he replied, between kisses.

'*The Lord of the Rings*,' she said, as he pushed her back onto the bed and kissed her neck. She arched her back as a shiver of pleasure ran down her spine, her hand grasping his hair. 'It's so...depressing,' she said, giggling, as his fingers tickled the contour of her side, before tracing the shape of her hip bone.

'It's inspirational,' he replied, firmly. 'Whenever I'm in the midst of a crisis...'

'...like now,' she teased.

112

'Yes, thank you, like now,' he said, nipping her ear in retaliation. 'I find it calming to realise that my problems are nothing in comparison to what those hobbits faced, and if you just keep going and keep going, you have at least a small chance of coming out victorious. I heard a great speech once about how persistence is basically the only difference between successful and failure. I agree wholeheartedly.' He looked adoringly down at her, pushing a stray strand of hair back off her face.

'I agree too,' she said, 'mostly, at least.'

'Well, you're mostly right then,' he smiled, mischievously. 'Now,' he said, turning suddenly more business-like, 'there's something I wanted to ask you.'

'Oh?' said Lulu, sitting up in anticipation. 'Sounds serious. I'm all ears.'

'How would you feel about painting me a mural?'

Lulu laughed. 'That's your question? Don't you have enough of my work already?'

'It wouldn't be for here, for me,' he said, reaching down to pick up his gin and tonic from the floor and taking a sip, building suspense.

'For your office building?' she guessed.

'Yes,' he replied, disappointed she'd stolen his thunder. 'Everyone else seems to be doing it, so I want to get in on the act too,' he said, pulling his best pouty face.

'You want to keep up with the Joneses?'

'Oh please, I am the Joneses,' he said, doing a pretend hair flick.

'Never do that again,' she warned, giving him a playfully shove.

'But seriously, it's a brilliant opportunity to make a statement,' he said, getting up and pacing as he continued. 'And, as well as a physical mural, I want it to be available digitally too. Everyone who uses our virtual reality technology will have it as their login screen, and I'll set it as the background on the work terminals too. It'll be fun.'

'Are you sure?' she asked, sitting cross-legged on the bed and following him with her eyes as he moved. 'I mean, I'm happy to do it, but do you really want to draw more attention to yourself at the moment?'

'Why not? The investigation won't find anything,' he said, more confidently than he felt, 'and the butler issue will be fixed soon. Our engineers are on it, and they're the best in the world; they'll fix it. And you only live once,' he added, as an afterthought.

'Okay,' she said simply, shrugging her shoulders.

'You'll do it?' he asked, surprised.

'Of course.'

A playful look painted itself across Guy's face. 'Will you bump me up the list, ahead of the guy from St Andrews who wanted you to paint him a mural?' he asked, crouching in front of her and giving her his best puppy dog look.

'That would compromise my professional integrity,' she said, in a mock stern voice.

'Well, we wouldn't want that,' he said, sending her a bold look. 'So we'll have to think of some other way to spin it...'

'What's in it for me?' she flirted.

Guy smiled, a broad, happy smile, knowing he'd got his way. 'I'm sure we can find some way to make it worth your while,' he said, triumphantly, before kissing her excitedly on the lips.

* * * * *

Thomas took a long, deep breath. He went over the evidence on his smart glasses, using his eyes and thoughts to control the images they showed him. He'd

114

been through it four times already this morning, each time playing over in his mind what he would say and how he would act. Thomas tried to imagine how Richard would respond, what questions Richard would ask him, and had prepared a story he hoped would be convincing. He went over it with a fine-tooth comb, trying to spot if there were inconsistencies, making sure everything fitted together coherently, making sure it was compelling in both content and delivery. A nagging voice at the back of his mind told him he'd missed something, or that Marvin would be a step ahead of him, or that Richard would see through it. But that voice was his constant companion, and if there was one thing he'd learned, it was that it could not be relied upon. His gut, on the other hand, was wholly dependable, and it was telling him to march confidently into Richard's office, and get this shit done.

He pulled off his smart glasses, carefully folded them, and put them away in his jacket pocket. He slowly rolled back his chair, inhaling deeply as he stood. He pushed in his chair in the fastidious way that only an accountant could, and headed across the open plan floor to the lift.

'Thomas,' said Marvin, stopping him dead in his tracks, 'do you have a minute?'

Thomas turned and looked behind him, to where Marvin sat, rigid, as always, at the work station he'd just passed. 'I'm afraid not, Marvin. I can do later this afternoon though?'

'Your diary says you're free now,' said Marvin, insistently, 'and it is rather urgent.'

'I'm afraid Richard's just requested that I go up and meet him,' replied Thomas, his tone smug, but his face blank, unreadable.

'Oh?' said Marvin, surprised. 'I'll come with you then.'

'Ah, I wouldn't do that,' said Thomas, firmly. 'He's requested a meeting with me only, and you know how he is.'

'He said that specifically?' asked Marvin, not bothering to hide the edge of mistrust.

'He did,' replied Thomas, lying through his teeth. Thomas had requested the meeting with Richard, not the other way around. 'And I really need to get going, otherwise I'm going to be late.'

* * * * *

Marvin watched Thomas go, barely noticing as a robot approached and handed him a rare sheet of paper. 'Thank you,' said Marvin. Although he couldn't deny the advantages of technology, there was nothing like a large printed sheet, upon which you could annotate freely. Paper made him happy; it was real and tangible and sedate, and, importantly, couldn't be hacked. He had a large collection of diaries, notebooks and fine writing paper at home, and relished scratching away with a fountain pen whenever he had some free time.

Of course, one did not admit these things in a workplace such as this. One was encouraged to "bring one's whole self to work", but one most certainly only did that if that whole self matched the corporate ideal. Marvin presumed there were other workplaces where the cultures were more inclusive and open, as they all spouted they were. But, these days, technology companies had the most complex accounting landscape of any industry, and that was what he looked for in employment: a good old-fashioned intellectual challenge.

* * * * *

'Ah, Thomas,' said Richard. Richard's colossal and lavish office took up three sides of the penthouse level, and had a series of areas in which Richard hosted employees, clients, and shareholders. The area you were allotted indicated a combination of how far up the food chain you were and Richard's mood on any given day. Richard got up from behind his mahogany desk. *Not very 'tech CEO',* Thomas thought, as always, shaking Richard's hand. He was ushered to a plush, relaxed seating area with sofas set up like they were in the Oval Office, complete with coffee table in the middle.

'Can I get you a drink?' asked Richard, his butler stationary in a far corner, waiting to spring into action when called.

'No, thank you,' replied Thomas. 'Thank you for dinner the other evening,' he started, although, of course, he had already thanked Richard digitally. 'It was great to meet Sabrina,' he said with an easy smile. 'She's quite a character.'

'Christ,' laughed Richard, 'that's one way to put it. She's always been a bloody handful, that one. Wish she would just get a job; I think if she had more to occupy her time, it might straighten her out a bit. But she won't be told; stubborn as a mule. Anyway,' he said, giving Thomas a stern look, 'what's all this about then? It's been a while since someone refused to let me know the purpose of a meeting ahead of time.'

Thomas didn't miss the undertone: *this had better be good, at least if you ever want to play tennis with me again...* 'It's Marvin,' said Thomas, looking down as though this were all a little embarrassing, or maybe just to keep it from being too obvious that his heart was thundering in his ears.

'Oh?' said Richard, disappointed. 'Go on then. What is it?'

'Well, it's delicate,' said Thomas, apologetically.

'Do get to the point,' snapped Richard, although he leaned forward a little in his seat.

'I may as well just show you,' said Thomas, pulling out his smart glasses and projecting onto the nearest wall. 'As we know, Marvin is a little odd, and kind of stuck in the past. Aside from his fixation with the old world and all things paper-based, he's also been helping small companies get around their tax responsibilities. Apparently, he thinks it's unfair that small enterprises are taxed at all, given their social contribution, and so, has become an expert at helping them dodge it. He even does it for free, like some kind of hobby.'

'Is it illegal?' asked Richard.

'Yes, some of it,' said Thomas, showing Richard communications from Marvin to the CEO of a small creative agency.

'He sets out the options for the CEO here,' said Richard, making the messages scroll with his own smart glasses as he read, 'and tells him the legal implications of each option, but he doesn't advise the CEO to follow the route that breaks the law.' Richard was gearing up to dismiss the message, and probably Thomas, out of hand.

'Yes, in this one,' said Thomas, hurriedly pulling up another document: the creative agency's annual accounts. 'But here, he said, highlighting an area of the accounts, 'they've followed Marvin's dodgy advice, and here,' he said, scrolling to the bottom, 'he's signed off on them, certifying that they've been completed accurately. Of course, to get around the AI checks after submission, they've lied in a number of areas. Marvin's really very good at this; he's turned it into an art form.'

'This is illegal?' Richard asked again.

Thomas nodded. 'Yes, entirely illegal,' he replied, confidently.

'Jesus!' exclaimed Richard. 'I thought we were safe with someone like Marvin, at least in the realms of staying strictly within the law. I thought the biggest risk with him was being bored to death.' Richard laughed loudly. 'However, it would look like I was wrong on that front too. I should ask him to regale us with some tax-dodging close shaves; I'm sure he must have some good ones.'

Thomas nodded. 'He would have had to learn his craft. I mean, from an accounting standpoint, he's pretty much a genius, but I bet he's had some fascinating near misses.'

Richard went quiet while he mulled over the evidence. He took his time, the extended silence considered by him to be totally normal, but considered by Thomas to be nothing short of excruciating. This was one area of hanging out with senior managers he hadn't quite become accustomed to yet: being comfortable with long, thick, thinking silences. He shifted uncomfortably, then chastised himself, telling himself to sit still and pretend to be relaxed.

Richard eventually looked up. 'Where did you get this information?' he asked, a dark shadow behind his eyes.

Thomas had his answer ready. 'Someone printed it out and posted it through my door,' he said, shrugging, as though he were equally perplexed by the whole thing. 'I scanned the paper for fingerprints, but there weren't any. And there was no DNA left on the sheets, nothing to help indicate where it had come from.'

'They probably got a robot to do it,' said Richard, 'whoever they are.'

'I keep trying to imagine who would have motive to tell me about Marvin's activities, instead of just shopping him to the police. I can only think it might be someone he helped avoid tax, maybe someone who's now being investigated. They wouldn't be able to expose Marvin to the authorities without admitting their own guilt. Or maybe he made himself a corporate enemy. Either way, I thought it prudent to keep this quiet. With all the heat we've had on the company recently, I didn't think you'd want another scandal. Sorry for the secrecy.'

'Of course, I completely understand,' said Richard, waving his hand as though it were a trifle. 'The question is how to handle his departure. There's no way we can keep him now,' he continued, thinking out loud. 'You have checked this out, haven't you?' said Richard, turning sharp eyes onto Thomas, pinning him under his gaze, searching for any malicious intent, or untruth, or general shiftiness.

Thomas was ready for this too; Richard had been around a long time, had seen his fair share of takedowns, and Thomas had never bothered to hide his ambition. And it had been, after all, one of Richard's biggest competitors who'd convinced him to employ Thomas in the first place. This was the problem with having to place your friends and family in companies belonging to friends, rather than your own; you never knew who you could trust or where their true loyalties lay. But Thomas knew he was almost over the line, he just had to dig in for the final push.

'Yes,' said Thomas, pulling up a webpage with his glasses. 'Here you can see the accounts were filed with Companies House, and they match the documents sent to me. I can't substantiate the messages, as I don't have access to his personal server, but I did ask a close friend of mine to approach him as a prospective client.'

'And Marvin was willing to help them break the law,' said Richard, knowing how the story would end.

'Yes,' said Thomas, simply.

'And this friend,' said Richard, looking intently at Thomas, his face a careful mask.

'Yes?' said Thomas, when Richard paused.

'He or she would be willing to go on record to testify?'

Thomas stopped, considering his answer; he hadn't expected Richard to ask this. He wasn't usually so much of a detail person. He considered giving a vague answer, as, the truth was, Thomas wasn't sure he could get his friend to testify. But Thomas could smell blood, all it would take was confidence from him. 'Absolutely,' he replied, 'although I shouldn't have thought it'll come to that. Marvin's going to want to keep this quiet and that's in our interests too.'

'Fine,' said Richard, reassured. 'Decision made. Go and find Marvin and send him up please. I'll tell him that he's fired, effective immediately. Thank goodness for the relaxed labour laws now everyone's entitled to UBI; it wasn't so simple to get rid of someone back when I first started, let me tell you,' said Richard, reminiscing. 'You had to pay people off, or "manage them out," God-awful process that was. Went on for months, took up more time than it bears thinking about, and all the while, you had to carry someone useless in your team. Much better now, thank the Lord. Anyway,' said Richard, getting up from his sofa, a clear signal to Thomas that it was time to leave.

'Ah,' said Thomas, trying to slow down his exit enough to ask the only real question he was interested in the answer to.

Richard laughed. 'Christ. Cutthroat to the core,' he said, clapping Thomas on the back. 'I'll announce you as interim CFO when I make the announcement about Marvin stepping down.'

Thomas' mind was racing. 'Thank you,' he said, carefully. 'But maybe it would be best to hold off making the announcement about me until the dust has settled around Marvin?'

'Why on earth would that help anything?' said Richard, suddenly suspicious. 'What angle are you working?'

Thomas flushed, cursing the involuntary reddening of his face. 'I don't have an angle,' he replied, trying to keep his voice conversational, trying to suppress the rush of blood in his ears. 'I just thought it might be less of a surprise for the rest of the accounts team if my appointment was made after they'd got over the shock of Marvin leaving.'

'Your appointment is as *interim* CFO,' said Richard, firmly, emphasising the possible temporary nature of the role. 'Announcing it will add a layer of stability and reassurance, showing there will be continued financial leadership here, and showing strong leadership and planning from me. Not announcing it will leave a big gaping question mark over our finances. If you'd be more comfortable with me appointing someone else, I totally understand,' he added, in a warning tone. 'I know it's a big step up for you, especially as you've only just been made deputy finance director.'

Thomas took the threat graciously. 'Of course, you're right,' he said, 'it's better to make both announcements together. I'll go and ask Marvin to come up here straight away.'

'Good. That's settled then,' said Richard, the warning still in his voice, letting Thomas know that he'd be under scrutiny for a while. 'Anton,' he said, to his butlerbot, 'put everything in place to terminate Marvin's employment with us, effective immediately.'

'Yes, sir,' Anton replied, the work done mere moments after it was initiated.

'We have legal basis to do this, yes?' Richard asked.

'Yes, sir, absolutely,' said Anton. 'I've double checked the evidence, and found a number of similar examples in other accounts approved by Marvin. Everything is ready to go as soon as you say the word.'

'Good. Go and get him then,' said Richard, dismissing Thomas, his tone still harsh. 'And Anton,' said Richard, sitting down at his desk, exhaling wearily, 'compile a list of possible replacements. Marvin's only been here for two bloody minutes, so try and find someone who's likely to have longevity, for Christ's sake.'

'Yes, sir. Of course, sir,' said Anton.

Idiot, thought Thomas, leaving Richard's office as quickly as was dignified, although not sure whether the word was more appropriate in reference to himself or his boss. He breathed a big sigh of relief as he entered the lift, leaning heavily against the hand rail, feeling as though he'd just come out of a boxing ring. He relaxed as the adrenaline ebbed away, considering how he would deliver the unfortunate Marvin his marching orders, playing the scenario over in his mind. It was almost a shame, Thomas mused, to see Marvin go; Marvin could have taught him a few tricks, he was sure. And now he knew about Marvin's criminal alter ego, he'd finally developed some respect for the surprising little man.

* * * * *

The lift pinged, and Thomas wondered why that annoying noise had never been changed. He walked out onto the office floor and surveyed the scene. There were robots mixed in with people, some who had literally just taken the place of workers, although considerably less of them were needed to get through the same volume of work. And, of course, the robots

123

were all linked up with each other, and with remote servers elsewhere, where the bulk of the real work was done. The robots themselves were mainly for inputs and outputs, and to improve the workplace experience for human employees. Management had mostly opted to make the robots look as human as possible, and interact with their fellow workers in the traditional way, doing everything they could to make the office environment feel comfortable.

And then there were robots who had face-like screens as heads, projecting the faces of co-workers who were working remotely, making it feel like they were actually there in the office. These robots wandered around between desks, morphing into different personalities, taking on the voice, and perfectly mimicking the mannerisms of the person on the screen. Many had been caught out having conversations about a colleague, not realising that the robot standing over their shoulder was streaming their conversation directly to that colleague. People had learned to be cautious, and the office was a less vibrant place because of it.

This floor, which had, twenty years earlier, housed only one function, now housed all support functions at the company. Human Resources, Legal, Accounting, Marketing, IT, Facilities, all sat on this one floor, and even then, it was mostly just robots. The company had given the engineers, creatives, strategists, project managers, sales teams, and general managers as much space as they could use on the other floors, but, even so, and with the addition of a pool in the basement, and a gym on the first floor, they had had to lease out many floors' worth of spare space to other companies. Office buildings all across the country, which had once been buzzing hives of activity, were now full of robots, or being converted into housing, or community centres, or, in some cases, had simply had to be knocked down.

People had free rein to work from home, from a holiday destination, or from wherever they happened to be. No longer did they have to check in with a manager to make sure it was okay to work remotely, nor did they have to work set hours, nor schedule holiday around the needs of colleagues. People could virtually do as they pleased. Job shares were often utilised for people who wanted high-powered jobs but without having to work full time. Both men and women took advantage of this, and people were measured on their ability to get work done, contribute to the team effort, and be available when needed, as opposed to physical hours spent in the office.

Companies couldn't, however, get away from the fact that the human-dominated functions operated far more effectively when people were situated together. Engineering, for example, was dominated by people, although of course they used AI to help them. Most of the engineers needed to come into the office to use the state-of-the-art facilities, and they developed much stronger relationships with the rest of their team as a result. Even human-dominated teams, where most people worked remotely, had higher morale than teams where robots dominated. You had a higher chance of finding someone you liked in a bigger group of real people, and human interaction would forever be a major part of what made a job enjoyable. Of course, for all functions, big meetings and workshop sessions still took place, where everyone had to physically attend, but these sessions were few and far between.

Thomas, knowing that deep down, Richard harked back to the 'good old days' on pretty much every topic, knew that it was worth trekking into the office whenever possible. He still worked from home regularly, but tried to ensure it coincided with when Richard wasn't about. That was one of the mistakes people made these days; they forgot that 'out of sight' can easily mean 'out of mind,' and chance encounters with the executive team around the building played a bigger part in promotions than pretty much anything else. Sure, if you did a good job in a big presentation, or invented something ground-breaking, you would be in management's good books for a while, but nothing could replace banter in the lift, or a conversation about a shared sporting interest in the canteen. The face robots had gone some way to combat this, as had the objective analysis the robots completed at regular intervals on each person's personal performance, but nothing could replace basic human proximity and interaction.

Thomas breathed deeply as he walked across the floor. It was soulless and depressing and he longed to be somewhere else; there was nobody here he could relate to. He spotted Marvin and made a beeline for him, interested to see how he would react.

'Marvin,' said Thomas, as he reached Marvin's work station.

'Come to deliver the bad news?' asked Marvin, chirpily, taking the wind out of Thomas' sails.

'Sorry?' replied Thomas, not sure whether Marvin already knew the message he was about to deliver, or whether he was referring to some other bad news.

'You went to see Richard, all secretive, smug and superior, although you thought you were hiding it masterfully, and now, on your way back, you've come directly to see me, a look of triumphant celebration not quite hidden behind your well-rehearsed corporate veil.'

'Um,' said Thomas, wondering who this man was and where Marvin, the timid, naïve, easy-to-manipulate accountant had gone.

'I've been around for long enough to spot people like you,' Marvin continued, basking in Thomas'

126

surprise, 'and I know you're plotting your way into Richard's job. He's too self-obsessed to see it; he'll probably be surprised when you make your move on him.'

'I don't know what you're talking about,' said Thomas, weakly, trying to pull together some semblance of composure.

Marvin laughed. 'Of course you don't. You're just an innocent little do-gooder from accounts. But, a word of advice, from someone who's been around for a while: all that matters, as humans, is our relationships with others. That's what makes us healthy, happy, fulfilled. When you reach the summit, looking down on all the ants below you, who will be standing there with you to admire the view?' Marvin turned and started towards the lift. 'And remember,' he said, walking away, 'those you trod on whilst scaling to those heady heights, won't be there to catch you when you fall.'

CHAPTER 9

'Lulu,' said Guy, smiling broadly, 'let me introduce you to Tony, my grandfather,' he said, excitedly, as an old man approached their table.

'Uh, hi!' said Lulu, standing up to shake his hand. 'Grandfather?' This was not what she'd been expecting when Guy had told her there was someone he wanted her to meet.

They sat in the roof garden café of Guy's office building in Bristol, which housed a strange mix of the old and worn, alongside the shiny and new. Solar panels and greenhouses filled with hydroponics surrounded them, robots silently tending the plants, but the planters outside, full of herbs and flowers, were made from reclaimed railway sleepers. There were old wooden benches dotted around amongst long swaying grasses, and reclaimed industrial-style tables and chairs to sit at. The café had a series of secluded, cosy spaces and felt like a cottage garden, which made it Guy's favourite meeting venue in the building. He'd even been known to drag people out here when it was freezing cold and blowing a gale. He said getting out of their normal, comfortable environments and being exposed to the elements for a while would do them good; blow away the cobwebs and help them see things from a different perspective. Guy was always putting in walking meetings for the same reason.

The greenhouses met pretty much all of the fruit and vegetable requirements of the workers in the office, the produce used in the kitchens to make a sumptuous variety of free meals. Guy and Lulu were sipping coffees and eating raspberry muffins and Tony ordered the same.

Tony laughed. 'Yes, you heard right! You would have thought being this whippersnapper's grandfather would afford me a little more respect around here, but Guy doesn't believe in special treatment apparently.'

'It's a pleasure to meet you,' said Lulu, sitting forward in her seat, bursting with questions to ask him.

'I was just explaining the fundamentals of AI to one of the new recruits; the young'uns think they know everything because they're masters of their online games, or they've built some software for something or other. But, you know, often, when faced with a problem, they have a shocking and callous disregard, or maybe lack of knowledge, I suppose, of the basic principles. It's fundamental to understand what everything rests on, and to take problems back to those principles, otherwise the products end up botched, with patchy code and structural flaws.'

'Thank you, Tony, for the lesson in AI,' said Guy, teasingly.

'You, my boy,' said Tony – he had only recently taken to calling Guy and those around his age 'my boy', but he was quite taken with the expression – 'learned everything you know, from me. Not your father; he was a *businessman,*' the word came out with a great deal of contempt, 'and as such, thought I, a mere engineer, was ten-a-penny, but you,' he paused, shaking his head, 'you, paid attention to my base principles, and it got you and the company where you are today,' he said, waggling his finger.

Guy laughed. 'Indeed, the success of the entire company is down to you and you alone,' he said, warmly.

'Quite right,' said Tony, smiling mischievously, before taking a bite of his muffin. 'These things used to be delicious before they took out all the sugar. Now they're perfectly ordinary.'

'And diabetes has been reduced by twenty percent,' said Guy, bantering, 'who would have thought? You see it's all about base principles.' Tony waved his hand, as though diabetes were a trivial matter. Guy continued, changed the subject. 'How are this batch of trainees getting on? Anyone worth watching?'

Guy's company, along with every other large tech organisation, took on new employees straight from school and trained them up themselves. There were universities with AI and robotics departments, but most of them had become broadly irrelevant since company taxation had gone through the roof. Instead of managers taking home massive bonuses with the profits, as happened in the early part of the century, companies, now not allowed to pay anyone over two hundred and fifty thousand pounds a year, poured most of their profits back into Research and Development and training, for which there were massive tax breaks. This meant that the pace of innovation was significant, with pretty much unlimited money behind it. Companies such as Guy's recruited the brightest and best, setting hacking competitions and robotics competitions, recruiting people who had already done a significant amount of inventing for fun by the time they reached working age.

'One of the girls, Jenny, seems to have a bit of something about her,' said Tony, moving his head from side to side as though considering it. 'As usual, most of them aren't as good as they think they are.'

Having a bit of something about you was high praise indeed from Tony, so Guy nodded with satisfaction. 'How's the retirement village?' he joked.

'Splendid, as always, thank you,' he replied, then spotted Lulu's perplexed expression. 'I live in a village built especially for, ha-hum,' he said, clearing his throat, pretending to be uncomfortable, 'those over a certain age.' He raised an eyebrow. 'However, although it might sound sedate and humdrum, I can assure you it's a veritable hotbed of activity. Many still work, although usually on a consultancy basis, here and there, you know. Most of the people in my village aren't short of a penny or two, so they just do it to keep their minds going. Anyway, there are plenty of social events, and fitness classes, and food festivals, and plant growing, and sheds full of kit to tinker with. We've got virtual reality rooms and all the rest of it, but I think most of us are bored of all that now, preferring a more 'in person' kind of life.

'I have the perfect balance. I come here four days a week, and spend the rest of my time growing vegetables there, whilst trying to avoid my wife! I've heard from friends that not all of us oldies are quite so lucky. I think in some retirement villages they just sit around doing things online, complaining that their families are too busy to visit in person, or indeed, virtually, but people never blame themselves when that happens, do they?'

'I thought that people, *over a certain age*,' she said, in her most diplomatic voice, 'weren't allowed to work.'

'A lot aren't, like those whose careers were in capped areas. Of course, the cap didn't exist when they chose their lines of work, so it's all a bit unfair really. But those of us lucky enough to be in uncapped areas, like me, are still allowed to work, if we can find someone willing to employ us. People mostly tend to do advisory roles, contracting back to their old companies. It can be very helpful to have someone around who wrote the original code, or made original manufacturing decisions. We can add a huge amount of colour, supplementing the documented records, which, especially in the early days, were often sketchy at best. Now the robots do all the documenting for us, but a lot of what we do today has its roots in work from years ago.'

'How's my grandmother?' asked Guy, changing the subject to spare Lulu the lecture that would likely follow.

'Oh, that old battle axe? She's fine, I think. She lives next door,' Tony explained to Lulu, when she gave him another confused look. 'I see her often enough, but she's a journalist, so she's always on some rampage or other. Anyway, some of us have work to do,' he said, abruptly getting up and giving Guy a playful squeeze on the shoulder. 'Guy, don't work too hard,' he said, with a glint in his eye, 'and Lulu, it was an absolute pleasure to meet you,' he said, before leaving them to it.

'Bye,' Lulu called after him, 'lovely to meet you too.' Tony waved a hand in farewell. She waited until he was out of earshot before asking Guy how old he was.

'One hundred and one,' Guy replied, laughing. 'He lives in the plushest of retirement villages. My father paid for it before he died, and now I pay him a salary significant enough for him to be able to comfortably afford it himself, but all he wants to do is work! He says it makes him feel useful, and like he has a purpose, and like he's not so old that he's over the hill.'

'Did he work for your father?' asked Lulu, trying to fit it all together.

'No. Dad and Tony didn't really see eye to eye and they had a big falling out when I was young. Dad liked Tony to be reliant on him, and in his debt, so Tony kept well clear. He had his own engineering consultancy. It did fairly well, but it never set the world on fire. Tony wasn't very good at getting clients; he was far more interested in playing around in the lab instead.'

'Well, I suppose working until you pop your clogs is as good a strategy as any, and what's the average life expectancy now? A hundred and thirty or something? I can't imagine sitting around, for what used to be a literal lifetime, doing nothing. And he's so full of life.'

'He's pretty much bionic,' chuckled Guy, 'but he's certainly vibrant. He says people his age who don't do anything die the most quickly. Now we've managed to keep our bodies alive longer, he says that's the only reason people die. They give up living, or maybe they run out of things to live for.'

'What about the ones who go on the longest?' asked Lulu, wondering if they'd found the secret to eternal life.

'Tony thinks it's the ones with strong family ties or a supportive community. Generally, he says, it's the ones with a purpose that keep going the longest. They feel needed and wanted. They're often the ones who give their time the most freely, and selflessly, who would never consider that they "should" sit down for a rest, or they "should" take it easy at their great age.'

Lulu nodded. 'I saw a documentary about how isolation still has a huge impact on wellbeing. I can't believe there's no tech solution,' she said, teasingly.

Guy chuckled. 'We're actually conducting some research into it at the moment. We've worked out how we can use AI to make people feel included without having to do a thing themselves. Just having a butler in the house helps, although it's not the same as living with a human. But we're also experimenting with the butlers booking their owners into community activities and then taking them there at the right time.'

'I guess if people are scared of going somewhere alone, it would feel less daunting if their butler's with them,' mused Lulu.

'And we're experimenting with introducing people in similar, isolated situations ahead of larger social events. They interact in virtual reality rooms online, and then hopefully attend real world events together, so they'll have a real person to go with and won't feel so alone.'

'Eternal life here we all come,' said Lulu, sarcastically.

'Don't worry, we haven't cracked it yet. People have often become isolated for a reason. They can have difficult personalities...' he said, throwing a meaningful look at Lulu. She swiped him on the arm, '...or can be stubborn, or have a deep-seated fear. You can take a horse to water, but you can't make it drink, and we're also looking into genetic and learned behaviours which lead to isolation.'

'Although,' said Lulu, cynicism in her voice, 'you'd think that maybe solving poverty, or eradicating disease around the world would be more important than keeping people alive indefinitely.'

'I couldn't agree more,' said Guy, 'but I've got more money to put into research than I know what to do with, and it's an interesting topic that could help improve a great number of people's quality of life.'

'I'm not saying it's not interesting,' she replied, 'but it's truly a first-world problem.'

'It is,' he agreed, 'and it's wrong that that expression still applies, given the tech we have today.'

'Indeed,' she said, her features dark.

'Come on,' said Guy, 'I didn't just bring you here to introduce you to Tony. I've got something else I think we should take a look at.'

* * * * *

Guy and Lulu walked out of the front entrance together, Guy turning left, then stopping. 'Here it is,' he said, lifting his hands and spreading them wide, towards the side of the building.

'What?' said Lulu, a little surprised, 'for your mural?'

'Yes,' he beamed.

'Um, you can't be serious?'

'What do you mean? I'm deadly serious.'

'But it'll be huge, and extremely prominent, and this is where you guys make announcements to the world. Every time you say anything to the press, the mural will be in the background.'

'Exactly,' said Guy, beaming.

'Are you sure?'

'Yes, absolutely. It will be amazing.'

She shook her head in disbelief. 'Okay, if you're sure,' she said, knitting her eyebrows in concentration as she starting to take photos on her smart glasses. 'Dimensions and building drawings please,' she said, to her glasses.

'Dimensions determined,' they replied, 'but I can't find building drawings anywhere.'

135

'Guy,' she said, all business-like, 'I'll need drawings for the building.'

'Done,' he said, pulling out his own glasses and giving them instructions. 'Now, I know a brilliant walk that starts here and ends at a Turkish joint a couple of miles away. Thought we could chat about the mural on our way to lunch.'

Lulu smiled and took his arm. 'Lead the way.'

CHAPTER 10

Guy projected a recorded news report onto the wall, the room quieting when the sound started. 'There have been four more reports of butlers developing feelings,' said Andrea, the news anchor, 'with no statement from the technology minister, or her office. Here's Humphrey Dellers, our technology correspondent, with more.'

The report cut to Humphrey, who was in someone's living room, with a crowd of people. 'Thank you, Andrea. I'm here with Sydney Peters, the owner of one of the rogue butlers,' he said, indicating towards an aging, slight gentleman, 'Madeline Jones, a technology expert,' he said, pointing to a young, glamorous woman, 'and Sunflower Davies, who is the leader of a technology-free community in Suffolk,' he said, pointing towards a middle-aged woman with out-of-control, greying hair, wearing a floaty, sack-like shirt. 'Firstly, Sydney, tell us what happened to your butler.'

'Well,' he said, slowly, 'I was just getting through the door. I'd been out for a walk, you see, because my daughter keeps telling me I need to do more exercise. And Dilly-Dally, that's what I call my butler, was just standing there, with his head down, in the middle of the room, not moving. I spoke to him, asking him if he'd finished all the jobs, I mean, of course he would have done, he's a robot for goodness sake, he does things exactly the same way every day. But it was more just something to say, you know, to try and work out what was going on.'

'And what happened then?' prompted Humphrey, nodding sympathetically, trying to encourage Sydney to get a move on.

'To start with, he didn't do anything. So I asked him another question, something about the weather outside, and then he lifted his head up, looked at me, and told me he needed a break. I mean, I suppose he's been working every day since my daughter rented him for me; I never really thought about giving him a break. Should I have?' he asked, looking at Madeline, expectantly.

'No,' she said, a little awkwardly, 'robots don't have feelings, and don't need breaks.' She gave a slight shake of her head. She was doing a reasonable job of keeping herself in check, but just below her TV façade, Guy could see a beast was trying to escape, wanting to shout, 'You're an idiot. Butlers are just code and bits of synthetic material.'

'And what did Dilly-Dally do then?' asked Humphrey, looking genuinely concerned.

'Nothing,' said Sydney, 'he put his head down, closed his eyes, and hasn't done a thing since. I called the emergency services and they came to take him away. I think they said they would take him back to the Department of Technology, investigate, and get back to me when they found the problem. But that was three days ago, and I haven't heard a thing. And my apartment's getting pretty messy; what am I supposed to do without my butler? They haven't offered to give me a replacement in the meantime or anything.'

'Do you think the company who makes your butler should supply you with a courtesy robot whilst yours is investigated?' asked Humphrey, sniffing the start of something controversial.

'Well yes, don't you think so? But the company in question, Cybax Technologies, hasn't even been in touch with me.'

'Cybax Technologies, if you're watching,' said Humphrey, 'we would welcome a statement from you.'

'But aren't you concerned about the safety of the butlers?' asked Sunflower, unable to contain herself any longer. 'I mean, they're going rogue and developing feelings, it's exactly what we were all worried about back at the beginning.'

Madeline all but rolled her eyes. 'Yes, Sunflower, let's bring you in here,' said Humphrey, as though he were still in control of the interview. 'Tell us about your community and why you live the way you do.'

'I live with a large group of similarly minded people, in an old fishing village here in Suffolk. We are committed to living tech-free lives wherever possible, living lightly on the planet, and turning our backs on the consumerism that has sadly taken over our society.'

'But you still use some technology, is that right?' asked Humphrey.

'Yes. We use technology where it helps us to be more self-sufficient and sustainable, so, of course, we generate our own energy from renewables, we farm our own food, and use modern technology, where appropriate, to help with this.'

'But you believe that too much technology is a bad thing?' encouraged Humphrey.

'Well, yes. We work with nature wherever possible. We grow fruit and vegetables in line with their natural growing cycles, meaning that we eat seasonally, and mostly grow things that thrive in our climate. We only use hydroponics in moderation. We reuse and recycle pretty much everything, and we never use virtual reality rooms, butlers to clean up after us, or technology to mindlessly play games online. We try to lead more balanced, natural lives.'

'What would your message be to those of us who lead lives filled with technology?' asked Humphrey. 'I have to say I'm guilty of this too, Sunflower.' Humphrey laughed in a well-rehearsed manner.

'The most important part of our existence is our community,' said Sunflower. 'We help each other in every aspect of our lives, from raising our children, to producing our food, to helping people through illness and hard times. We try to minimise our use of technology, and instead, focus on what makes us human; relationships with others.'

'So what do you think about the reports of butlers acting strangely?' asked Humphrey.

'I think it was inevitable that this would happen eventually. Whether the butlers are learning to be human, or have been hacked, this technology is dangerous. Technology is fine, in a limited capacity, but bringing these things into our homes is like welcoming in a ticking time bomb.'

Madeline was shifting beside Sunflower, clearly itching to get involved. 'Madeline, as a technology expert, how would you respond to that?' asked Humphrey.

'Firstly, I would like to reiterate that these butlers have not done anything dangerous or harmful to anyone.' She paused briefly to emphasise the point. 'There are overrides in every butler to prevent any action that would harm a human, or an animal. There has never been an instance of any robot injuring a human. Yes, people have tripped over them or hit them and hurt their hand, but, even when attacked, butlers do not retaliate, they simply shut down.'

'So you don't think the robots pose any kind of threat?' asked Humphrey.

'I think that trying to use recent events as proof that butlers are dangerous, or like "ticking time bombs", is both inaccurate and unnecessarily inflammatory. Inciting panic is not helpful to anyone, and will not help us get to the bottom of this. Even Sunflower has said that her community both recognises the utility of AI and uses robots in their lives. Robots have transformed our lives for the better, it's as simple as that.'

'And what do you think is the most likely explanation for recent events, Madeline?'

'We don't currently understand what caused these glitches, but my money would be on code being accidentally deployed from inside Cybax Technologies. The best course of action is to stay calm, report any unusual activity immediately, and wait for the authorities and Cybax to do their job.'

'But do you think it's possible that the butlers are developing feelings?' asked Humphrey.

'No,' said Madeline, firmly. 'Butlers are made up of good old-fashioned code. They don't have feelings. If they did, through some kind of machine learning, develop feelings, we could reprogram them to remove the code responsible and instruct them not to develop 'feelings' in the future. People are forever getting confused between the development of artificial general intelligence, or robots which can genuinely think for themselves, and narrow AI, like butlers, who can only act within certain parameters. We are still decades away from creating something that can really think for itself, that has feelings, and that could theoretically be a danger to society. Whatever the current problem, there will be a rational explanation, and it will be fixable.'

'There you have it,' said Humphrey, smiling his end-of-segment smile, 'stay vigilant, but don't panic. Back to you in the studio, Andrea.'

Guy ended the projection. 'What do we know so far?' he asked, looking around the board table at the group of people, and robots with faces of people, who were joining from elsewhere. Benji had gathered the defence minister, technology minister, their close aides, representatives from the team investigating the unusual activity, two of Guy's engineers, and their respective public relations leads. PR was one of those areas which should be automated, but it was hard to teach a robot to tread the nuanced line between a spun truth and a lie, or that sometimes they shouldn't answer the question they'd been asked. Consequently, PR still employed a healthy number of humans, although a lot of the tracking and analysis was done on an automated basis, as was a great deal of story and opinion seeding.

The minister for technology, Tina, gave them a summary. 'It's been over a week since the first reported case,' she started, 'and my team have been trying to find the source of the "emotions" in the butlers' code. The problem is, so far, we haven't been able to find anything that looks remotely relevant. After the first couple of days, we realised we were going to need help from your team, so we reached out to your engineers.'

'Benji let me know,' said Guy. 'And? My understanding is that we couldn't find anything unusual either?'

One of Guy's engineers shook her head. 'No. We haven't been able to find anything out of the ordinary.

There are six butlers under investigation now, and we've tested them all. They seem to be fine.'

'Is it in dispute whether the butler owners are telling the truth?' asked the defence minister, Rebecca.

'No,' replied the engineer. 'All of the butlers' activity logs and video recordings are intact. They clearly show that the strange behaviour did take place.'

'So what are the options?' asked Rebecca.

A member of the investigating team spoke up. 'A prankster hacking into the butlers and altering the code for fun, before wiping out any evidence. Someone working alone, or in a small hacking group who's maliciously hacking into the butlers, testing the art of the possible. Or, hackers from another country, testing the water and trying to spread suspicion and fear.'

'This might sound like a stupid question,' said Rebecca, 'but we're sure the butlers aren't actually spontaneously developing feelings?'

She flushed at the ripple of snickering that washed around the table.

'I can't see how that would be possible,' said Guy, sending harsh looks at his people. 'If they were developing feelings, through some kind of machine learning, then there would be evidence of it in the code. Given that there isn't any, I think we can rule that option out. And,' he said, frowning, 'for the avoidance of doubt, no, the butlers are not becoming sentient. They're robots. They're made of simple code. That message needs to be clear and consistent from us all,' he said, sternly, looking around the room for agreement. The ministers nodded.

'So what's the most probable option at this point?' asked Tina.

'We have no idea,' said the lead investigator, 'but, whatever the cause, it means the butlers are vulnerable to attack, and when it becomes public knowledge that there's a known way in, it's going to attract a flock of hobby hackers trying to see if they can find it.'

'Okay,' said Guy, 'have we found out how they're getting in?'

'Not yet,' said the engineer, shaking her head.

'Is there anything else I can do to help?' asked Guy. 'More people? Anyone we can reach out to who used to work for us who might have an idea?'

'If there is anyone, we can compel them to help if needed, given that it's very much in the interests of national security,' added Rebecca.

'There are a couple of people who might be useful,' replied the engineer. 'I'll get you a list.'

Tina nodded. 'And if there's anything else you need, let the investigating team know, and I'll approve it. We need to contain this before it gets out of hand.'

'Which brings us to PR,' said Guy, everyone's heads swivelling to the end of the table where the PRs had congregated. 'How are we going to handle this?' He looked expectantly at his head of public relations, Michele Anderson.

Michele breathed in, taking a considered pause before responding. 'As I see it, the options are, one: tell everyone the truth and advise them to switch off their butlers until further notice – not ideal in terms of the inevitable fallout.

'Two: say we're all working together in a highly collaborative way, and that we're homing in on the problem. Everyone should continue as normal, as there's no evidence that there's any threat. Essentially this is a continuation of the communications strategy utilised by the Department of Technology to date, but we'd add confirmation of Cybax's involvement. People will accept this for a short time, but the press will continue to apply some heat and the grace period will only last for so long.

'Option three: we keep Cybax's involvement so far quiet. Tina's department issues a statement saying they can't find anything suspicious. The next step, according to protocol, is for Tina's department to reach out to Cybax and conduct a full-blown investigation, to see if we can jointly find the source of the problem. This buys us a bit more time, but would, in all likelihood, be spun to the detriment of both Cybax and Tina's department by the press.

'Obviously, this isn't great timing, given the investigation already underway by Iva's department.' Michele paused, thinking. 'And there's plenty of video footage, which has already gone viral, of six separate and seemingly unconnected incidents, so there's not much chance of trying to cast doubt on the whole thing. A fourth option would be to imply that we think some test code was accidently released as part of a software update. On the plus side, this may reassure people, because it takes focus away from the idea of an external attack. On the other hand, it would be difficult to explain why only six robots have been affected. Equally, if there were to be another incident, we'd look like fools and would be accused of lying.'

'What's your gut telling you?' asked Guy.

'Honestly, the threat doesn't seem big enough to justify telling everyone to turn off their butlers. It would cause hysteria, and I don't think that's warranted at the moment. So, we try and buy ourselves more time. I don't think another investigation is in anyone's interests, so we say we don't think that's necessary or required in this instance. We say we're collaboratively working on the problem and will report back when we know more. It's also the straightforward, honest truth, which means when Iva comes sniffing around, there'll be nothing for her to spin.'

'Fine,' said Guy. 'I don't see that we have much other option. Are you happy with that, Ministers?'

Tina and Rebecca nodded. 'As you say, I don't think there's anything else we can do,' said Rebecca. 'I think it's time to get GCHQ involved too. I'll inform them of the potential threat and see if they've got anyone who can come and work with us. God, can you imagine if this originates from Russia?'

'The stuff of nightmares,' said Guy, reflectively. 'Let's hope it's a disgruntled ex-employee, or a teenage hacker whom we can buy off by promising them a job.'

CHAPTER 11

Iva looked out of her office window in London, the view terrible, nothing like the offices of those they investigated. She watched as a delivery hive drove past, drones, like bees in reverse, picking up packages from the automated truck mothership and delivering to pre-designated points in people's homes and offices. It was a flurry of activity as perfectly coordinated drones came and went at lightning speed, carrying all manner of packages and letters as the truck rolled ceaselessly down the street.

Iva thought, wistfully, of the old Royal Mail, and the friendly postman who had come to her door every day when she'd been little. Her family had always given him a present at Christmas, and they'd had a little chat each day. All gone now. The drones were faster, cheaper, and never took sick days or holidays. Iva liked that her purchases were delivered the same day, but it was transactional and impersonal: the price one paid for hyper efficiency. The drones could say 'Good morning', and even make conversation when required, asking where the package should be delivered if it wasn't obvious, but it just wasn't the same.

She watched as a butler came out of a house and walked to the designated delivery point in someone's garden. The protective cover, which had opened when the drone delivered, and closed immediately afterwards, now automatically peeled back, the butler picking up the delivery and taking it inside. Iva thought of the new dress which would be hanging on her wardrobe door, ready for her to try on when she got home. She'd seen it in a shop window on her way to work and used her smart glasses to order it. All she'd had to do was put them on and think *buy*, and tech had done the rest. Her glasses had suggested the right size, and had even offered her the option of purchasing accessories from other stores to go with it. These had been selected based on a complex algorithm using, amongst other things, data from her past purchases, recent trends, and the store's recommendations.

If she decided she didn't like the dress, which her glasses had indicated would be unlikely, her butler would pack it up and send it back for her, and the money would be refunded back to her account without Iva having to lift a finger. *Consumerism at its height*, thought Iva, both loving and hating it. *He would have loved it.* She pulled out her smart glasses to look at an image of a man in his early twenties, leaning casually against an academic building.

Iva jumped as Mila tapped on her office door and walked in. 'Am I interrupting?' she asked.

'No, I was just contemplating the double-edged sword of our modern era,' she said wistfully, before walking to her desk and sitting down. 'How can I help?'

'We've analysed the data Benji submitted regarding the working hours discrepancy at the Exeter factory,' said Mila.

'And?' asked Iva, holding her breath, but knowing from Mila's body language it wasn't good news.

'We can't find anything out of the ordinary. The data's consistent with Guy's story and we have no evidence that anyone's been paid for work in excess of their annual hours allowance.'

'I bet if we were conducting this investigation in December, the story would be different,' said Iva, cursing that she hadn't waited just a little longer before launching her attack.

'Maybe,' said Mila, 'but this means we have nothing, and time is running out. I take it there's been no contact from your source?'

Iva shook her head. 'You would know about it if there had been,' she said, irritably.

'And was there any fallout from your attempted arrest of Guy and those he was meeting?' asked Mila. Iva scowled; how did she know about that?

'No. None of them put in an official complaint, but Francesca Miller, Guy's lawyer, was in contact to say if there's any more harassment of her client or his business associates, she'll file a lawsuit.'

'So what now?' asked Mila. 'Where do we go from here?'

'We step up the search for another mole. We interview everyone who works for Guy, both domestically and at Cybax. We look especially hard for any disgruntled current or ex-employees. We offer them anything they want to turn on him. We make it known that we're generous to both informants and their families, and make it clear that protecting the anonymity of our sources is of utmost importance to us.'

'Even though we'll most probably want them to testify?' asked Mila, with a concerned frown.

'We can cross that bridge if we manage to get to it. The most important thing is to find some dirt we can work with. We'll worry about the details later. And, in the meantime, we all have to hope that the original mole gets back in touch with something concrete.' Iva put her head down and began to read something on her computer. Mila exhaled loudly as she turned and left the room.

* * * * *

Gerry and Penny Watson, Thomas' parents, walked back into their small, Victorian, worker's terrace house in Exeter. It was pretty from the outside, the red bricks and climbing roses making it look cosy and cottagey in the sunshine. They entered, however, a dark and gloomy space, the curtains drawn and the smell of smoke hitting them like a slap across the face. Their two eldest sons lounged on the sofas, smart glasses on, playing some kind of starship commander game.

'There's one on your tail,' said Sam, urgently. 'Head for the asteroid field and I'll circle back to cover you.'

'Roger that,' said Ben, turning his head and presumably heading for the asteroid field.

Gerry and Penny looked at each other, rage building on each of their faces. Penny marched over to the curtains and threw them open, light streaming into the small and cramped space. She went first to Sam and then to Ben, ripping their smart glasses from their faces and throwing them across the room, onto an armchair. She picked up two of the empty beer cans that had been casually discarded on the floor and threw one at each of her lazy, good for nothing sons.

'Hey,' said Sam, angrily, standing up and moving towards his mother. 'We were in the middle of a game. We were about to beat the Andrews brothers and become the highest scoring pair in the universe. We've worked our butts off for this.'

'The highest scoring pair in the universe?' mocked Penny. 'Back in the real world, where it matters, you're about the lowest scoring pair I know. Look at you,' she said, indicating the mess strewn across the room. 'You're both grown men, lying about, crap everywhere, smoking weed, like grungy teenagers. Who do you expect to clean up this mess? Hey? Because it's not going to be me anymore. I've had enough of running around after you ungrateful, lazy scroungers.'

'Come on, mum,' said Ben, the more laidback of the two, sitting forward in his seat. 'What else are we supposed to do? There aren't any good jobs, and it's not like we need to work; UBI gives us enough money to live on.'

This was too much for Gerry. 'Aren't any good jobs?' he repeated, harshly. 'So the jobs we do, to keep this house going, to pay for you to sit around on the sofa, playing computer games like a pair of children, aren't good enough for you?'

'No,' said Sam, shrugging his shoulders as though this were obvious. 'We're clever. We're almost the best in the StarGaze universe. You get a lot of respect when you're in that position. We don't want to do menial work where we're at the beck and call of *robots*,' he said, emphasising the word as though it were disgusting.

'And anyway,' said Ben, 'we give you some of our UBI, so it's not like we don't pay our way.'

Penny laughed, a cruel, hard laugh, the kind that indicated something bad was coming. 'We can no longer work extra hours at the factory, so you're going to have to do more than just give us some of your UBI.

You're going to have to get *menial* jobs, and help us cover the debt repayments.'

'No,' said Sam, squaring up to his mother. 'As you said, we're adults. You can't make us do anything we don't want to. It's not our fault you decided to have a third child. It's not our fault you decided to try and give us everything, living beyond your means to do so. It's not our debt.' Sam was on a roll, clearly enjoying the sound of his own furious voice. 'We didn't make you do any of it, so it's not our responsibility to bail you out now you can't keep breaking the law to pay for it.'

'How dare you,' said Gerry, astounded. 'You're drunk and high; that can be the only explanation.'

'Why don't you ask your favourite child, Thomas, to pay for it? He's rich enough. He wouldn't even notice such a *paltry* amount,' said Ben, calmly, although with hatred in his eyes. 'And, if you think about it, it's all his fault anyway. If you hadn't had him, you wouldn't have had to cover all the costs for three children, with only the UBI meant for two.'

Gerry shook his head. 'For Christ's sake. Yes, we had three children, because we weren't willing to have an abortion. That made money tight, but we gave all of you everything we could. Only Thomas, though, was willing to get off his arse and work for something. He didn't complain about doing menial work. He worked hard. He looked for opportunities, and he took them. Why did you two turn out so differently?'

'You introduced Thomas to Guy, your idol,' said Ben. 'That's why he became successful, because you put your favourite son, and only your favourite son, I might add, in a position where he could do well.'

'And if you'd shown any interest, we would have done the same for you,' said Gerry, his face a bright shade of red. 'Instead, you've turned into jealous, indolent, bitter people, who do nothing but sit around in your parents' house, playing computer games.'

'And anyway,' said Penny, 'we might have asked for Thomas' help, but you know full well we're not on speaking terms at the moment.'

'Not our problem,' said Sam, his face a blank, impenetrable, heartless mask.

'Well then,' said Penny, fury taking hold, 'you are no longer our problem. I've had enough of supporting you. You're ungrateful, idle, and have never had to lift a finger to help anyone but yourselves. That's partly my fault, I know, so now you can take your UBI and go and look after yourselves.'

'What?' said Ben, the wind taken out of his sails. 'You can't do that. Where would we go?'

'Not my problem,' said his mother again. 'Hopefully this will shock you into taking some responsibility and thinking about people other than yourselves. Maybe this will make you understand all the things your father and I do for you that you take for granted. We've mollycoddled you for far too long, so now it's time to try something different. You can't even change a tire for goodness sake; it's embarrassing.'

'People don't change tires any longer,' said Ben, as though his mother were a moron. 'You ask a robot and they do it for you.'

'Exactly,' said Penny, 'you always think there's going to be someone else to do everything for you. Well, that stops today.'

'We know about your extra hours at the factory,' said Sam. 'We'll turn you in.'

'Get out of our house,' said Penny, shaking with rage. 'You're no longer welcome here, and if you so much as think about turning us in, you'll never be welcome again.'

* * * * *

Richard and Thomas sat in their autonomous car on the way to Bristol University. Bristol was known as a hub of both creativity and technology, and had been for decades. Richard had jumped on that bandwagon early, sponsoring the university when it had led the way in several fields of technological research. Unfortunately, these days, companies led the way, and Richard was yet to find an appropriate way to terminate his expensive relationship with the university. It was also an annoying drain on his time, as he had to turn up to this event and that opening, making it look like he gave a damn.

Universities had reverted to their original purpose, which, he thought, was a good thing. Those who attended focused on pure, hardcore academia: researching, developing and furthering knowledge in their areas of interest. Richard thought it was good that people studied English Literature, or History, or Philosophy, but it had little relevance to him or his company. Far fewer people attended, and the ludicrous practice of the early 2000s, where successive governments had perpetuated the insane idea that it was good to get as many people to university as possible, was thankfully over. All it had led to was massive debt, a chronic skills shortage, and unmet expectations. There had been too many graduates, most of whom had no real, distinguishing, desirable skills, and when they'd completed their three- or four-year romp through university life, and realised they still couldn't get a high-paying job at the end of it, they hadn't been very happy.

Companies had finally taken ownership of the problem, because they struggled to find employees with the skills they needed. They'd started their own training programmes, or part-funded industrywide training colleges, where students got hands-on experience of real-life problems, as well as being taught the actual, hard skills they needed.

Over time, people realised these programmes were the way to get a well-paid job, and they became hugely oversubscribed, especially as they often paid students to attend. Universities became less relevant, and everyone agreed it had been a bad move to try and use universities, which had never been intended as training grounds for employment, for that purpose.

It took the government a while to catch up, but they did eventually, and managed, after considerable lobbying from all angles, to entirely overhaul the primary and secondary education systems as well. Now, as much credence was given to artistic endeavour, creative pursuits and helping people find areas of real interest, as to maths, English, coding, critical thought, and leadership. Students were taught about financial management, online dangers, mental health, and the importance of community. They were told that they might not ever get a job, which was why it was important to find their passion, and use the financial freedom afforded under UBI to pursue it.

Of course, wealthy parents, dying for their children to get a job without a working hours cap, paid career consultants ludicrous sums of money to help find the route through which their child was most likely to be financially successful. Whether this was best for the child or not was irrelevant; they would thank their parents later (of this the parents had no doubt).

The most prestigious universities were, naturally, still doing a roaring trade. A degree from Oxbridge had never been in greater demand, especially as people had more time on their hands, and courses were free, paid for by the government. But, the degrees were in demand from people pursuing their genuine interests, and often later in life, once they'd managed to work out what their interests actually were. Many other universities had either closed down, turned into skills colleges, or partnered with companies to help deliver their internal training programmes.

Bristol was a prestigious enough university that it was still in high demand, and they still managed to churn out some good research every now and again, so it wasn't a bad thing to be associated with them. However, Richard planned to hand the running of the relationship over to Thomas; let him spend his time handing out prizes and cutting ribbons. Richard had a tennis forehand to work on.

'You haven't announced my appointment as interim finance director yet,' said Thomas, casually.

Thomas and Richard were facing each other in the car, on plush, cushioned seats. Richard always chose spacious town cars, with seats facing each other and a table which could be raised in the middle, or lowered down to become part of the floor. This meant he could work in comfort when he travelled, and it was a good, mobile meeting venue. It had a fridge, and compact tea and coffee maker too.

'No,' replied Richard, continuing to look out of the window at Bristol's impressive gorge.

'When do you plan to?' asked Thomas, watching Richard carefully.

'I'm not sure,' said Richard, still refusing to look Thomas in the eye. 'It depends on the applications I receive in the next few days for the replacement FD position.'

'Oh?' asked Thomas. 'How so?'

Richard finally turned to look at Thomas' face, meeting his eyes with a cold, dark stare. 'If I find someone good, who can start immediately, then there will be no need to appoint you as interim FD at all. It will allow for a smoother transition.'

'Will it?' asked Thomas, smiling lightly, clearly amused.

'What's so funny?' asked Richard, beginning to anger at Thomas' impertinence. He was nettled not only by his smug facial expression, but his body language was all wrong too. He was lounging back in his seat, legs crossed, arm out, as though he were talking to a peer in the country club, not trying to convince his boss to give him a promotion.

'It's probably for the best,' said Thomas, ignoring Richard's question.

'What is?' asked Richard, confusion taking hold of his features. 'You don't want to be FD?'

'Not any longer,' Thomas replied, cryptically, taking his time, clearly enjoying the upper hand.

'And why is that?' asked Richard, twitching with irritation.

'Because there's a bigger job I've got my sights on.'

'There is only one bigger job,' said Richard, his face turning red with rage. 'My job.'

'Yes,' said Thomas, calmly looking at Richard. 'And that's the job you're going to give me.'

* * * * *

Richard told the car to stop. He knew something significant was about to come out of Thomas' mouth, and he didn't want to be anywhere near the press that would be awaiting them at the university when it did.

Richard paused for a moment, taking a deep breath and getting a hold on his emotions. Thomas was clever, measured; there was no way he would act in this way unless he knew he had an ace. This was going to require careful attention, and for him to get himself under control. He'd seen this happen before, the transition from employee to rival, and underestimating your enemy was never a good idea; many a CEO had been toppled that way. His arrogance, which had thus far shaped his relationship with Thomas, had no place here.

'Okay,' said Richard, evenly, respectfully. 'What's this about?'

'You're finished,' said Thomas, 'of that, there can be no doubt.' Richard held his breath. 'All there is left to discuss is how we deal with the transition. We can do it amicably, or we can do it in a way that will be embarrassing for you.'

'But that embarrassing route might jeopardise your succession,' said Richard; he was not dead and buried yet. 'What have you got?' he asked, openly.

Thomas paused, drawing the silence out, Richard unused to being treated this way. 'You've been having multiple affairs, keeping multiple mistresses, and, what do you call them? Misters? Male mistresses? Either way,' said Thomas, 'it would be humiliating for you, and your family, if evidence of these affairs should come out.'

'Mortifying,' agreed Richard, 'but not necessarily terminal.'

'No,' agreed Thomas. 'But if anyone found out about the robots, or the virtual reality rooms you like to visit, it would be a different story.' Richard gasped. 'I know, I know,' said Thomas, as though he agreed it was desperately unfair, 'you thought you were there anonymously. The problem is, nothing's really anonymous any longer; there's always a way to be traced.'

'How do I know you have proof of any of this?' asked Richard, but he knew in his gut this final attempt to save himself was futile.

'Shall I show you some footage?' asked Thomas, enthusiastically reaching for his smart glasses, as though nothing would give him more pleasure.

'Show me,' said Richard, grimacing, but he'd be a fool if he didn't make sure Thomas had what he claimed.

'What would you like to see?' asked Thomas, glasses on, flicking through the files. 'Ah, here's a particularly depraved one; you're in a room full of underage girls,' said Thomas, projecting the image onto one of the empty car seats.

'They're computer simulations,' said Richard, weakly, 'and they're fifteen; practically of legal age.'

'Do you think the press would feel compelled to grant you any leeway based on that fact?' asked Thomas. 'Would you like me to show you more?' he asked, continuing to project as he flicked through the files.

Richard bowed his head in defeat. 'No. That won't be necessary. You've got it all planned out?' he asked. Thomas nodded. 'Tell me.'

'You'll announce your resignation and me as your successor. You'll tell the world this has been planned for a while. After the investigation by Iva, you decided the corporate world is no longer for you and you want to spend more time enjoying your life: playing tennis, spending time with your family, whatever. You will stay for three months to guarantee a smooth transfer of power, but, in reality, you'll be powerless from this moment on. I will call the shots, starting immediately. You will meet with the shareholders, reassuring them, talking up my appointment. You will do everything you can to make sure the company is not adversely affected by this transition.'

Richard nodded, slowly, taking in Thomas' demands. 'I would like a ceremonial role,' said Richard, requesting, not demanding, which was unusual for him. 'I've given my life to this company. I've built it into what it is today. Whatever you might think of me, or my methods, that's God's honest truth. And aside from the fact I don't want to cut all ties, it would look strange to the investors, journalists, anyone who knows me, if I did. People would start digging for the real reason why I, suddenly and without any real explanation, had departed my company. I'm known for my staying power, so the press would smell a story.' Richard paused to gauge Thomas' reaction, and Thomas nodded.

'I'm not asking for any power or authority,' Richard continued, 'but it would need to be a respected position, or it won't be credible. I'd suggest chairman,' he said, confidently but not insistently, before waiting for Thomas to make the next move. Richard had witnessed enough of these situations to know he wasn't entirely without power. He was a very public man, with a big personality, and plenty of influential friends. If Thomas exposed Richard, Richard would be sure to take Thomas down too, so it was important that all sides were happy enough.

'Okay, fine,' said Thomas, 'but it will be an entirely ceremonial role; cutting ribbons, attending charity events, that sort of thing. And, if you get too big for your boots, you'll find yourself suddenly deciding that you want to step down completely,' said Thomas, his eyes cold, Richard believing every word. 'I don't care if it looks suspicious.'

Richard nodded. 'Fine,' he said, resignedly.

'And I'll need a significant number of shares,' said Thomas.

'Yes,' said Richard. 'It would look suspicious otherwise. Anything else?'

'I don't think so,' said Thomas, 'but I'll let you know if that changes.'

'I just have one question,' said Richard, almost wistfully.

'Yes?'

'I went to great lengths to ensure my anonymity. Where did you get that footage?'

'You know I can't tell you that,' said Thomas, with an infuriating smile. 'Suffice it to say, it's unlikely that anyone else will find it.'

Thomas instructed the car to continue on its journey and they pulled up outside the university a few minutes later, the chancellor rushing forward to greet them. They climbed out of the car and he made a great fuss over Richard, virtually ignoring Thomas. They chatted for a few moments outside, smiling for the cameras, before the chancellor ushered them towards the door. 'After you,' said Thomas to the other two, smirking, as they reached the entrance.

'No,' said Richard, meeting Thomas' dangerous eyes. 'I insist. After you.'

The chancellor looked from Thomas to Richard and back again, then followed them through. 'Thomas,' he said, hastening after them to catch him up, 'tell me, what is it you do?'

CHAPTER 12

Guy took hold of Lulu's hand as they got out of his car, Lulu giving him an 'are you sure?' kind of look, Guy replying with a silent 'I'm game if you are'. They smiled at each other and Guy squeezed Lulu's hand as he led her towards the crowd.

They were visiting a community project that Guy sponsored. It was for people who had either retired, or who had never wanted, or been able, to get a job. The idea was that it was a physical, real-world centre, where people could gather, practice hobbies, and form meaningful relationships, and it had been a great success. They grew vegetables the old-fashioned way, with the younger members seeking growing tips from the old-timers, rather than instantly reaching for their smart glasses. They made things in the woodwork shed, they sewed, made hats, knitted, cooked, sang, painted, photographed, held book groups, hosted speakers; you name it, they did it, and it had managed to appeal to people across all ages and backgrounds.

They were hosting an open day today, to attract new members, show the world what they did, and raise money for some additional kitchen supplies, a few woodworking tools, and a new greenhouse. Guy had paid for and overseen the site's development, making sure it was fully kitted out and making it feel homely and as far from technology as it was possible to be. The community still benefitted from the odd butler here and there, but generally, the place was run by humans for humans, and to carry out very human activities.

The most powerful part of the project was the relationships people formed. It got those, who would otherwise be isolated, sitting at home watching television, or plugged into a virtual world, out into a community, giving them something meaningful with which to fill their time. Even if all they did was make a couple of cups of tea, chat with a member or two, and sit and read a book, being a part of something bigger than themselves was important. Having other people with whom to share the courgettes they'd personally grown, or hat they'd made, resulted in a sense of achievement and pride that they could never achieve at home, alone. This connection to other people was so powerful, that the health benefits were considerable. Why the UK ever thought the nuclear family was a good idea, Guy would never know.

Guy and Lulu entered the centre's garden, to be greeted by the happy sight of a large horseshoe of tables, covered with white tablecloths, and an array of craft projects and tasty treats atop them. There was all manner of things for sale: artwork, cakes, vegetables, books, bird boxes, mechanised clocks, and they were doing a roaring trade, the place packed with people. It reminded Lulu of a country village fete, in both setup and atmosphere, and she couldn't help but feel her spirits lift as she took in the bunting, hanging lights, bales of straw, and smell of barbeque. That was something they still hadn't cracked, thought Lulu, along with at-home dry cleaning: making the online world smell real.

Guy left Lulu admiring some artwork at one of the tables closest to the entrance, and took to the makeshift stage. It had been constructed by the woodworkers, and, although it looked rickety, he was pleased to find it sturdy underfoot. People crowded round, a hush falling over them as they waited expectantly.

Guy beamed. 'Hello,' he said, looking around at the crowd, taking in their faces. 'For those of you who don't know me, my name is Guy Strathclyde, and this project is extremely close to my heart. I am delighted to see so many people here today, and so many wonderful stalls filled with so many unique things. I'm particularly excited to sample Mrs Galby's millionaire's shortbread; I have it every year and can tell you it's the best I've ever tasted. Mrs Galby, you'll have a rush on now, so make sure you save me a slice!' The crowd laughed, and Guy waited for the noise to die down before continuing.

'When we first started this project, many thought it was a strange thing for someone like me to become involved with. Surely I want to see everyone sitting at home, communicating through technology – preferably my technology!' Another chuckle from the crowd. 'But, although I'm more than happy for people to buy the things we create at Cybax, it's my wish that the technology we sell also be used to enhance real relationships. I want it to free us up from the parts of life we don't want to be burdened with, so we can spend more time with other people, enjoying the parts of life we love. For me, and I know for many of you here today, community and real in-person relationships are those parts of life I love,' he said, flicking his eyes towards Lulu. She smiled, feeling her cheeks heat.

'So, it gives me great pleasure to announce that we're going to open another centre, just like this one, in York. That will bring the total number of centres to date, to five. And, I might add, there is strong and growing demand for places like this all over the country, so I don't anticipate York to be the last, not by a long chalk. And, should you wish to, you can also become a member of the centres' online community. It doesn't collect any data from users, there are absolutely no adverts, and nothing on there is available to anyone who's not a member. So, next time someone in York needs to make millionaire's shortbread to blow one's socks off, you'll be able to tell them Mrs Galby's the lady for the job.' Guy finished to raucous applause, grinning at the audience, the homebrew beer clearly going down a treat.

Guy came off the stage as the centre's choir shuffled on. The pianist began with gusto, and the choir started belting out 'All that Jazz' from the musical *Chicago*. Guy was full of energy as he approached Lulu, taking her hand again as the journalists pounced.

'Mr Strathclyde,' said a young woman with ginger curls, eying their hands with interest, 'could we take a photo for the article? Perhaps with Miss Banks?' She pushed them together and stepped back to take a photo on her smart glasses without waiting for an answer. Guy put an arm around Lulu and she looked up at him in surprise. He looked down and smiled, and she smiled back, neither of them noticing, or caring about, the pack of journalists capturing the moment. They'd be all over the internet in minutes.

* * * * *

Guy looked intently at the lady telling him about her travel agency business. She'd been a teacher, before the standardised AI programme had been brought in, and her job had been one of those made redundant.

She had subsequently travelled the world, using nothing but her UBI to pay for it, visiting all manner of places, and vlogging as she went. She'd garnered a decent following and people had started to approach her, asking her where they should go on their next trip, and she'd been happy to oblige.

As her following grew, she was given free virtual stays in top hotels and resorts across the world, but she found the whole thing sickening. They wanted her to promote their hotels, or attractions, based on nothing more than a virtual tour. She'd found it so impersonal and plastic, that she refused to talk about any of them, instead, only talking about places either she, or someone she knew, had personally visited.

'Of course,' she said, Guy nodding along, giving her his full attention, 'you still need to get someone to play the algorithms for you, you know, so you show up in searches and on social media sites, and in virtual reality rooms. Maybe the kids all know what to do, but we weren't taught that stuff when we were at school. You have to make sure you appear in the right place at the right time, or something like that, so I just produce the content, and I give it to my daughter to promote online. Not that I really care, I've never been one to care about money, or the number of people following me, I just do it because I love it, and it keeps me busy.'

* * * * *

Lulu had graduated to a stall selling artwork, munching on a decadent piece of chocolate rocky road as she meandered her way around the stands. 'I love your work,' she said, genuinely, to the man behind the table.

'Thanks,' he said cagily, causing Lulu to look up and see why.

'Where did you find the inspiration for this one?' she asked, pointing to an abstract seascape at the front of the table.

'Portsmouth,' he said monosyllabically, giving her a hostile look.

She was going to let it go and move onto another stall, but knew she'd forever be curious about his hostility if she didn't ask. 'I'm sorry,' she said, looking him directly in the eye. 'Have I done something to offend you?'

'Ha!' the man laughed, as though it were obvious what she'd done. 'You famous modern artists are all the same.'

'You don't like my work?' she asked, taken aback. 'That's why you don't like me?' *It wouldn't be the first time*, she thought, although she'd assumed it would be more inclusive here than that.

'That's a fabrication though, isn't it? To call it *your* work?'

Lulu's temper flared. 'What did you just say to me?'

'You know what I mean,' he shot back.

'I am entirely responsible for my own work and always have been. I would never take credit for something someone else created.'

'But it's fine to take credit for something a robot created on your behalf?' said the man, crossing his arms firmly in front of him. 'We, here, take time to hand-paint all of our work. We don't use AI to help us. We don't apply effects or instruct robots to paint this or that in our name.'

'And you think I do?' asked Lulu, shaking with pent-up fury.

'You all do,' he said, as though it were an indisputable fact. 'And you walk around taking all the credit for something some computer code created.'

'I have no idea why you think that,' said Lulu, 'but you should check your facts; it might prevent you from making false accusations. I have never, and have no intention of ever using robots in my work, at all. My studio is virtually a technology free zone. I paint everything by hand. I use projectors and rulers. Occasionally I use things I've printed from the internet; things like news articles that have been written by robots, or artwork that has been created by robots, and I incorporate them into my work. But, if you'd bothered to do any research on me before flinging accusations, you would know that I use these materials to help me comment on how meaningless I think stuff created entirely by computers is.' She turned her back and went to look for Guy, silently chastising herself for feeling the need to justify her methods to someone as ignorant as him.

* * * * *

Mila and Iva arrived at the community project. They were leaving no stone unturned in their quest to find a new mole; maybe there was a disgruntled member who could tell them something. And Iva wanted to rattle Guy, to show him she was still very much on his case. They walked around the crowded space, looking at the stands, Mila sampling some fudge, which incurred a frown from Iva. Not that she'd ever admit it, but Iva had a lot of respect for Guy, starting a project like this. She thought people needed to spend more time together, doing real things they enjoyed, and Guy had made it happen.

Iva watched as Guy spotted Mila, walking up to her and giving her a kiss on each cheek, her frosty reaction telling him this wasn't a social visit. 'Lovely to see you, Mila,' said Guy, happily, although keeping it business-like. 'How are you and Iva enjoying the day?'

'We only just arrived,' said Mila, officially, 'but it looks like it's been a great success. You've attracted quite a crowd.'

'It's a testament to the dedicated people who run the centre,' said Guy, matching her tone. 'They're the ones who make everything happen and they've done a brilliant job.'

'Guy,' said Iva, sauntering over to join them, holding out her hand to shake his. 'How lovely to see you again.' She held his hand for just a beat too long.

'Likewise,' said Guy, taking back his hand. 'If you'll excuse me though, I must go and retrieve my millionaire's shortbread.' He smiled with cold eyes.

* * * * *

Guy fumed. It was one thing for them to come after him in the corporate world, but they'd crossed a line coming here, trying to imply this project and all the work the members did was somehow tainted.

He was walking towards Mrs Galby's stand, when a commotion by the entrance caught his attention. A cluster of people was forming around something, and Guy went over to see what was going on, as did Iva and Mila. He worked his way through the crowd, reaching the front to see a butler, one of Cybax's butlers, sitting on the ground, legs bent up to its chest, rocking back and forth. Guy acted immediately, rushing forward to turn the robot off at its hard switch, then picking it up and carrying it towards the exit, Lulu joining him.

'You need to say something,' she whispered, 'otherwise it looks like you're trying to hide something, or cover something up.'

Guy nodded. He could practically feel the smart glasses of half the crowd already recording his actions. Some would be live-streaming to news channels already.

He took a deep breath and turned around. 'Sorry,' he joked, 'where are my manners? Leaving without saying goodbye! I'm going to take this butler straight back to Cybax HQ, where I'll request the investigating team from the Department of Technology join me. Unlike in the other cases of butlers acting strangely, I'm hopeful that I managed to turn this one off in time, meaning we'll be able to see what, in the code, caused this strange behaviour. I would urge anyone who experiences similar strange behaviour from a butler to immediately do the same.'

Guy was about to leave when an afterthought struck him. 'Nobody asked the butler to act in this way, did they?' He said it as though it would be a highly entertaining ruse if they had, but, of course, no one came forward.

* * * * *

Thomas' brothers, Sam and Ben, had left their parents' house a week before. They'd been convinced their parents would relent after a few days of cooling off, so had stayed with friends, sleeping on sofas. But, after a week of radio silence, they were starting to realise that maybe they'd misjudged the situation; maybe they were going to have to find somewhere else to live.

'We could just call them,' said Ben, as they flicked through apartments for rent on their smart glasses.

'These places are tiny, and will take up most of our spare UBI. I don't think we'll even be able to afford a butler.'

'We can't call them,' said Sam. 'We'd only be proving them right, showing that we can't look after ourselves, and we'd end up having to get jobs and give all the money we earn to them. If we're going to have to get jobs, better to keep the money ourselves.'

'What's the point, when we'll have to spend it on stuff that Mum and Dad normally pay for? It's not like we'll have any more disposable income. If anything, we'll have less,' said Ben.

'Look, you can crawl back to Mum and Dad if you want, but I'm not coming with you. Maybe it is time we moved out; it'll be good to have our own space.'

'If you say so,' said Ben, unconvinced, but, as ever, happy to go along with his brother. 'How about this one?' He showed Sam a two-bed apartment with a balcony overlooking the river.

'Done,' said Sam. 'I can't be bothered with any more searching. Phone the agent and tell them we'll take it.'

'At least it's furnished,' said Ben, 'but we'll need to buy bed linen and cutlery and that sort of stuff. How much money do you have in your account?'

'Nothing,' said Sam, shrugging. 'I spent it all on the horses.'

'Are you kidding? You're expecting me to cover the whole deposit and pay for everything else as well?'

'I can take out a loan,' said Sam, waving his hand in irritation.

'Are you serious? Haven't you learnt anything from Mum and Dad's situation?'

'They did it over a prolonged period of time,' said Sam. 'I only need some money to cover me until my next UBI payment comes in, and that's in a few days.'

'Fine,' said Ben, sulkily. 'Get the loan. I'll contact the agent.'

* * * * *

Ben and Sam walked into their new apartment, each with a couple of bags of clothes slung over their shoulders. They put the celebratory beer they'd bought in the kitchen, opened the small, under-counter fridge, and then reality set in.

'The fridge isn't working,' said Ben, frowning.

'Um,' said Sam. 'Where's a butler when you need one?'

'We haven't ordered it yet,' Ben replied.

'That's what we should do then. I'll order one now, and it'll be here by the time we've finished our first beer.'

'Okay,' said Ben, handing Sam a beer and sitting down on the sofa. 'There's no television,' he said, realising this had been an oversight.

'Just project something from your glasses,' said Sam.

'The quality won't be anywhere near as good, and it's hard to message people and project at the same time.'

'You'll have to do one or the other then,' laughed Sam.

Ben huffed. 'Turn the light on, would you. It's a bit dingy in here.'

Sam flicked the switch. 'Not working,' he said, flicking it back and forth a couple of times to prove the point.

'Have you ordered the butler?' asked Ben.

'Yes. But I'll see if I can find the circuit board. Maybe the electricity's off.'

'Okay,' said Ben, taking a gulp of his beer.

Sam rummaged around the flat, looking in every cupboard, which didn't take long, but found nothing. Eventually, he gave up and slumped on the sofa, taking a swig of his brother's beer. He put his head back, resting it on the sofa, and noticed some boxing above the front door. 'Ah ha,' he said, triumphantly, grabbing a chair and climbing up to take a look. 'Yep,' he gloated, 'found it. The electricity's off.' He flipped the switch to turn it on, and a voice spoke from the smart metre in the kitchen.

'UBI reference number, please,' it said. Sam jumped down, walked the few paces to the kitchen, picked up the smart metre, and told it his reference number. 'Please hold the scanner up to your face,' said the voice. Sam did as he was asked, holding the smart metre up so it could take a picture of his face. 'Thank you,' said the voice. 'You have been linked to this address for gas and electricity. Is there anyone you would like to add, to share the bill?'

'Yes, definitely,' said Sam, taking the smart metre over to his brother and thrusting it at him. 'There you go, Ben.'

Ben reluctantly took the device and gave it his details. 'Thank you,' said the metre, and Ben threw it down.

'I'd forgotten about energy costs,' said Ben, worried. 'We're really not going to have much money. We might have to cut down on some of our game subscriptions.'

'Don't be ridiculous,' said Sam. 'We need those subscriptions. What would we do with our time otherwise?'

'Or maybe the streaming services,' said Ben. 'We have a lot of those, and we don't even have a television.'

'We'll have to buy one, then,' said Sam, his tone becoming hostile. 'We'll find a way to make it work.'

Ben took a deep breath. He picked up his glasses and started searching for a job, just as the doorbell rang. 'That'll be the butler,' said Sam, happily, running for the door.

'We can't afford it,' said Ben. 'We have to send it back.'

'Don't be ridiculous,' said Sam, harshly, 'who doesn't have a butler?'

'Well, I'm not paying for it,' said Ben. 'If you want it, you'll have to pay for it yourself.'

'Fine,' said Sam, letting the butler in. 'But you can't use it to do anything for you. You'll have to do your own washing up, your washing, your ironing, your cleaning, tidying, parcel retrieval. All of it, you'll have to do yourself.'

'Yes, I will,' said Ben, flicking through his online subscriptions and cancelling a few. Once he had a job, he wouldn't have time for all of them anyway.

CHAPTER 13

T.J. lounged on a sofa in Lulu's studio. The space was cavernous; it used to be a church, and had a massive window at one end, taking up practically the whole wall. At some stage it had been converted from stained to clear glass, with a view out across the harsh Devon moorland.

Lulu handed T.J. a gin and tonic. 'To you and your miraculous rise to the top,' she said, holding up her own drink and clinking his glass before slumping down next to him.

'Why thank you,' he replied, taking a sip, then leaning his head back on the sofa and looking up at the ornate ceiling. 'I can't quite believe it. It's what I've been working for, for so long.'

'And that's why you deserve it,' said Lulu. 'Hard work and persistence pay off every time.'

T.J. smiled. 'With the help of a bit of luck.'

'A bit of that never hurts,' she agreed, thinking about her own luck, which had given her the life she now lived.

'We've both done the impossible,' said T.J. 'Scaled to the top of the tree from the dirt at the bottom.'

'The improbable,' Lulu corrected, giving him a 'get it right' kind of look.

'The improbable,' he agreed, with a conciliatory smile.

'How are your brothers?' she asked, changing the subject. 'I heard on the factory grapevine that your parents kicked them out?'

'I don't know,' said T.J. 'As you know, I don't speak to any of them any longer, although Ben sent me a message telling me that Mum and Dad are in financial trouble.'

'What?' she said, shocked. 'Why? They always seemed so responsible and sensible.'

'They had three kids,' he said, shrugging. 'They borrowed money to pay for stuff. They use pretty much all of their income just living, or at least they did when my brothers lived at home, and they've been working illegal extra hours for years to pay off the debt. That's why we fell out, actually, because I didn't agree with them breaking the law. If people found out, it would reflect badly on all of us.'

'What?' said Lulu, not believing this was his primary concern, and reeling at the information he'd just given her. 'They work illegal hours at the factory? Guy's factory?'

T.J. laughed. 'Yeah. Loads of them do. They've been doing it for years. I thought you knew. Maybe that could provide good fodder for a new painting,' he said, amused with himself.

'I'd heard rumours, but I never thought your parents would be involved. What do they do in the extra hours?'

'Oh, I don't know. This and that. They produce extra robots,' he said, halting abruptly when he realised what he'd just said.

'What is it?' asked Lulu.

'Nothing,' said T.J. 'I just realised something. Nothing important.'

'Are you going to pay off their debt?' asked Lulu. 'It's not like it's from gambling or lavish holidays, and you directly benefitted from it.'

'I didn't ask them to put themselves in that position,' said T.J., bristling.

'But even so, it can't be that much, especially if they've been paying it off for years. You could help them. Do it anonymously if you don't want them to know.'

'No,' said T.J. 'I don't want to help them. I think it's around a hundred thousand and I don't have that kind of money to just throw away.'

Lulu raised her eyebrows, not believing the words coming out of T.J.'s mouth. 'Helping your parents would be throwing money away?' she asked.

'Would you do it for your parents?' he threw back, eyes flashing viciously.

'That's totally different, and you know it,' she snapped, getting up off the sofa, and moving away.

'Okay, okay, I'm sorry,' said T.J., 'I'll think about giving some money to my parents. Happy now?' he said, indicating that she should sit back down.

'Fine,' said Lulu, taking a large swig of her drink and telling herself to let it go.

'How's the boyfriend?' asked T.J., changing the subject as she sat down.

'The one you hate?' asked Lulu, sceptically.

'Yes, that one,' he said, amused.

'Fine thanks. Great, actually,' she said, pausing for a second. 'Why don't you like him anyway? I bumped into your parents the other day and they said he helped start your career.'

T.J. shook his head, as though she wouldn't understand. 'Best not to start down that route,' he said. 'No good can come of it. I shouldn't have brought him up. But, Jesus, since when has there been so much stuff we can't talk about? It's never been like this.'

'I know,' said Lulu. 'Let's just draw a line under it all and get back to the way things were.'

'Fine by me,' said T.J. 'Come on, let's hug it out.'

Lulu laughed and rolled her eyes, but scooched over and gave him a hug. He left his arm around her and she rested her head on him, enjoying his familiar warmth. She grabbed a cushion and put it in his lap, laying her head down on it, like they had a hundred times before. T.J. smiled, stroking her hair. For a while, it felt like maybe it could be as it always had been, like they could be best friends and confidants, like what had happened the other day in the park hadn't happened. But, of course, it had.

Lulu sat up, suddenly awkward.

'What is it?' said T.J., taking hold of her hand.

Lulu pulled it away and moved to the other side of the sofa. She took a deep breath. 'We can't do this anymore,' she said, her tone resolute.

'We can't be friends?' he asked, laughing, although Lulu could see he knew what she meant.

'Don't,' said Lulu. 'You kissed me the other day. I don't want to give you the impression that anything's going to happen between us, and lying on the sofa like this kind of gives that impression.'

'Lulu,' he said, 'don't do this. We've been friends forever. Don't let him come between us.'

'It's not Guy,' said Lulu, gently. 'It's you and me. We're not the same people we used to be. We've been growing apart for ages; you know it as well as I do.'

'What do you want me to do?' he pleaded. 'I'll do anything, whatever you want. I can't not have you in my life...I love you.'

'And I love you too,' said Lulu, 'but only as a friend. And I will only ever love you as a friend. But if I met you now, I'm not sure we'd even become friends. Your parents need you and you won't help them.' She was starting to get agitated.

'Is that what this is about?' he asked, aghast. 'I'll transfer the money to my parents now.' He pulled out his smart glasses.

'I thought you "didn't have that kind of money",' she said, angrily. 'You've just proven my point. The T.J. I knew growing up would have helped his parents because he wanted to. And the only reason you're saying you'll do it now is because you want to appease me.'

T.J. didn't respond. There was no way to refute her accusations. 'But you're the one I want with me at the top of the mountain,' he eventually said, head in his hands.

'What?' exhaled Lulu. 'You're not making any sense.'

'Lulu, I need you. You're the only one I've ever cared about.'

'Maybe some time without me will encourage you to connect with other people then. I think you should go.'

'Lulu...'

'There's nothing you can say,' she said, walking in the direction of the door.

He followed her, picking up his coat. 'Okay,' he said, 'but maybe once you've had a chance to cool off, we could talk.'

'No. And don't call me,' she said, opening the door to find Guy coming up the steps on the other side.

'Thomas?' said Guy, shocked. 'How do you two know each other? Wait. Is Thomas your muse?'

'He *was* my muse,' said Lulu, firmly.

'Sell-out,' hissed Thomas, sneering at Guy as he stormed past.

Lulu ushered Guy in and closed the door, sinking down to the floor, her back pressed against the wood, her body shaking.

'God, Lulu,' said Guy, rushing to her side. 'What's going on?'

Lulu shook her head, still shaking. 'T.J. isn't who he used to be. I've known it for ages, but he seemed harmless enough. Then he kissed me the other day, and I knew I'd have to put an end to it. And then he came here today, telling me he'd just been made CEO of his company, all smug and arrogant, and I realised I didn't even recognise him any longer. Then he told me about his parents: they work in your factory, and they can't cover their debt repayments because their extra hours have been ended, presumably because of the investigation. And he said he wouldn't help them out, like they meant nothing to him. They gave him everything. Did you ever meet them? Penny and Gerry? They're lovely; they'd do anything for anyone.'

Guy hung his head. 'Come on,' he said, 'let's get you somewhere more comfortable.'

He helped her up and led her to the sofa, settling her there. 'I'm making tea,' he said, 'seeing as you don't seem to have a butler to ask.'

'No butler in here,' she said. 'Almost tech-free zone, remember?'

Guy rummaged around in the kitchen and made two mugs of tea, heaping a spoonful of sugar into Lulu's and stirring it well. 'Here you go,' he said, handing her a mug and sitting down at the other end of the sofa. 'I had no idea you even knew Thomas.'

'Everyone used to call him T.J. growing up. It was only when he started in the corporate world that he changed it to Thomas.'

'I've known his parents for years,' said Guy. 'I managed the factory in Exeter for a while, when I was working my way up, and got to know them and Thomas then. Gerry and Penny have always been too kind for their own good, but I didn't realise they were in that much debt, not any longer at least. They asked me to help Thomas at the start of his career, and I asked Richard to give him a job. Richard looked over his profile and decided to do it; not illegal, but borderline. Thomas started in the finance department and has been working his way up there ever since.'

'It seems he's managed to work his way right to the top now,' said Lulu, cynically, taking a sip of her tea.

'Yeah. That is strange,' said Guy. 'Richard would never just give up his business.'

'He told me not to tell anyone,' Lulu replied. 'Said they were still working out the details of the transition.'

'Thomas must have something on Richard,' said Guy, 'and they don't want the world to know, so they're going to try and make it look as above-board as they can. Happens a lot.'

'Shady commercial world,' said Lulu, scathingly.

Guy shrugged. 'I guess so.' He took a sip of his tea. 'I gave Gerry and Penny extra hours because I found out about the debt they were in. And it fitted well,' he said, slowly, 'because I needed trustworthy, hardworking people to help me with an off-the-books project. They've been working extra hours for me for

181

years; I didn't realise cancelling the hours would affect them so badly, not that I had any other choice.'

'Because of the investigation?' asked Lulu. Guy nodded, darkly. 'What's the side project?' she said, quietly, not sure if she wanted to know the answer.

Guy took a long, slow breath, standing up and walking around. 'I will tell you,' he said, 'but I can't yet. I really hope you believe me when I say it's not something for profit or personal gain. It's charitable. But, in order to protect the other people involved, I have to wait until our latest project is complete. I promise I'll tell you everything then.'

'And when will that be?' she asked, her tone edgy.

'It was supposed to be done already, but because of Iva's investigation, we've had to delay. We're going to wait until it's over, which shouldn't be much longer. She hasn't got anything on me, so she's only got another few days before legally she has to stop.'

'But if she knew about this side project?' asked Lulu.

'I'd be finished,' he said, without hesitation, 'and probably put in jail.' Lulu raised her eyebrows. 'But I promise, unless I've totally misjudged you, you would approve.'

'I think you should go,' said Lulu, shaking her head in disbelief. 'Twice in one day. It never rains, but it pours.'

'Lulu,' said Guy, begging with his eyes.

She shook her head. 'If and when this whole thing is over, and you can be honest with me about it, then maybe we can start seeing each other again. But until then, I'm not interested. I don't want to be in a relationship with secrets. If you don't trust me enough to tell me what's really going on, then maybe we shouldn't be together after all.'

Thomas was furious. Guy had done it again. He was always there, one step ahead, stealing his thunder, ruining his dreams. He'd had enough; Lulu was his and he wasn't going to sit back and let Guy have her. He pulled out his smart glasses and thought, *call Mila*. A few moments later, the call connected.

'Thomas?' said Mila, surprised.

'Where are you?' he asked.

'In London. Why?'

'And Iva? Where's she?'

'Here too,' said Mila, hesitantly. 'Thomas, what's going on?'

'I need to talk to you both, but it should be in person. I'm in Devon. I'll jump on the hyperloop and will be with you in a couple of hours, max. Tell Iva it's important.'

'Thomas,' said Mila, hesitantly. 'I know you and Guy have a turbulent relationship, and Guy doesn't seem to realise there are issues between you, which must be frustrating, but are you sure you want to do this?'

'I think you need to work out where your loyalties lie,' snapped Thomas, knowing she would do whatever her job demanded, no matter what.

'It's not my loyalties I'm concerned about,' said Mila, hotly. 'See you when you get here.' She terminated the call.

Iva was waiting for Thomas in the lobby, tapping her foot nervously as the minutes ticked by. She knew he could get cold feet; he was a high-profile informant and it had happened to her before. She would need him on the record, and willing to testify, and he'd had plenty of time to cool off on the journey up. She started pacing, hating the waiting, running through every scenario in her mind. What if it had nothing to do with Guy? What if it was all a big ruse? What if he had nothing significant? She was almost out of time, and she needed something big. What would he want in return for the information? She'd been around long enough to see it all; nothing could surprise her any more.

Thomas walked quickly into the building. He looked around and headed for the reception desk, Iva intercepting him before he could make it there.

'Mr Watson,' she said, warmly, knowing the best way to get someone like Thomas to cooperate was to treat him with respect, to act as though the king had come to inspect the department. 'So kind of you to come. Do come right this way. I've got a pass waiting for you.'

Thomas smiled. 'Thank you,' he said, as she held the security door open for him. They got in the lift and Iva handed him the pass.

'Just fingerprint it please,' she said, in a way that was more than a request, but not quite an order, like it was a simple formality over which he had no choice. He did it without even thinking. Iva noticed the twitch of Thomas' mouth as he realised he'd made a mistake. If he changed his mind and wanted to back out, it would be harder now; Iva could prove he had been in the building, and she had the recording of his phone call with Mila too.

'Let me get you a drink,' said Iva, as she led Thomas into her office and gestured towards one of the comfortable looking chairs.

'No, thank you,' said Thomas, keen to get to it.

Iva sat in the other chair, strategically placed at an angle to both ensure they could talk comfortably and to make Iva seem open and non-threatening. 'What can I do for you, Mr Watson?' she asked sweetly, happy to oblige his unspoken request to get a move on.

'I want to tell you about Guy's illicit activities,' said Thomas, evenly.

Iva tried not to show any reaction, but the corners of her lips twitched up and a light came to her eyes. 'Please,' she said, sitting forward in her chair, 'go ahead.'

* * * * *

Thomas looked around for any signs of Mila. He knew she would be here somewhere, watching and listening to his account in a room close by. He wondered how she would react to what he was about to say. *I'll probably marry her now*, he thought, absently; Lulu would never forgive him for what he was about to do.

That gave him pause, more than anything else had. Would Lulu ever forgive him if he didn't do this? Should he wait and see? *Too late now*, he thought, knowing deep down they could never go back to the way things were anyway; Guy had ruined everything.

'Where to start,' said Thomas, cruelly. 'Guy's been paying people for illegal extra hours, my parents included, since he took over his company. He lavishes unlawful perks on every employee, only getting away with it because he gives them to everyone and not just those at the top. He's been hiding money, siphoning it out of the company for years, which I've helped him do – I'll obviously need my part to be overlooked if you want me to testify to any of this...' He said the last part as though it were a minor point.

'I'm sure we can make that happen,' said Iva, reassuringly.

Thomas nodded. 'He's been helping the Defence Department wage cyber warfare on other countries, using his robots to illegally gather intelligence, and he's been spying on other departments too. How do you think I got into your system to message you?' He smiled at the lie. He'd actually stolen Mila's computer when she was in the shower. Like an idiot, she'd left it open and logged in, and he'd managed to get to it just in time before the automatic lockout kicked in. He hadn't found another time to send more tip-offs, as she'd been more careful since his first break-in. He wondered if she suspected him, but she'd never given any indication that she knew.

'That was you too?' asked Iva. 'Using Guy's tech?'

'Yes,' said Thomas, only just considering that he might have to prove these lies later down the line. 'I don't have access to the tech now though,' he added, quickly, 'as Guy moved his secret facility after your raid in Exeter, and he won't tell anyone where he moved it to.' Thomas breathed an inward sigh of relief as Iva seemed to accept this.

'Go on,' she said, now openly eager.

'As I was saying, he was helping the Defence Department defend against Russian attacks, but they decided to turn the same tech inward, and spy on other government departments.' Thomas wasn't actually sure that Guy was doing this, but Guy and Rebecca, the defence minister, were always so cosy, that he was sure something was going on. At the very least, it would send Iva off on a bigger chase after Guy's investigation was over, meaning hopefully she would leave him well alone.

'Why's he been doing all of this?' said Iva. 'Extra hours, siphoning off money?'

'He's been investing in other countries,' said Thomas, pausing for a few moments to let the gravity of his words sink in. 'He thinks it's unfair that other economies have been devastated by the tech revolution and economies like ours haven't done anything about it. He sees the sparks of competition kindling in Eastern Europe, and he's doing everything he can to help them. They're already allowed to buy our tech, so they can reverse-engineer it to a certain extent, but Guy's also loaning engineers, giving them money, and founding his own companies. He thinks increased international competition will lead to positive changes in our quality of life. He says he wants to combat some of the shadows from the light of technology, and thinks the way to start this is to help more people benefit from it.'

'You're accusing him of breaking international trade agreements?' said Iva, almost open mouthed.

Thomas nearly laughed at her expression. He managed to keep himself under control, settling for a self-satisfied smile instead. 'Yes, I am,' he replied. 'But far worse than sharing knowledge across borders, he's also been committing treason by distributing tech in rural Africa. He says he can't bear that people still die of disease and famine, and can't accept that, given the tech we have today, people still don't have access to clean drinking water, or knowledge about contraception, or access to education. He's been dropping worker drones and water drones for years. That's what the extra hours go towards, and what the money pays for, and why he's so nice to his employees, to try and keep everyone happy so no one informs on him.'

'Well, it's worked,' said Iva. 'We couldn't find a single lowly factory worker willing to say a bad word about him; totally unheard of.'

'Because he keeps them sweet,' said Thomas. 'And socially, they'd be ostracising themselves. A lot of those people rely on the extra hours; they've got used to living beyond their means, and Guy provides them with a way to pay for it. If someone informed and everyone else found out, their life wouldn't be worth living.'

'Wow,' said Iva, taking it all in. 'Guy is giving tech to Africa?'

'Yes,' said Thomas. 'Which, in case you're not up to date with international trade agreements, is off limits because China "owns" most of Africa.'

'I know, I know,' said Iva impatiently, 'they've been paying significant sums to African dictators for decades to gain access to their metal mines. The dictators take the money and build themselves palaces, while the people still don't have water, or real roads, or reliable food supplies.'

'And Guy thinks it's morally abhorrent that British tech aid is limited because of a commercial worry that China could get hold of the robots and reverse engineer them,' said Thomas.

'You can't blame the government for worrying,' Iva shot back. 'If China found a way to do it, they'd undercut the UK and once again become the manufacturing centre of the world.'

'Come on,' said Thomas, not able to contain his contempt for the idea. 'The government's paranoid, and it's hurting the economy. We're not allowed to sell anything to anyone who might possibly, maybe, one day resell to China. And the devices all have GPS trackers, which make them shut down if they enter prohibited territories, and there's a self-destruct mechanism if the tech's tampered with in any way. It's comprehensive stuff.'

'How did Guy get the robots to Africa without them shutting down?' asked Iva.

'He disabled the GPS mechanisms. The anti-tamper precautions remain intact, but he's still committing treason.'

Treason,' repeated Iva, triumphantly.

* * * * *

Mila left work late that night, having listened to Thomas' full interview and then gone through it in excruciating detail with Iva afterwards. Iva had managed to convince Thomas to go on the record, so long as he received full immunity, and so long as his part in helping Guy hide money was omitted from the investigation. Thomas had given a full statement, altering some of his allegations about the Defence Department spying on other departments, she noted. As soon as Thomas had signed his statement and was safely out of the building, Iva had called the whole team together to plan their attack.

'We've got enough to bring him down,' said Iva, visibly high on the thrill of her investigation's new circumstances. 'Thomas has given me financial records which clearly show what's been going on. We know which facilities offer extra hours, although Thomas won't give us the identity of specific individuals within those facilities, apart from his parents, oddly, not that I'm going to give him the satisfaction of going after them. Small fry and family feuds I have no interest in.

'We know who was helping Guy to export robots illegally,' she went on gleefully, 'but what we don't have is the robots themselves. Now, this isn't required, we have enough, but it would be the icing on the cake, and it would give us much better press coverage. Picture the footage of our raid on an illegal facility,' she said, caught up in her own imagination. 'So much better than a boring old trail of money.'

Mila felt sick as she helped plot Guy's demise. The only good thing about Iva's greed was that at least there was some time for Mila to warn him. She hadn't been planning to help him; she'd convinced herself that she would follow the rules and do her job. But when she'd heard what Guy had been doing and why, she couldn't help but support him. The department was meant to catch bad guys: people breaking the rules to further their own aims, people who were greedy and selfish. It wasn't meant to prosecute people who were breaking the law to try and bring an end to famine and disease. And she agreed with Guy; it was ludicrous that poverty was allowed to exist when they could easily erase if for good, if only everyone worked together.

So, when she left work, instead of sacking off drinks with her childhood friend, Sabrina, and her crowd of socialites, as she usually would have, Mila met them at a swanky bar in Mayfair. She ordered herself a Bramble, then cornered Sabrina.

'Mila!' said a tipsy Sabrina. 'You came! I didn't think you would!'

'Hey, Sab,' Mila replied, inwardly rolling her eyes; she was not in the mood for drunken exuberance. 'I need to ask for a favour.' She knew this would come back and bite her eventually, but carried on anyway.

'Of course,' said Sabrina.

'I need you to go and see Guy, in person, and tell him that he's finished. Thomas came to work earlier and informed on him.'

'That guy who works for Daddy?' asked Sabrina, snapping out of her carefree performance, showing the razor focus that Mila had always thought was wasted on life as a socialite. Mila nodded. 'I met him at The Club,' she said. 'Found him detestable from the moment I first saw him.'

'Really?' asked Mila, wondering how her own judgement had been so off.

'Really,' she replied, firmly. 'And judging by something Daddy said yesterday, I think Thomas has found a way to oust him too.'

190

'He has,' Mila confirmed, thinking back to Thomas' bargain with Iva, where he'd told her about his new appointment and made her promise to leave him alone. Iva had agreed without hesitation. She'd replied that she and Thomas were the same. They'd worked their way up from nothing, and they deserved their positions; she was only interested in prosecuting the real bad guys. Mila had baulked at that. She'd been privy to Iva's outrageous discrimination with regard to the cases she pursued, but she'd never actually heard her say the words out loud.

'Christ,' said Sabrina. 'I'll do whatever you want. Poor Guy doesn't have a bad bone in his body. All he's ever wanted since we were kids was to make the world a better place.'

'I know,' said Mila, 'which is why I'm putting my career on the line to warn him about what's coming.'

'Okay,' said Sabrina, 'I'll go now. What specifically should I say?'

'Tell him Thomas has informed on him. Tell him Iva knows about Africa and Eastern Europe. The only reason she hasn't already sent someone to arrest him is because she's trying to find the robots.'

'Cryptic,' said Sabrina flippantly, immediately shaking her head in apology as Mila sent her a dark look. 'Okay, sorry. Thomas informed. Africa, Eastern Europe. She's trying to find the robots.'

'He needs to leave immediately, if he doesn't want to go to jail.'

'Christ,' said Sabrina again. 'Poor Guy.'

'I know,' said Mila. 'Go, now. We don't have any time to lose. He's in Devon with the artist.'

'Okay. Don't worry, I'll be there by midnight.'

'Thanks, Sabrina. Here's her address,' she said, handing Sabrina a rare piece of paper. 'I owe you one.'

'Don't be ridiculous,' she replied. 'This is what friends are for.'

* * * * *

Sabrina got into her autonomous car and it took her to the hyperloop. It submerged into the ground and she felt the familiar jolt as they sped off into the darkness. They emerged at Exeter, her car immediately heading for Dartmoor, to Lulu's old converted church. Dartmoor was bleak and barren, and Sabrina had never understood why people chose to live here. The moors could boast none of the vibrancy and convenience of the city, no glamorous people to sit and watch and take clothing clothing-related inspiration from. She imagined numerous groups of tourists, rambling about the place, marvelling at the unspoilt expanse of scrubland, but walking-chic wasn't really her style. She looked out of the window as she raced towards her destination. The stars were more beautiful here, she would admit that much.

She arrived at the church and jumped out of her car, banging on the door, which, weirdly, didn't seem to have any kind of digital bell or entry system. She banged and banged and eventually the door opened, a bleary-eyed Lulu peering out at her.

'I need to see Guy,' said Sabrina, getting straight to it.

'Who are you?' asked Lulu, taken aback by the socialite clad in skimpy dress and heels, smelling of cocktails and expensive perfume, on her doorstep in the middle of the night.

'That doesn't matter,' she said. 'I really need to speak to him. He's in trouble. Is he here?'

'He's not here,' she replied. 'I kicked him out earlier.'

'You kicked him out? Guy? The biggest catch this country has to offer?' Sabrina couldn't imagine a move so ludicrous; Guy was everything she dreamed of.

Lulu gave her an incredulous look. 'Yes. He deserved it,' she said.

'Do you know where he is?'

'No.'

'Can you call him? Ask him to come back here?'

'Why don't you just call him?' asked Lulu, confused.

'It would be traceable,' she said, 'and difficult to explain.'

'Whereas all the cameras that caught you coming down here? They're, what? Not able to trace your journey?'

'They are,' she replied, 'but they're not able to hear my voice, or, for the most part, see my face. All they can prove is that I came to Dartmoor in the middle of the night, to see my good friends Guy and Lulu.'

Lulu huffed. 'Fine. I'll message him.'

'A call would be better,' said Sabrina. 'Just don't say anything about me, and don't sound distressed. Just say he needs to come back because you want to talk, or something.'

Lulu picked up her smart glasses and instructed them to call Guy.

'Lulu?' said Guy, picking up immediately and sounding surprised.

'Hey,' she said awkwardly. 'Listen, can you come back tonight? I think we should talk.'

'Uh,' said Guy, 'of course, I'll come back now. I'm in Exeter, so I'll be there soon. Is everything alright?'

'I'm fine,' she said. 'See you soon.'

* * * * *

193

Guy knew something strange was going on when he saw the high-end car outside Lulu's house. He rushed to the door and hammered the knocker. Lulu answered almost immediately, her face a mask. 'What's going on?' he said. 'Who's here?'

'Someone called Sabrina,' she answered, shaking her head. 'Says she needs to speak to you urgently.'

'Lulu, we should talk,' he said.

'No, we shouldn't,' she replied. 'I have no idea what's going on, but it doesn't look good.'

'Guy!' said Sabrina, joining them by the door. 'I have a message for you.' She looked pointedly at Lulu as Guy stepped inside and closed the door behind him.

'It's fine,' he said, ushering them all through to the main living space. 'You can say whatever it is. I have a feeling the time for secrets is over.'

'Mila came to see me,' she said. 'Thomas informed on you. He's told Iva everything. About Eastern Europe and Africa. The only reason she hasn't come to arrest you already is because she's trying to find the robots. I have no idea what all that means, but Mila said you would.'

'Unfortunately, I do,' said Guy.

'Fine. Well, in which case, my work here is done. I'll leave you to it,' she said, making for the exit. Then she turned back. 'Actually, there is one more thing.'

'What?' asked Guy, wondering what she could possibly have to add.

'That little shit, Thomas, has managed to take Daddy's job. Please find a way to make him pay.'

'Sabrina, at the moment, I need to find a way to stay out of prison.'

'Just in case an opportunity presents itself,' she said, shrugging. 'After all, it was you who introduced him to Daddy in the first place.'

Guy let the remark go. 'Thank you, for warning me,' he said.

'Any time,' she called over her shoulder.

'Lulu,' said Guy, hesitantly, when he heard the door shut, 'there are some things I need to tell you.'

* * * * *

Lulu sat down at the table; this didn't feel like a sofa conversation. 'What's going on, Guy?' she asked.

He pulled out a paint-splattered wooden chair and sat too. 'It's a long story,' he said, 'but essentially, I've been helping other economies create commercial tech that can compete with the UK and US. And I've been sending illegal tech aid to Africa. I didn't tell you earlier, because firstly, I didn't want to make you an accomplice, and secondly, I wanted to protect the others involved. I trust you, implicitly, but I wouldn't want any of the people I've been working with to divulge my involvement to anyone, regardless of who they were, and I wanted to extend them the same courtesy. However, our mutual friend Thomas has put an end to all that.'

'I read about mysterious technology being delivered to rural areas in Africa,' said Lulu. 'I never thought it would be you.'

'There are people dying,' he said, simply. 'I visited Africa when I was younger, just before my brother died. I was thinking about a role in politics, in international aid. What I saw there made absolutely no sense to me. We have so much tech over here, doing such silly, meaningless things for us: ironing our shirts, vacuuming our homes, cutting our grass, delivering us endless stuff. Over there, there are still areas where they don't have clean drinking water, or enough food, or basic education. So, when I got back, I started a private

195

engineering project with Tony to create two different types of robot that we could send to Africa. The hardware had to be reused from existing robots, or the manufacturing process would have attracted too much attention, but changing the software allowed for the appropriate modifications.'

'What modifications?' asked Lulu.

'We coded them to take more initiative. The water robots, for example, had to find the closest well, determine which communities used it, and then create the best daily delivery route and schedule. That alone had mind-blowing implications: children who hadn't been able to go to school, instead having to fetch water for their family, could finally learn. Overnight, water wasn't something they had to worry about any longer. It was simple and used tech that wasn't ground-breaking, but made a huge difference to whole communities.'

'What did the other type of robot do?' asked Lulu.

'They were butlers. We coded them to be workers: to prepare fields, plant crops, fix huts, educate the villagers about disease and contraception, and broadcast educational content and news programmes whenever appropriate. They tapped into the international internet satellite network and everything was powered using solar.'

Guy took a long pause, trying to assess Lulu's reaction, but she didn't give much away, just motioning impatiently for him to continue. 'What happened?' she asked. 'How did it play out?'

'The first drop was terrifying. We shipped only one of each type of robot, using drones to deliver them to the most remote location we could find, trying to avoid detection. We just dumped them and let the locals and the robots figure out the rest together. We watched the whole thing live on video footage taken by the robots. Their reaction was fearful at first, especially of the butler. The water robot was less intimidating, and they could understand it more easily, but a robot that looked like them must have been terrifying. I didn't even think about that beforehand; stupid, I know. I was just so excited to see what kind of difference we could make and to learn from the first drop so we could make them better for the next one.

'The adults were cautious, but the children would run up and have a look at them when they thought no one was watching. The water robot got straight to work, following one of the kids to the local well. The kid saw it fill itself up with water, and walked back to the village with it, shouting loudly to everyone that he'd brought back enough for them all. People came rushing out of their houses, the adults sceptical, but the child recounted what he'd seen, and drank the water himself to show them it was true.'

'Trusting of him,' said Lulu.

'That's kids for you!' Guy replied, recalling the image of the delighted child. 'Luckily that settled it for most of the villagers, but some of the older residents took a few more days to come around; I guess they were convinced when they saw the others didn't get sick.'

'And then what happened?' asked Lulu.

'The change was amazing, but took longer than we'd expected. For weeks, the kids walked to the well with the robot, making sure it was coming back with water. After a while, they trusted that it would do, and stopped going with it, and that's when great things started happening. Instead of staying at home to help out, most of the kids started walking to the not-so-local school. The butler also had a role to play in that, picking up a lot of slack for the villagers. And both the water robot and the butler could work through the night, as there was endless sunshine to recharge them

197

during the day. It really is incredible the amount a butler can get done at full speed. We limit them in UK homes to make them more palatable, but when they're going for it, they're basically just a blur.

'We learned from the first drop, made some modifications, and then sent more out there. We repeated the process a number of times, sending only a pair at a time, as that's all we had the resources to create. But when I took over the company, the world was my oyster and we've been ramping up production ever since.'

'That's what the extra hours have been for?' asked Lulu, everything falling into place.

'Yes,' said Guy. 'There are a couple of people in each facility who know the truth about what's going on, and they keep a cover story going for the others. They make sure the correct chips go onto the production line, and that none are accidently left there at end of the shift, that kind of stuff. Penny and Gerry have been overseeing operations in Exeter for years.'

'Who would have thought it,' said Lulu. 'Gerry and Penny, ringleaders.'

Guy laughed. 'They're brilliant at it,' he said. 'That's part of the reason why I helped out Thomas. I figured if he was anything like them, he'd be a great asset.'

'But it turns out he's not,' said Lulu, 'or not any longer at least.'

'Thomas was one of four key people making sure the operation continued,' said Guy. 'He talked a good game, saying he cared about the work we were doing. Although it seems as though that was all just a story to string me along. He took care of the financial side, siphoning money from Cybax to pay for it all.'

'He was probably lining his own pocket at the same time,' said Lulu, thinking of the lavish lifestyle Thomas enjoyed.

'Maybe,' said Guy, shaking his head. He had trusted Thomas, but then, so had Lulu.

'And that's why the GPS trackers were disabled,' said Lulu, surprising Guy with her knowledge. 'I used to work in the factory in Exeter,' she reminded him. 'One of the guys was trying to show off, bragging that he knew how to disable the secondary GPS trackers. I don't think many realised the full implications of it, but I always felt uncomfortable, not knowing what was really going on.'

'I made sure to leave the self-destruct mechanisms,' said Guy, 'in case they were tampered with, so the likelihood of reverse engineering was remote. In fact, given the sophistication of the mechanisms, along with the intellectual property protections covering our inventions, I don't see how China could ever be a threat anyway, unless they came up with new tech of their own. The government don't see it that way of course, and I've never pushed the issue too hard in case it led to increased scrutiny.'

Silence settled over them as Guy gave Lulu time to consider what he'd said. 'Thank you for telling me, even if it took news of your impending arrest,' she said eventually, a playful smile on her lips.

'My impending arrest...,' repeated Guy, only now starting to think about the implications. 'I need to make a phone call,' he said, pulling out his smart glasses and telling them to call Benji.

'Benj,' said Guy, lightly, 'I was thinking we should have watermelon ice cream at the meeting on Monday, to celebrate.'

'Watermelon ice cream?' said Benji, his tone even. 'You know I hate that.'

'I know, but sometimes we have to do things for other people's benefit,' said Guy, pretending to scold him.

'Fine, I suppose I can put my own feelings aside,' replied Benji. 'Oh, Guy?'

'Yep?'

'The butler you brought in from the community project has been analysed, both by our engineers and the government guys. We found some rogue code with a showy tag, and GCHQ have tracked it back to a teenage hacker in Slough.'

'Thank God for that,' said Guy. 'I take it the teenager has been offered a job with us?'

'Yeah, but unfortunately GCHQ got in there first. Our software team have closed the door though, so no one else should be able to get in.'

'Great. Get the PR team to spin up a story, and make sure you collaborate with the government.'

'Already done,' said Benji.

'Always a step ahead,' teased Guy. 'I've also been meaning to tell you that we've decided to promote you to chief operating officer.'

'What?' said Benji, his surprise palpable.

'Yeah. The board agreed it a couple of days ago. I'll sort out the details. Just remember the watermelon ice cream, or the position's off.'

'Harsh,' said Benji. 'But I suppose I can live with that.'

CHAPTER 14

'Thomas!' said Mila, shocked, as she walked into her apartment. 'I didn't realise you were planning on coming over tonight,' she went on, her tone icy.

'I thought we could celebrate,' he said, giving her a kiss on the cheek and handing her a glass of champagne before retreating to the sofa. 'Not only have I got a new position as CEO, but Iva's agreed not to investigate me. It couldn't have worked out any better if I'd tried.'

Mila stood steadfast by the door. 'That's how you see this whole mess?' she asked.

'Mess?' laughed Thomas. 'I wouldn't call it a mess. I'd call it a dream come true.'

'Backstabbing the man who gave you a leg up in the first place? You wouldn't be anywhere near where you are today without him.'

'He's breaking the law,' said Thomas, with a shrug. 'He had it coming.'

'Like you've been doing too?'

'I only did it because Guy put me in such a difficult position; abuse of his power really.'

Mila's face turned severe. 'Do you believe that? Or are you just trying out a new line? Because we both know you only do things that further your own ends.'

Thomas halted. 'Mila, what's going on?' he asked. 'Is this because I didn't come to you? Did you want to be the one to bring Guy down? Is that it?'

Mila laughed, shaking her head in disbelief. 'Are you kidding me?' she said, taking a few steps towards the sofa. 'Do you actually believe that's a possibility? That the reason I'm angry with you now is because I'm *jealous*?'

'You're ambitious,' said Thomas, confused. 'And bringing down Guy would be a big coup, so yeah, I think it's possible.'

'Thomas, let me explain something to you,' she said, sitting in an armchair and leaning forward, putting her champagne to one side. 'The reason why the rich stay rich is because they work together; they help each other out. They do business deals, they network at parties, they give jobs to each other's children. Sometimes they fall out, but everyone knows about it. What they do not ever do is pretend to be someone's friend, use them for their own purposes, and then backstab them.'

'I wouldn't say...' Thomas tried to interrupt, but Mila held up a hand to stop him.

'Guy was ostensibly your friend and mentor. He let you into his inner circle and involved you in projects that only his most trusted were privy to, projects which, as it turns out, were only trying to make the world a better place.'

'He had it coming,' said Thomas. 'I did what anyone in my position would have.'

'What you've done,' Mila continued, undeterred, 'is prove that you can't be trusted, not by anyone. From this moment on, the club you've tried so hard to become a part of will reject you. You're too dangerous, too reckless, too selfish. Nobody can do a deal with you; you'd run off to greener pastures at the first sign of a problem. You have no loyalty and no integrity. Not only have you just signed Guy's death warrant, but you've signed your own as well.'

Thomas' blood ran cold. He'd never thought of it like that. He'd assumed that as soon as he reached the top, he'd be safe, that he would gain respect and entry to the social circles he craved to be part of, simply because of his title. He hadn't thought about the possibility that they wouldn't want him, that they'd reject him, that they'd have morals.

'But they're all breaking the law left, right, and centre,' said Thomas. 'I haven't done anything different.'

'Most of them aren't really breaking the law,' said Mila. 'Most of them just push the boundaries a bit. They give jobs to people that arguably they shouldn't, they lavish perks on their employees, which arguably contravene the pay cap. But the important point is that it's all grey. They very rarely cross a line they know there's no defence against. That's why even Richard got to keep his job after his investigation: because there was nothing concrete enough for Iva to secure a conviction. And now you've taken down one of the genuinely good guys.'

'It's your job to take down people like him,' said Thomas, trying to deflect the conversation away from himself. 'No wonder Iva's always looking over your shoulder.'

'It's my job to catch people who are breaking the law, yes,' said Mila hotly. 'But I'd rather catch people like you, who are siphoning off money, or illegally accessing government files and using them to blackmail corporate CEOs, for nothing but their own personal gain.'

Thomas reddened. *She did know*, he thought. 'I don't know what you're talking about,' he said, fire sparking behind his worried features. 'I've never done anything like that.'

'Oh stop,' said Mila. 'I know you accessed my computer; I'm not an idiot. I thought you might try it, so I left my computer unlocked that time, and told my butler to record your activity.'

'That's illegal, unless you tell me you're going to record me.'

'Luckily, I work for the Enforcement Office, so I have special powers.'

'Which you've abused in recording me,' said Thomas, his body rigid, muscles held by fear.

'No, I haven't,' said Mila, evenly.

'I won't take back my testimony against Guy,' said Thomas, starting to panic. 'Iva would come for me; I'd be finished.'

'You're finished anyway,' said Mila. 'Weren't you listening to what I said? You'll be ousted from the CEO club as soon as you officially join it.'

'I will not,' said Thomas, his mind telling him to take back control, to take a deep breath and think. 'What do you want?' he asked, after a few moments of silence. Iva had agreed not to pursue him for his crimes, but there was no guarantee the protection would be honoured by Mila. Even if Iva managed to get him an official pardon, it would only cover the things he'd told her about, and there was plenty more hidden away in the depths of his past, not to mention the other side projects he was working on. Until now, he hadn't even considered that Mila might cause him a problem; he'd been toying with the idea of marrying her, for Christ's sake.

'I want you to put down your champagne, pick up your coat and leave my apartment. After that, I never want to see you again.'

'You're not going to try and blackmail me?'

'Some of us don't operate in the shady way that you do,' said Mila, giving him a disgusted look.

'So you won't prosecute me then?' said Thomas, feeling the clamp of worry around his brain ease a fraction.

'I didn't say that,' she said flatly.

'So you are going to prosecute?' he asked, the vice returning with even greater force than before.

'I didn't say that either,' she said. 'I said I would like you to leave my apartment, you absolute piece of shit.' She pointed to the door. 'Or should I ask my butler to escort you out?'

'Your butler can't do that,' said Thomas, trying to find a way to look at it without showing his concern.

'Again, my butler has special abilities, given my job. It's possible that someone like you could get angry and come to my apartment to try and attack me, so Matt's allowed to defend me, although he's not allowed to attack, of course. So,' she said pointedly, 'should I ask Matt to show you to the door?'

'No, don't be ridiculous,' said Thomas, putting down his champagne and reaching for his coat. 'I'm not going to give you the satisfaction of letting you throw me out of your apartment.' He tried to give off an air of confident control, his actions too hasty to be convincing.

'Bye, Thomas,' she said, watching as he walked to the door. 'Don't contact me again; you won't like the consequences if you do.'

* * * * *

Benji got out of his taxi and walked the last half mile to the building to which he'd so recently relocated the robots. *All for nothing*, he thought, his head down, shoulders slumped, as he considered the risk they'd all taken, for no good reason. The only saving grace was that at least everything was easier to destroy here than it would have been in Plymouth.

He ducked down a side street and walked to the end, to an inconspicuous grey door in a dull and dreary wall. He put his hand on a barely noticeable scanner and the door immediately sprang open. He stepped through, then pushed it closed behind him, looking around the small, blank space to make sure everything was as it should be. He stood still while a face scanner checked he was authorised to be here. Once that beeped, a keypad appeared in the wall, and Benji punched in an eight-digit code. The inner door slid open to reveal a cavernous warehouse, filled with crates ready to be shipped.

So close, thought Benji, as he surveyed the vast effort that would now never be utilised. He sighed at the risks so many people had taken, the costs involved, the emotional toll it had taken on them all. If this had happened a year ago, just after their last successful shipment, it wouldn't have been so bad. There would have been ten or twenty crates to get rid of, and, although he would have been sad because of the squandered effort and wasted potential those crates represented, he would have consoled himself, because at least the warehouse wasn't full. At least the warehouse didn't look as it did today.

Today, it was packed full of crates. Full of millions of pounds' worth of tech. Full of thousands of hours' worth of effort. Full of multiple life sentences' worth of law breaking. Full of hundreds of remote villages' worth of aid. And it was all going to go up in smoke. *All for nothing*, he repeated silently to himself, anger coursing through him as it had at regular intervals since Guy's watermelon ice cream call.

He'd thought about doing something radical, about trying to make the shipment without Guy's authorisation, but he knew it was too risky, and, worse, could leave an evidence trail that would send them all to jail. Guy had always been careful to ensure he was the only one who could be implicated in the event that someone found out what they'd been doing. If Benji tried to take matters into his own hands, he could inadvertently sign arrest warrants for them all. He walked over to the small security office in the corner of the warehouse, and tapped on the door.

'Hi Billy,' he said, his voice glum.

'Hi,' replied a five-foot-tall woman with peroxide blonde hair tied back in a ponytail. 'It's a sad day,' she said.

'How do you know?' asked Benji, suddenly on high alert.

Billy gave him a 'Come on now' look. 'You asked me to clear the warehouse,' she replied. 'No exceptions. "Make absolutely sure nobody is inside the building", remember?'

Benji nodded.

'That can mean only one thing,' she said, 'and it's devastating, for everyone involved.'

'I know,' said Benji, thinking that he'd have to promote her. 'Devastating,' he replied, not knowing what else to say. 'But we may as well get it over and done with. Is everyone out?'

'Yes,' said Billy. 'I've double checked and triple checked. There's no one here but you and me.'

'Fine,' he said, sighing again. 'Have you got your key?'

'Right here,' she said, holding it up and walking, with Benji, to the newly installed control panel. Benji looked at it with regret. *Complete waste of time,* he thought, remembering bitterly the trouble and costs involved in installing this system at such short notice. They put their physical keys in the mechanisms and turned them together. A sensor pad appeared, and they both put a hand on it, before each typing in a code. Benji pressed a button to confirm the instruction. A light started blinking, and a countdown timer appeared.

'Time to get out of here,' said Billy, picking up her bag and heading for the exit, Benji swiftly following behind.

They left the building, ensured both doors were fully sealed behind them, and then headed back to the main street. They crossed the road, entered the nondescript newsagent on the other side, and waited, pretending to browse the glossy magazines. Benji marvelled that any paper publications had managed to survive the tech revolution, but they had. Some things just looked and felt better in print. Flicking through pictures in a magazine was a ritual that some people craved, and if people were willing to pay for it, there was always someone willing to provide it.

They waited the full five minutes, which passed with agonising leisure, each of them nervously checking their smart watches at frequent intervals. Eventually, they heard a low rumble, then saw the column of fire, like an upside-down rocket engine raging out of the top of the building. Benji looked nervously at the building's walls. He had employed the best engineers to fit the protective inner casing, but if it failed, the whole building would come down, and take half the street with it.

'Oh my God,' shouted the shopkeeper, pulling out his smart glasses and calling the fire brigade. Benji and Billy walked outside to get a better view, their faces pained. All that potential, up in flames.

* * * * *

'Lulu,' said Guy, stroking the hair back off her face, carefully watching her expression in the morning light. They were at Guy's house by the sea, having decided the previous night it would be safer there than at Lulu's tech-free home. His bedroom suite took up half of the back of the house, complete with the most incredible view over the sea.

'It must be amazing in here when it's stormy outside,' said Lulu, looking at the flat calm water from where she lay on the bed. It felt wrong for the sea to be so docile at such a turbulent moment in their lives.

'Lulu,' repeated Guy, leaning back against the headboard.

'When are you going?' she asked, knowing they'd put off this conversation for as long as was safe.

'Today,' he replied, watching intently for her reaction. 'Benji's just destroyed the facility. The authorities will be picking over the wreckage as we speak, and when Iva gets wind of it and realises we've destroyed the robots, she'll come straight for me. There's no reason for her to hold off any longer.'

'But without the robots, she doesn't have any proof,' said Lulu, shaking her head, trying to think of anything that would mean he didn't have to go.

'She's got Thomas, and he has all the financial records,' Guy replied, taking hold of her hand and playing with her fingers. 'There's no future for me here.'

'Who'll take over your company?' asked Lulu. 'Who'll continue the work you've been doing in Africa?'

'Benji will be COO, and he'll handle things until the board can recruit a new me. As for the African project,' he said, regretfully, 'that will cease to exist.'

'It can't,' she said, 'what about all those people who'll die without your help?'

'I'm going to Africa,' said Guy, gently. 'I'm going to do what I can to help them develop their own technology, but it'll be slow going, and I'll be a fugitive, and I won't have anything like the resources I have here.'

'What about me?' said Lulu, tears in her eyes. She wasn't sure what she'd expected, but this wasn't it.

'Come with me.'

'What?'

'Come with me,' he repeated, his expression telling her he meant it.

'Become a fugitive too?'

'You wouldn't have to be a fugitive. You could legitimately move to Africa. You could say you're looking for new creative inspiration, somewhere life is completely different from here.'

'But I'd give away your location. It would be the first place Iva would look for you.'

'But luckily, since the West refuse to share their tech with African countries, most African countries refuse to cooperate with the West. Even if she did find me, the likelihood of her being able to have me extradited is extremely low. And it's a risk I would willingly take to have you there with me.'

'Jesus, Guy, I can't believe this. Yesterday this wasn't even on the horizon and now you're asking me to give up my life and leave the country?'

'I know it's a lot to take in, but you can take as long as you need to decide. I'm going today; I've got to get out before Iva gets here, but you can come and join me anytime. I know roughly where I'm going, but not exactly. I'll be in contact with Benji, so he'll help you find me.'

'You're not telling me where you're going?' she asked, feeling as though Guy had just slapped her across the face. 'You don't trust me?'

'Of course I trust you,' said Guy, looking down into her eyes. 'But you're going to be one of the first people Iva takes in for questioning when she realises I've gone. She'll interrogate you, threaten you, tempt you, throw everything she can at you to make you tell her where I am. And she'll use lie detector technology.'

'Oh,' said Lulu.

'I don't want to put you in a position where Iva knows you're lying to her. Then you'd either be done for obstructing the course of justice, or have to tell her my location.'

'Okay,' she said, relief flooding through her. 'But how come you're going to tell Benji? Won't you be putting him in the same position?'

'I'm not going to tell Benji,' said Guy. 'I'll find a way to get in contact with him once I'm out there.'

Lulu sat up to face him. 'Should I tell her I know you're going to Africa?'

'Yes, if it comes to that. I'd prefer she doesn't know anything, but if you have to, you can tell her that much.' Lulu leant back next to him and Guy dropped an arm around her shoulders.

She pressed herself into the warmth of his body, breathing him in, revelling in him. She wondered when she'd see him next. He kissed her, sliding her down onto the bed, his lips caressing hers, her mind flooded with him, blocking out everything but him. 'Come with me,' he murmured. 'Today. Now. Don't stay here. Don't think about it, just come and be with me.' She pressed a hand to his cheek, stroking her thumb across his lips. It would be so easy to say yes. He held her gaze with hopeful eyes. 'I love you,' he said.

Lulu smiled, euphoria coursing through her. 'I love you too.'

'Then come with me,' he implored, fingers tracing up her neck, into her hair. He pressed his forehead to hers, closing his eyes. 'Please, come with me.'

Lulu's mind raced. The silence stretched and Guy opened his eyes, looking at her expectantly, hopefully. 'Guy,' she started, her voice hesitant. 'I will come with you, but,' she added quickly, as she took in Guy's reaction, 'not today.'

'Oh,' said Guy, shoulders slumping with rejection.

'There's something I have to do here first,' she said, pulling him back to her as he tried to sit up, to put space between them. 'Then I'll come and find you. I promise. I love you.' Her eyes held his, trying to make him understand that she meant it. 'No matter what happens, I will come and find you. I want to be with you; there's nothing I want more.'

'What do you need to do? Can I help?'

'No,' she replied, firmly. 'You just concentrate on getting out of the country. That's your job. My job is something else entirely.'

* * * * *

Guy kissed Lulu goodbye on the jetty at the bottom of the cliff below his house. He pulled himself away, climbing into the waiting boat, then powered out to sea. Guy hadn't told Lulu anything else about how he would get to Africa; he'd said he couldn't travel as normal, obviously, Iva would have made sure of that, but he'd had a contingency plan in place for some time, knowing deep down that eventually he'd have to use it.

Today was that day, she sighed, as he raced across the flat calm sea.

Lulu turned and climbed the steep steps back to the house. She asked a robot to make her a coffee, sat down, and waited, looking out over the sea and wondering how long it would take for Iva to turn up. Guy's boat disappeared, and she hoped he was far away before Iva realised what was happening.

Would Iva go to Guy's office in Oxford first, or Lulu's house in Devon, or would she come straight here? Lulu got her answer more quickly than she would have liked. She was on her way for a swim to try and clear her head, when the front gate alarm screamed through the silence. Guy had told her not to hang around here, had urged her to go back to Devon, or anywhere that had nothing to do with him, but she'd always had a reckless streak, and she wanted to see the look on Iva's face when she realised Guy had slipped through her fingers. The one Iva had been trying to bring down for her entire career, gone beyond her reach.

Lulu opened the gate, then went to the front door to watch as they arrived. A convoy of four large vehicles pulled up and bodies in black uniforms started pouring out, moving like ants around the side of the house as well as in through the front door. Iva stepped out of the front car, accompanied by Mila, who was projecting a warrant using her smart glasses.

'He's not here,' said Lulu, evenly, 'although, according to that,' she said, indicating towards the warrant, 'you're allowed to search the place and seize what you want, so I'm sure you'll have a thorough rootle around anyway. Can I get you a tea or coffee?' she asked, sweetly.

* * * * *

213

Mila eyed Lulu suspiciously. Had she worked out that Mila was behind Sabrina's tip-off? Was she planning to tell Iva? She didn't know the artist, didn't understand her motives, and that worried her.

'Where is he?' asked Iva, her voice snapping, as though she were some kind of military general and Lulu a lowly soldier.

Lulu raised an eyebrow. 'I'm afraid I'm not sure.'

'Arrest her,' Iva said to Mila, furiously. Mila stayed rooted to the spot.

'Who tipped him off?' Iva spat, closing the gap between them so her face was only inches from Lulu's. 'Who told him?' she repeated, slowly, trying to intimidate.

'I'm afraid I have no idea what you're talking about,' said Lulu, her features an impenetrable mask. 'Tipped him off about what?'

'You're playing a dangerous game,' said Iva. 'I will arrest you for perverting the course of justice.'

'In relation to what?' asked Lulu, irritated. 'Why are you here?'

Iva looked suddenly unsure. 'Take her to the kitchen,' said Iva, 'and stay there with her.' Her eyes followed Mila, her face full of suspicion.

Iva's enforcers searched Guy's beautiful home, pulling everything apart, taking pictures off the walls, seizing all tech, recording everything on their smart glasses so they could pick over it all later. Lulu winced as she saw her pictures being handled with rough, uncaring hands.

'He's not here,' said one of the men to Iva, when they were convinced they'd searched every nook and cranny.

'And he's not at any of his other known residences, or offices, or favourite projects, or hangouts.'

Iva turned to Mila, her stare accusing. 'Well?' she demanded.

Mila refused to buckle under Iva's hostile gaze. 'I thought he'd be here,' she said, shaking her head. 'It made the most sense from what I know of Guy.'

'Where is he?' said Iva, rounding on Lulu. 'Where has he gone?'

'I'm afraid I genuinely don't know. In fact, he refused to tell me, because he didn't want to put me in an awkward position. Can someone please tell me what this is all about?'

Iva ignored Lulu's question. 'Who tipped him off?' she demanded, hitting the table with her palm. 'How has this happened?'

Lulu shrugged, but didn't say a thing.

Iva rounded on Mila. 'It was you,' she accused. 'I knew it was a bad idea to let you stay on this case. I knew you'd be loyal to your roots, just like the rest of them. You're fired.'

'Iva,' said Mila, with more confidence than she felt. 'You can't fire me, because I've done nothing wrong. It's illegal to fire someone on a whim, so if you really want to do this, it will cost you your job.'

Iva looked Mila directly in the eye. 'You. Are. Fired.'

'I'll be leaving then,' she said lightly. 'My legal team will be in touch.'

There was something about the way Mila said 'legal team' that made Iva shudder. Mila's family were formidable, their resources were considerable, and Iva would be a fool not to be at least a little intimidated by her threat.

'I'll come with you,' said Lulu. 'I need to go to Bristol, so we can share a car at least part of the way.'

'No,' said Iva, 'I won't allow you two to travel together.'

'You just fired me,' said Mila, 'so I am no longer under your command. And you have no legitimate reason to arrest Lulu, unless there's something I don't know?'

Iva shook her head and waved her hand in frustration before walking out of the room. 'Didn't think so,' said Mila, under her breath, as she and Lulu headed for the door.

CHAPTER 15

Lulu pulled up at the Glen Murray retirement village. It was like something out of *The Stepford Wives*; everything perfectly manicured, the grass a lush, flawlessly cropped green, the trees pruned into immaculate shapes, the road's surface smooth and without blemish, the white picket fences a blazing fresh white, and the variously sized but almost identical clapboard houses dotted around the plot, all pristinely clean and tidy.

Lulu rolled down the window of her autonomous taxi, and, to her surprise, found a real-life woman sitting in the little hut by the gate.

'Hi,' she said, brightly. 'How can I help you?'

'I'm here to see Tony Strathclyde,' she said, 'although he's not expecting me.'

'No problem,' said the middle-aged woman with badly dyed hair, 'it's rare for our residents to turn away a visitor; most of them don't get them as often as they'd like. What's your name?' She gave her smart glasses a silent instruction to call Tony.

'Lulu Banks,' she replied.

The woman did a double take. '*The* Lulu Banks?' she asked, trying to get a good look at her through their respective windows.

'Yes,' she sighed, with friendly reluctance.

'Lovely to meet you,' the woman said, smiling and taking the hint. 'Ah, Mr Strathclyde, I have a visitor for you.' She paused and frowned at what was obviously a sharp rebuff from Tony. 'Of course, Mr Strathclyde, I totally understand, it's just that it's Lulu Banks, not a window salesman.' This clearly did the trick as the lady smiled broadly. 'Yes, certainly, Mr Strathclyde, I'll send her up right away.'

The lady turned back to Lulu. 'He would be delighted to see you,' she said, beaming, as though she'd done Lulu a tremendous favour. 'You can go through.' The barrier lifted.

'Which house is Mr Strathclyde's?' Lulu asked.

'Oh, sorry, I assumed you knew. He lives in one of the penthouse flats in the main house at the top of the drive. Just ask for him at reception if he isn't already there to meet you.'

'Thank you,' said Lulu, then told her car to drive on.

The car travelled noiselessly over the smooth tarmac, winding its way along the meandering road, taking far longer than would have been necessary, had the road been straight. Once they passed through the first collection of cottages, the road straightened out, turning into a tree-lined avenue, which ended at an impressive-looking manor house, which, again, was in immaculate condition.

Her car reached the large turning circle in front of the house, and a man in a uniform approached, opening the door for her and offering her his hand.

'Thank you,' she said, taken aback by all the human help about the place.

'This way please, Miss Banks,' he said, politely. 'Mr Strathclyde is waiting for you in the orangery. 'Do you have any bags you'd like me to carry?'

'No, thank you,' she said, bemused by the parallel universe she seemed to have stepped into. There was certainly tech here, of that there was no doubt, but none of it was visible. *Must be how the residents like it,* she thought. *Must remind them of their youth, back in the good old days.*

'Just through here,' said the human butler, showing her through a side door into a magnificent orangery, a number of lush green plants and comfortable seating arranged artfully throughout.

Tony was sitting on a low wicker sofa at the edge of the room, overlooking a beautiful rose garden with an impressive water feature and square pool in the centre. There was a woman with him, who seemed about his age, with stylish short grey hair, wearing an expensive-looking full-length summer dress. It was bright yellow and dragged attention to her, but she wore it with confident poise. *Must be Tony's wife,* Lulu concluded.

Tony saw Lulu approaching and sprang to his feet. 'Lulu!' he exclaimed, throwing his arms wide in welcome. She reached him and kissed him on each cheek.

'It's lovely to see you,' she said, thinking again what a lucky man Guy was to have a grandfather like Tony.

'The pleasure is all ours,' he replied, turning to introduce her to the woman at the table. 'And this,' he said with an arm flourish, 'is my beautiful wife, Isabella. Iz, this is Lulu, Guy's...friend.'

Isabella raised an eyebrow as she flowed elegantly to her feet. She held out an effortless hand and waited while Lulu reached over to shake it. 'It's a pleasure to actually meet you,' Isabella said cryptically.

'Iz, stop it,' said Tony, ushering them all into seats. 'Do excuse my wife's personality.' He sent her a silencing sideways glance. 'She can't help herself.'

'Do excuse my husband's irritating ways,' countered Isabella, 'he doesn't realise how rude he is.'

'Iz, Lulu has not come all the way here, in person, to watch us have a domestic, legendary though they are; you could probably use one as inspiration for a painting,' he laughed. 'Sixty years together is a long time.'

Tony stopped talking, but Lulu wasn't sure how to respond, so she waited for one of the other two to pick up the conversation.

'Anyway,' Tony went on, 'where are our manners? What can we get you to drink? Tea, coffee, something stronger?' He gave her a sly smile.

Lulu wasn't sure what it was about the older generations, but they had a strange obsession with drinking at lunchtime. She'd always found it gave her a terrible headache and made her want to sleep the afternoon away. She laughed. 'Some water would be great.'

Tony signalled for a human butler to come over, and ordered Lulu's water and two cups of tea. 'Are you sure we can't get you anything else? Cake? Toast? Some lunch? Have you had lunch yet?'

'Honestly, just some water would be great,' she replied. She hadn't been able to eat anything since Guy had left. The stress and emotion had put her on edge. There would be plenty of time for eating when her work was done, when she and Guy were lying on a beach, sipping elaborate fruit juice concoctions from a pineapple. Or at least that was the version of her future she liked best, from the endless scenarios she'd run through in her mind.

'What can we help you with?' asked Isabella authoritatively, as the butler retreated with their order. 'I'm sure you haven't come all the way out here for a social call.'

I didn't come out here to see you *at all,* thought Lulu, prickling at her tone, but told herself to focus on the matter in hand. 'No,' she said, 'I came here to tell you there's a warrant out for Guy's arrest. Thomas Watson, you know, the one Guy helped up the ladder?' They both nodded, pained expressions on their faces, so she continued. 'Well, Thomas decided, for whatever reason, to inform on Guy. He went to Iva Brooksbank, the one who's been running the investigation into Guy's business affairs,' she added, not knowing how much Isabella knew. They nodded again. 'He told her everything about the Africa project, and the Eastern Europe project.'

'Has the new facility been destroyed?' asked Tony, suddenly all business-like and focused.

'Yes,' replied Lulu, biting her lip as she thought about all the investment, physical, mental, emotional, and probably financial, that Tony had made in that venture.

'Christ,' said Tony. 'It couldn't have come at a worse time. The warehouse was brimming full of robots.'

'I know,' said Lulu. 'Benji wasn't happy about it, but everything was successfully destroyed, so there's no evidence that can be used against Guy, or the others involved, whoever they are. However, Thomas has given Iva the full financial records, and he's told her in detail how he siphoned money from Cybax to pay for the projects. Guy's hoping the other partners are safe, but he doesn't know for sure. He never thought Thomas would betray him.'

'Always too trusting, that one,' said Isabella, accepting her tea from the butler. 'I told his mother that, when he was a boy. He never wanted to see the bad in people, even when it was staring him in the face.'

'Yes,' sighed Tony. 'But that won't help us now. Did he get away? She hasn't caught him?'

'I think he did,' she replied, gloomily. 'He took a boat from his house on the coast, but he wouldn't tell me any more of his plan, so as not to put me in a difficult position.'

'So that's it?' asked Isabella. 'Guy's gone and he didn't ask you to go with him?'

'Iz,' said Tony, 'that's between Lulu and Guy. It's none of our business.'

'It is our business,' she replied hotly. 'Guy is our only remaining grandson, and the only one of our children or grandchildren to have successfully developed a heart. He's given it to her,' she said, accusingly, a hint of a French accent sneaking into her voice, 'and I can't imagine he would have left without asking her to go with him. So she must have said no.'

'Don't jump to conclusions,' chastised Tony.

'Well then?' demanded Isabella, rounding on Lulu. 'Did he ask you to go with him?'

'Yes,' she said, matching Isabella's hostile tone, 'and I intend to join him. But there are a few things I have to do first. One of those was to come here, to tell you the truth about what happened.' She took a deep breath to calm herself. 'Guy and I won't be able to contact you, possibly ever again, so he wanted me to make sure you knew the true story, and to tell you he loves you two more than anyone else in the world. He said to tell you that if you need anything at all, Benji will help.'

'We'll be fine,' said Tony, dismissively. 'Look at where we live. Our biggest problems in life are what to order for supper, and the early-morning yoga class being too full.'

'Be that as it may,' said Lulu, 'if you need anything, you know where Benji is.'

'Good old Benj,' said Tony.

'What about Mila Carter?' asked Isabella. 'Wasn't she working for this Iva woman?'

Lulu nodded. 'Yes, she was. But when she found out what Guy had really been doing, she tipped him off. That meant he could destroy the robots and get away in time. Iva suspected she was responsible, and fired her because of it.'

'She can't do that,' said Isabella, enraged.

'Iva doesn't have any evidence,' Lulu agreed. 'Mila's got her family lawyers on the case.'

'Iva should be quaking in her boots then,' said Tony, a twinkle in his eye. 'I'd put money on Iva having just issued her own P45.'

'P45?' asked Lulu.

'You youngsters,' said Tony, laughing. 'It's the piece of paper they used to give someone when they left a job.'

'Oh, I see. Obviously they don't have to do that any longer.'

'No,' agreed Tony, 'it's all linked up, online, like it should be.'

'I think Iva realised she'd acted a little hastily. But she did it in front of a whole team of people, and Mila said then and there she was going to sue her, so it would've been difficult for Iva to back down without losing a lot of face.'

'Well done, Mila,' said Isabella, warmly. 'I always liked her fire; she would have been a splendid addition to the family.'

Tony's eyes went dark. 'Indeed, she would have.'

They sat in silence for a few moments before Lulu picked up again. 'Guy doesn't think you're implicated anywhere, Tony, and you were never in any meetings with Thomas, so he doesn't think there's any trail back to you. But he said to warn you, as there's still a chance there could be. Who knows what Thomas got up to? Or Iva could pretend she has something on you to try and intimidate you into cooperating with her.'

'Over my dead body,' spat Isabella. 'If she tries that I'll do a special exposé on her. See how she likes that. In fact, I have a good mind to do one anyway.'

'Might be best not to bring unnecessary heat onto ourselves though, darling,' said Tony, squeezing her hand warmly. 'And anyway, after that business with her fiancé, I don't think I could condone something so nasty.'

'Oh I suppose you're right,' she conceded.

'The business with whose fiancé?' asked Lulu, confusion written across her face. 'Iva's? She has a fiancé?'

'Had a fiancé,' said Isabella, quietly.

'What happened to him?' asked Lulu, reading the meaningful look between them and knowing there was something they weren't telling her.

'He died,' said Tony.

'Whilst working for our son,' added Isabella.

'Iva wanted an inquiry. She insisted there was something untoward in the way he died. She had a whole file on it,' said Tony.

'But our son paid off his family, and because she was only the man's fiancé, she had no legal rights to do anything other than obey his family's wishes.'

'My God. Is that why she wants to take down Guy so badly?' asked Lulu, finally understanding the ferocious hatred in Iva's eyes.

'I imagine so,' said Isabella, shrugging.

'She was supposed to take a job working for Cybax when she graduated from Plymouth, but after the incident, she went and did a post-grad at Oxford, and then became an investigator. Her whole career is about avenging her fiancé,' said Tony.

'Our son always was a bit of a blunt instrument,' said Isabella, shaking her head. 'Should have brought Iva in, not sent her packing.'

'And now Guy's paying the price,' said Lulu, sadness settling on her.

'We've all paid the price for our son,' said Isabella darkly.

Lulu stayed and chatted for another half an hour; she enjoyed their company and found their relationship intriguing. She never knew if Isabella was going to blow up, or agree wholeheartedly with what Tony was saying, and Tony humoured and respected her in equal measure.

'You know relationships like ours take time to bloom,' said Isabella, catching Lulu watching them. 'It took us a good two decades to work out how to live together.'

'And then another two decades to work out it would be better if we didn't!' added Tony.

'My point,' said Isabella, giving Tony a chastising look, 'is that if you do decide to go to Guy, make absolutely sure it's what you want. Guy's not frivolous when it comes to matters of the heart, and it's better to end it now if you're not entirely sure. You're going to be exiles, and that won't be without its baggage. It's going to hang over you every day, niggling away at you, worrying you, making you wonder if it's your last day together before someone hands Guy in. It's quite an emotional weight you're going to have to carry. It's not a load to take on without serious consideration.'

'Oh Isabella, stop trying to put her off,' said Tony crossly. 'If you ask me, jump in with both feet and don't look back. Who cares about the issues; you only get one life, so you've got to live it. If it doesn't work out, it doesn't work out, but you'll always regret it if you don't give it a go.'

'And now you see why we can't live together,' said Isabella, dismissively. 'We can't agree on a damn thing.'

'And yet we're still madly in love,' said Tony. 'Baffling, isn't it?'

* * * * *

'Thomas,' said Penny, throwing the door open and wrapping her arms around her son. 'It's so good to see you.'

Thomas awkwardly patted his mother on the back, pushing her away moments later. 'It's nice to see you too, Mother,' he said, looking around the small, square, terraced house with disdain.

'Mother?' she laughed, in surprise. 'You're formal all of a sudden. What happened to Mum?'

'I guess I've grown up,' he replied.

Gerry rolled his eyes, stepping forward to shake his son's hand. 'Thomas,' he said, inclining his head. 'Come on in.'

'You're a bit later than expected,' said Penny lightly, 'so I hope you don't mind if we eat straight away? It's just that your brother has a new job; it's up towards Bristol, and he's working this afternoon.'

'Ben?' said Thomas, surprised to see him. 'I thought you and Sam had moved out?' They took their seats at the table, and helped themselves to the roast pork with all the trimmings that was waiting.

'We did,' said Ben sheepishly, as he heaped potatoes onto his plate, thinking of Sam, now alone in that apartment, 'but it didn't work out.'

'Why on earth not?' asked Thomas, with a hint of condescension. 'Could you pass me the applesauce? This isn't the healthiest lunch, is it?'

Everyone ignored Thomas' reprimand; they'd learned from experience that no good could come from biting. Ben answered his first question instead. 'Because I got a lesson about the cost of living the life I live,' he said, honestly, 'and got a front row seat to the unveiling of Sam's true self. He's borrowing money to keep living as we did here: gambling, gaming, and has hired a butler to do everything for him. He can't afford it on top of rent, groceries, socialising, and all the other little costs that unexpectedly add up. Every time I brought it up, he either got aggressive, or told me to pay for everything. He said he'd pay me back later, but short of winning the lottery, I don't see how that's ever going to be possible, and he's going to run out of credit very soon.'

'I can't imagine they've given him any kind of decent credit limit,' scoffed Thomas. 'I mean, his only income is UBI and he has no credit record, having always lived here and never having had to pay for anything. And he's already used up the limit, you say, Ben?'

Ben inwardly rolled his eyes at Thomas' pompousness, but let it lie in the interests of cordial relations. 'Yes,' Ben replied. 'Not sure what he's going to do when the money runs out, but anyway, I reined in my spending, refused to pay for any of the butler, and got a job. To my surprise, I really enjoy working. I'm just working as an attendant at one of the plush old-people complexes, but I like the sense of community there. I like that people have time to stop and talk. I like real, in-person conversations; there's something richer about them. I like that I've got a reason to get out of bed, that I'm good at my job, and I like earning money. It's empowering.'

'Crikey,' said Thomas, 'quite the convert.'

'Thomas,' said Penny, her tone sending a clear warning, not even looking at him as she loaded her fork.

'Bro,' said Ben, shrugging, 'it might not be the swanky gig you've got, but everyone has to start somewhere, and I'm a few years behind you. Who knows,' he joked, 'in five years' time, I might be running the place.'

'Ha! Maybe,' Thomas laughed. 'Like me, you mean,' he continued, before sitting back expectantly.

'Um, what?' asked Gerry, through a mouthful of crunchy crackling. 'Amazing crackling, by the way, Penny.'

'Thanks,' she smiled, wiping some stray gravy from her lips.

Thomas sat up taller in his seat, preening his feathers. 'Richard's just named me as his successor. I'm Pixbot's new CEO,' he said, puffing out his chest, proudly.

Penny raised an eyebrow and Gerry put down his knife and fork. They sent each other a meaningful look. Ben kept eating, as he already knew the news; Lulu had come to see a couple of residents at work and had told them all about it. He'd been listening in, of course; he'd always found her interesting, but he was a few years older and had hung out with a different crowd back when they were kids, and they hadn't seen each other in years.

'What've you got on him?' asked Penny flippantly, as though it might be a joke.

'I'm sorry?' coughed Thomas. 'I tell you I'm going to be CEO of one of the biggest, most successful tech companies in the world, and you ask me that? Not even a word of congratulation?'

'Congratulations,' said Gerry heartlessly. 'But seriously, the only way you could have got that man out of that job is if you're blackmailing him, and everyone will know it. Even that Rottweiler Iva- whatsit couldn't topple him.'

'After the ordeal Iva put him through, Richard has realised that he wants to spend more time enjoying life: playing tennis, seeing his friends, going on holiday. I've been a loyal and dependable employee, and, seeing as he had to fire his whole top rank after the investigation, I was the obvious choice as his successor.'

'Because there was no one else?' asked Ben, scraping up the last of his gravy with his knife, which he then put straight into his mouth.

Thomas shuddered. 'Because I'm the best man for the job,' he spat, putting down his knife and fork with a clatter. 'Honestly,' he said, with a pained expression, 'I can't believe you're doing this to me. I decide to let bygones be bygones and come all the way *here*,' he said as though his parents' home was beneath him, 'and you can't even do me the courtesy of saying well done when I tell you my news.'

'Well done,' said Penny, her tone almost mocking. 'Is that why you're here? Because you have no one else to give you praise and adoration?' Thomas looked as though he'd swallowed a wasp. 'When you cleared our debts, I thought you'd finally developed a heart, or missed us, or had realised that the whole point of human existence is our relationships. But it looks like I couldn't have been more wrong.'

'Cleared your debts?' said Thomas, confused. 'I didn't. Those are your debts, not mine, and I thought it was good for you to have them hanging around your necks. That it might help teach you a thing or two about fiscal responsibility.'

Gerry balled his fists and Penny gave him an encouraging look. 'How dare you,' said Gerry, standing up, his body tensed in fury. 'You come here, to our home, and you talk to us like this? We were ready to put the past behind us and move forward as a family, but obviously all you want is a fan club. Well, here's the thing, Thomas,' he said, spitting the name as though it were poison, 'we are not your fans. You're selfish and arrogant and conceited and rude and condescending and full of your own ludicrous self-importance. We couldn't care less if you're a CEO or unemployed. All we ever wanted was for you to be a good person and to find something meaningful and enjoyable to fill your time. We hoped you'd found that when Guy took you under his wing, but it seems as though it only completed your corruption.'

'And you even turned on Guy,' added Ben, despising his brother more than ever, and enjoying seeing his parents finally give him what for. 'You've turned on everyone who's ever helped you and that's made you think you're an evil mastermind. The reality is that everyone can see through you, and you have no one left to give you the adoration that you need.'

'What do you mean?' asked Penny. 'About turning on Guy?'

Ben turned to face his mother. 'Thomas went to Iva and informed on him. He told her everything about the Africa project, and all the robots, whatever that means. As I said, I only know what I overheard at work. Apparently, Guy had to destroy everything.'

'What?' asked Penny, going white. She rounded on Thomas. 'You did what?'

'He was breaking the law, committing treason, and so, might I add, were you.'

'He was helping starving people in Africa.'

'He was breaking the law,' repeated Thomas.

'How did you even know about it?' asked Gerry, his face a cold, angry mask.

'Someone had to skim off the money to pay for it all,' Thomas said with a shrug.

'What?' Penny said again, banging the table with her fists to vent some fury. 'Guy let you into his inner circle. He trusted you, and no doubt paid you for your services, and you betrayed him?'

Thomas looked at her like she was an idiot. 'He was breaking the law,' he repeated, slowly, as though she hadn't understood when he'd said it the first two times.

'And so were you, you despicable little excuse for a human being,' Penny hissed. 'But I bet you're not taking responsibility for your own illegal actions. Surely if you were so outraged, you would have turned down any role in it, and gone to the authorities straight away. But you didn't, did you? You profited from it for as long as you could, and then used it to get Guy out of the picture, knowing you could never be half the CEO he is.'

'You've never understood business,' said Thomas, in his most patronising tone.

'Get out,' Penny whispered, suddenly calm. 'You're a monster and I never want to see you again.'

'Don't be ridiculous,' said Thomas, full of pomp. 'I'm your son, the only son to have made anything of himself; you're not going to disown someone like me.'

Gerry gasped in shock. 'You're living a delusion,' he said, trying to make Thomas understand. 'You might want to see someone about that. And if you do, then maybe we would talk to you again, but we don't care about your position in some company. We care about you as a person, and unfortunately, you've turned into a horror show. I'm sorry, but I'm afraid we don't want any part in your life any longer.'

'You will regret this,' said Thomas, a look of dawning realisation crossing his face; they were serious. 'You were working illegally at the factory for Guy. Iva's going to come after every single worker who did extra hours, and I'm not going to do a thing to protect you. You'll have to take your fate along with the rest of the ants.'

'I think it would be best if you left now,' said Gerry, flashing a disbelieving look at his wife. He walked to the door, opened it and waited for Thomas to leave.

'You will wish you hadn't done this,' said Thomas, furiously getting up from the table, toppling his chair over backwards.

'On the contrary,' said Penny. 'I have a feeling it will be the best thing we've ever done.'

CHAPTER 16

Lulu turned up at the airport with two large bags full of possessions. Benji had told her not to take too much stuff or it would look suspicious. As it was, there was a high chance she and all her baggage would be searched, over and above the usual automated checks. She'd brought a few clothes and some toiletries, but she reasoned wherever she was going, she would be able to buy new things, so she'd given over most of the available space to her painting supplies. She wasn't sure rural Africa would have much in the way of her usual paints and brushes.

She waited, as she'd been instructed, outside the Chutney Café, but she wasn't sure what she was waiting for. She'd only been there for a minute, when a skinny, barely noticeable guy in his late teens handed her a magazine. 'You dropped this,' he said, thrusting it into her hand before walking away.

She frowned in surprise, but accepted it, then went into the coffee shop, ordered an Americano, sat down, and pretended to casually flick through the pages. Stuck to the back cover was an old-school mobile phone. She detached it as subtly as she could, turned it on and tapped the envelope icon that indicated there was an email waiting to be read. *Can't remember the last time I used one like this,* she thought, as the email opened, *or the last time I was sent an email for that matter.* Everyone used messaging services through their smart glasses now.

The email was a confirmation and e-ticket for a flight to India. Lulu had been expecting a flight to Africa, so wondered for a moment if the teenager had given the magazine to the right person. *Of course he did,* she chastised herself, *how many people just turn up at the airport and wait for someone to contact them?* The whole thing seemed ludicrous to her, like something out of a film.

E-tickets had long been almost irrelevant, because the airlines had access to biometric information about their passengers, so all you had to do was use a fingerprint and face scan to register for your flight and again to go through security and then again to board the plane. It would seem that this ticket wasn't assigned to anyone in particular, so she had to go to an automated check-in desk and assign the ticket to herself. It wouldn't show up on her banking app, should anyone be monitoring that, and the only trail would be through her biometric and passport data, which was difficult for anyone to get hold of, unless the police suspected you'd done something illegal, or that you were a threat to national security. Nevertheless, the authorities would be able to track her, should they want to, so Lulu wondered how Benji planned to get around that; the last thing she wanted was to lead Iva straight to Guy.

Once she'd been biometrically linked to her ticket, Lulu went to the bag drop, where she used her fingerprint to deposit her luggage. Usually this would have been sent ahead in a separate autonomous car, to a separate area, meaning passengers didn't have to haul their bags into the airport, but seeing as she hadn't known what code to put on her luggage, she'd had to do it the old-fashioned way, garnering several pitying looks as she struggled with her ungainly load.

Her luggage was whisked away to be scanned and loaded, leaving Lulu free to enter security, again, with a press of her finger and scan of her face. The days of putting all your personal possessions in little trays and walking through metal detectors were long gone. Security was now just a pod, like a kind of vacuum chamber.

Lulu stepped into a scanning pod, and to her immense relief, it quickly let her through to the other side. She was taking an atmosphere flight, where the plane would travel high in the Earth's atmosphere, able to travel much faster than a traditional plane, given the reduced air resistance. It would only take a couple of hours, after which she had no idea what she was supposed to do. She hoped that would become clear once she arrived. The flight was boarding, so she hurried to the gate.

* * * * *

Iva was sitting in her office in London, going through everything they had to date on Guy, still fuming that he'd managed to get away without leaving a single breadcrumb for her to follow. She'd still take the case to court, and he'd still be convicted, but she wouldn't have the satisfaction of seeing him led away and visiting him behind bars.

Iva jumped as her smart glasses went crazy, beeping and vibrating around in circles on the desk. She played the message they wanted her to receive. 'Alert for Lulu Banks,' said the message, 'she is currently at Heathrow Airport, about to board an atmosphere flight to India.'

'Send a team to arrest her,' said Iva, without hesitation.

'We have no grounds on which to arrest her,' said the robot.

'I don't care,' said Iva, furious, knowing that Lulu, the one person who could lead her to Guy, was about to slip away from her too. 'This is it. If we let her go, we'll never find Guy Strathclyde. Arrest her,' she repeated, full of authority.

'I am afraid that the robotic team are unable to arrest Lulu Banks, given there are no legitimate grounds on which to do so. Please gain authorisation to override the protocols. Until then, I am unable to assist you.'

Iva let out a primal scream, throwing her smart glasses across the room. There was no way her boss would give her authorisation to arrest Lulu; as the robot had said, there were no legitimate grounds. *Fucking robots,* thought Iva. *Everything has to be black and fucking white, no room for judgement.*

Iva jumped up, retrieved her smart glasses, and ran to the lift, ordering a car to meet her at the front door. The car was waiting for her by the time she got there. 'Hyperloop to Heathrow,' she said urgently. 'As fast as you can.' Though, of course, the car *always* travelled as fast as it could, within strict safety parameters, which, even in an emergency, couldn't be broken. *I miss the old days,* thought Iva, sitting forward and tapping her hands together, nothing else for her to do but sit and wait.

* * * * *

Lulu nervously looked around. Benji had given her strict instructions: exact times she should turn up, exact places to stand, an exact order in which to do things. She'd got the impression that if she did any of it wrong, the whole trip could be in jeopardy. She had remembered everything and done it perfectly, of that she was sure, but that didn't prevent her from worrying.

She was the last person to board the plane, getting to the gate just before it closed. She pressed her finger to the scanner, stood in the designated spot for the face scan, and boarded, taking her aisle seat and strapping herself into her harness.

She willed the doors to close, for the attendants to work faster, for there to be more urgency about getting underway. The attendants, who on this expensive airline were still human, were joking around at the front of the plane. Even if they worked faster, it wouldn't make a difference because the plane was operated by a robot. They'd done away with the pretence of a human captain almost a decade before, so the plane would leave the gate exactly when it was scheduled, and would take off at precisely the time the software said it should.

The doors closed and Lulu exhaled, not realising she'd been holding her breath. They were still on the ground, but at least they were making progress. The attendants started talking over the speakers, telling the passengers what to expect from their weightless flight, detailing what to do in an emergency. *Some things never change*, thought Lulu, remembering back to her first flight when she was a kid.

The plane started moving and Lulu felt her spirits lift. *Almost there,* she thought as the attendants sat down and put on their harnesses. They taxied to the runway, on time, as ever, and took off, much to Lulu's astonished relief.

* * * * *

Iva didn't even get as far as the hyperloop by the
time Lulu's flight took off. For all the brilliant
developments in transport, getting across cities at rush
hour could still be painfully slow going. The old tube
network in London had been upgraded where it could
be, but it had to stop every two minutes to let people
on and off, so there was no getting away from its
laborious speeds, and it didn't always take you exactly
where you wanted to go. This meant people still
travelled overground, and for all the developments in
autonomous vehicles, which improved the flow of
traffic, and for all the increases in flexible and remote
working, which reduced the volume of people, there
were still just too many people trying to move around at
the same time in a finite amount of space.

Iva's smart glasses summoned her once more.
'Yes?' she snapped.

'Lulu Banks' flight has just departed Heathrow on
schedule,' said the annoying robot. 'It is due to land in
Delhi in two hours.'

Iva was about to say, 'Track her when she arrives,'
but knew she didn't have the authority to make that
happen, and had no grounds on which to gain the
authority either. 'Fuck,' she said, out loud, cutting off
the transmission, before hurling her smart glasses across
the car.

* * * * *

Lulu landed in India, got off the plane, collected
her luggage, and entered the arrivals lounge. She looked
around, trying not to be conspicuous, although not at
all sure what she should be doing. She decided the best

238

option was to sit in a café and wait. She trusted that Benji would have a plan. But, before she even got that far, a plump middle-aged woman approached. She was wearing a headscarf and holding out her arms as though Lulu were a long-lost friend. *Just go with it,* Lulu told herself, hugging the woman back.

'New ticket in pocket,' the woman said, in a strong Indian accent. 'Wig in bag. Flight take off in forty minute, need get going.'

'I need to change my hair?' asked Lulu, surprised. 'The robots will recognise my face anyway.'

'Yes, but people not. No robots.'

The lady pulled back, patting Lulu's arm before walking away. She wasn't sure she fully understood, but followed the instructions as best she could. She tried to make it look as though being hugged by a total stranger were an entirely normal occurrence, and headed to the rest rooms to don her wig before repeating the same check-in and bag drop process that she had in London.

This time her flight was to Baghdad, where a similar thing happened, but she was also given new identity documents along with a new wig and coat, then to Madagascar, where she was driven (in a banged-up old manual car) to a boat, which took her to the African mainland. From there, she was loaded into a Toyota pickup, which drove for almost a full day before depositing her in a vegetated area at the edge of a village full of huts, right next to the coast. The truck drove away and she took off her wig, reasoning the blonde mop was more conspicuous than her natural colour.

She looked around, disorientated, wondering if she should sit tight and wait or explore the place a bit. She'd been deliberating for a couple of minutes before curiosity got the better of her, but just as she was scanning around for a good place to stash her luggage, a tall, lean, tanned man came walking out of the foliage.

'How do you like your new home?' asked Guy, striding towards her.

'Guy?' she asked, not sure if she really believed it.

'In the flesh,' he laughed, scooping her up into his arms and pulling her to his chest. 'I've missed you,' he said, leaning down to kiss her.

'It's been what? Two weeks?' she laughed.

'Yes, but I miss you after two hours, so two weeks felt like an eternity,' he said, kissing her again.

'Well, I suppose I missed you a little bit too,' she said, smiling mischievously.

'Only a little bit?' he asked, pretending to be offended. 'I might have to send you back.'

'Don't you dare,' she ordered. 'I think I'm going to like it here.'

'There's not much in the way of tech,' he said, his tone hesitant.

'Sounds blissful,' she replied, looking up into his eyes. 'Are there drinks in pineapples?'

'Ha! There can be if you want there to be.'

'Come on then, hurry up and show me around.'

They each took one of Lulu's bags and Guy led them into the village. They walked through an open area in the middle, past a collection of small market stands and what looked like a bar, a few of the villagers turning to watch as they went. Lulu smiled and waved, and they waved back warmly, but they didn't avert their gaze. Guy led her to a small, nondescript hut on the far edge of the village and dumped her bag on the packed ground outside. 'Welcome to my humble abode,' he smiled, pushing open the flimsy door with a halting flourish, having to unhook the floor matting before it would open fully. 'It's going to be an adjustment,' he said, his brow furrowed in worry, trying to work out what she made of it all.

'Guy,' she said, dumping her bag and looking up at him. 'I love it.' She kissed him enthusiastically, pushing him backwards into the single room inside.

* * * * *

Lulu and Guy lay on two makeshift sun loungers on the beach. Guy had made her a cocktail in a pineapple, as promised, and they lay back and listened to the waves lapping against the sand.

'This is heaven,' said Lulu, rolling over to face Guy, smiling broadly.

'I know,' he laughed, 'but I'm worried it might get boring after a while.'

'Why would it?' she asked. 'I've got enough art supplies to last me for ages, and we've got money, so when I run out, we can find somewhere to buy more. I've got you, and there's enough to do here to keep us busy, although I did spot a few robots around the place; I take it that was your doing?'

Guy laughed. 'Guilty. We put robots here in the last wave of drops. That's part of the reason I decided to come here. The locals showed particular interest in them and an aptitude for understanding them. I thought I might be able to teach them a thing or two.'

'So that explains all the electrical kit in the hut next door,' she said. 'Just couldn't help yourself, could you?'

'Again, guilty as charged,' he said with a smile. 'But just think of all the things we could build that would help them.'

'I know, I know,' said Lulu. 'And it will keep you busy.'

'Which is important to me.'

'It's important for everyone,' she replied, reflectively. They sat for a few moments in silence, enjoying the heat and the breeze and the sea, Lulu thinking of her bizarre journey over here. 'I keep meaning to ask you, why all the costume changes on the way here, yet only one identity change? The robots can recognise me regardless of my hair colour or clothes or travel documents.'

'Yes, they can,' replied Guy. 'But not all countries have the tech we do. No finger scanners from Iraq onwards, right?' he asked. Lulu nodded. 'So that was the end of the robot tracking. Iraq has some cameras around, but they're not linked up to sophisticated identification software, not yet at least. Similar in Madagascar, so if Iva was tracking you, she'd need to put in a fair amount of legwork to do so, although, as you say, if she managed to get hold of any video footage, she could easily run it through software available to her in the UK to identify you. But the chances of that are slim. Not only does she have no legal grounds to track you, even if she did, there's no guarantee that each jurisdiction you travelled through would cooperate with her, especially for something so comparatively trivial on the international crime scene.'

'And the money?' asked Lulu. 'I moved everything I could into the account Benji told me to. How was that moved? And how can we access it without raising suspicion?'

'Blockchain,' Guy said cheerfully. 'Thank God for the well-established, international, illegal money-moving method that is currencies on mutually distributed ledgers,' he joked.

'Come again?' said Lulu, frowning and shaking her head. 'That was all gibberish to me.'

'Since the turn of the century, there have been cryptocurrencies. Since their inception, they've been used by drug dealers and other criminals to move money around, because there's no way of tracking and identifying individuals and their transactions.'

'So we're akin to drug-dealing criminals now?' joked Lulu.

'Only if there's something you're not telling me,' Guy shot back, with an inquisitive eyebrow raise.

'But how can we buy things if our money's all in a cryptocurrency? Do they use it to buy and sell stuff out here?'

'The company we're using have created a way to use real currencies in their transactions as well as virtual ones.'

'But wouldn't governments have something to say about that?' asked Lulu, surprised. 'Surely that can't be good for them in terms of regulation and oversight?'

'The Western governments all tried, unsuccessfully, to close the platform down,' he replied, 'and they put limits on the amount of currency the platform is allowed to buy, but if individuals like you or me decide to deposit our money into the vaults of a virtual, offshore bank, the government can't legally stop us. The more people who do that in each currency, the greater the number of currency swaps the platform is able to do, and therefore the greater the number of international transactions.'

'Who uses it, apart from criminals?' asked Lulu.

'Businesses, wealthy individuals trying to hide money, either for themselves or to give it to their kids, anyone needing to transfer large sums of money between countries...'

'Do people get away with it?' she asked. 'Hiding money?' Concern and outrage were equal in her tone.

'Sure, some people do. But if the Inheritance Department becomes suspicious, if a family can't account for large sums of money at the time of a wealthy person's death, then the department has powers to seize and access all correspondence belonging to the deceased individual. They can also question, with the aid of a lie detector, the family of that person. If they're found guilty, then the full inheritance is forfeit, and the family is left with nothing at all.'

'Harsh,' said Lulu. 'I like it.'

'Some people still manage to get around it, by not telling their family anything, and setting up an automatic notification at a point long enough after their death for the authorities to have concluded any investigation. But it's still risky and stressful and most people don't think it's worth trifling with.'

'Is what we're doing illegal?' asked Lulu.

'What you're doing isn't,' he said, reassuringly. 'You're essentially just using it as a regular bank account and you're entitled to move money anywhere you want. Your money's accessible from anywhere in the world, free of charge, although subject to published exchange rates. It's stored in an online account, and you can access it whenever you want, although if you go over a certain limit, you'll have to pay an import tax. They still mostly use physical money here, so we'll need to go to a bank to withdraw funds if you want to spend it locally, but if you want to buy anything online, you just spend it as you normally would.'

'From my smart glasses? How will that work?'

'Your new glasses,' he said, 'will connect to the web of internet satellites, just like they would at home. The only difference is that you're paying from a different account, and the account won't track every transaction detail. Your account is identified only by a series of codes, which also means if anyone gets hold of those codes, they can access your money.'

'So it's not as safe as conventional banking?'

'Not if you're lax about keeping the codes secret and separate.'

'It's like an old Swiss bank account then? Where identities are secret?'

'Exactly. The authorities hate it, but there's not much they can do about it without becoming a totalitarian state.'

'Crazy,' said Lulu, 'I had no idea.'

'Most people have no reason to know about it,' said Guy. 'And that's the way it should be. Governments need to have visibility and control over where their currency is and make sure no one is manipulating it. It's much better for almost everyone to have a conventional bank account at a bank that reports to the government. But for anyone like me, a fugitive on the run, it's handy to be able to hide my identity but still keep some money.'

'How did you move it? Weren't your accounts frozen at the beginning of the investigation?'

'Yes, but I've been putting money away for a rainy day for some time now. There's nothing illegal about using the crypto banks, but I made sure to set it up in a way that transactions out of my conventional bank accounts didn't look suspicious. Luckily, I didn't get Thomas to help, although I did consider it.'

Lulu raised her eyebrow in agreement. 'But we can't just buy things and have them delivered here,' she said, waving her hand around. 'It's not exactly crawling with delivery drones.'

'I know. Collecting things will be more of a challenge, but there are towns, just not close. We'll have to do it the old-fashioned way and make long trips to get things.'

'Oh God, look at us talking about buying things. We're sitting on a beach in Africa, and can't help but think like Western consumers. What do we really need anyway?'

Guy smiled. 'Good point. Anything we do need, like medicines or food, the robots are already programmed to get for the village upon request; they've got detachable flying drones they can use to go and make pickups.'

'And there are people in the towns who know what to do with a flying drone?'

'People adapt to new opportunities surprisingly quickly,' said Guy. 'Especially when there's a seemingly endless supply of money from an international crypto bank linked to the drone.'

Lulu shook her head. 'It's kind of sad,' she said, 'money really does make the world go round.'

'We don't have to think about that any longer,' said Guy, climbing onto Lulu's lounger, Lulu adjusting so she could cuddle in next to him. 'We're in heaven, remember?'

'Yes, we are,' said Lulu, squeezing him tighter.

'I just hope Thomas gets his comeuppance,' said Guy. 'I don't normally hold grudges, but I just can't get over what he did.'

'I know. I paid off his parents' debt just to spite him,' Lulu replied.

Guy looked at her. 'You didn't?' he asked, surprised.

'I did,' she replied, sitting up. 'Why the reaction?'

'Because I paid off their debt too!'

'No!' she laughed.

'Yes,' he said, laughing too.

'Lucky Penny and Gerry.'

'Well, if anyone deserves it, they do.'

'With a son like Thomas, that's certainly true.'

'What did you have to do before you could come out here anyway?' asked Guy, realising he still didn't know.

Lulu smiled, a sly smile. 'Just a little tribute to my muse,' she said innocently.

CHAPTER 17

Mila walked into her department's main office, or at least, the department to which she hoped she would belong again after this meeting. She was escorted up to the fifth floor, a strange experience, given that until recently she'd had free rein to move around as she pleased. She was deposited outside the director's office, and waited patiently to be summoned inside.

After ten minutes, Mila becoming nervous and irritated in equal measure, the door opened and Iva walked out with Albert, the director.

'Mila?' said Iva, surprised. 'What are you doing here?' Iva looked from Mila to Albert and back again. 'Oh,' she said angrily, 'the old boys' network strikes again. Didn't you go to university with Mila's father?'

'Yes, I did,' said Albert, a warning in his tone. 'Last time I checked, it wasn't a crime to go to university with someone.'

'Of course,' said Iva, through gritted teeth, stalking away.

'Mila,' said Albert, his tone turning friendly, 'do come in.'

Mila walked into Albert's bland, square office. There was no artwork on the walls, nothing bright and colourful, only charts and filing cabinets.

'Every notebook I've ever had is in those filing cabinets,' said Albert, following Mila's gaze. 'I still use a notebook, you know. I think there's something powerful in the connection between the actions of one's hands and the thoughts in one's head. I know smart glasses make us more productive, but sometimes I can't help but jot things down.'

Mila smiled. 'I love to flick through real pages,' she replied, as though she were admitting a terrible secret. 'There's nothing like being able to see them turning back and forth; it makes our brains work differently, I'm sure.'

'And the feel of the paper is so reassuring,' added Albert, taking the seat behind his desk and motioning for Mila to sit across from him.

She sat down. 'Thank you for agreeing to see me today,' she started.

'Of course,' he said. 'I have to say I was surprised when I heard Iva had let you go.'

'Without legitimate grounds,' she added. Albert nodded, but didn't say anything, indicating Mila should continue. 'I have a case that I'd like you to consider prosecuting,' she said, reaching into her bag for her smart glasses and projecting onto the wall. 'As you know, Iva's methods have been questionable, since the beginning of her career as your senior investigator. Her dealings with Guy back then pushed the limits of acceptability, and she's never stopped.'

'Iva gets results,' replied Albert. 'And she doesn't cross the line, not to my knowledge anyway.'

'I'm afraid she has been crossing the line,' said Mila firmly. 'Aside from inappropriately and groundlessly firing me, she has broken numerous other laws on her vendetta against Guy Strathclyde and anyone who comes from a privileged background.'

'I'm assuming you wouldn't be telling me any of this unless you had proof?' asked Albert, sighing reluctantly.

'Of course not,' she said, pulling up the first piece of evidence through her glasses. 'Here I'm showing you records from the IT department of correspondence that took place between Thomas Watson and Iva. Thomas used my computer without my permission or knowledge to access our systems. Here,' she went on, pulling up some video footage from her butler, 'is Thomas waiting until I'm out of the room, running to my laptop, and accessing the network using my account. He's clever enough to mask that the message was from my computer and tips Iva off about the facility in Exeter. He also spends some time rummaging around our intelligence database, and steals a large quantity of information relating to Marvin Edwards, Pixbot's former CFO, and Richard Murphy. He later uses this information to blackmail Richard out of his job, having already done the same to Marvin. Iva has promised Thomas a full pardon for all of these crimes.'

'She doesn't have the authority to do that.'

'No, she doesn't,' replied Mila. 'In addition to this, Iva neglected to report the system breach to anyone, but assured me that she had. She requested a routine login change, but didn't tell anyone the real reason why. My supposition is that she was hoping her mysterious source would contact her again, and she wanted to make sure the door was open when they did. Of course,

I made sure I never left my computer unlocked in Thomas' presence again, so he never got a chance.'

'That could have meant our IT system was compromised,' said Albert, shaking his head. 'Our entire database could have been leaked.'

'Yes. It doesn't bear thinking about,' agreed Mila. 'My butler alerted me, so Thomas didn't have long, and I checked which files he'd stolen, so I knew he'd only taken reports relating to Richard and Marvin. But if someone had managed to find a back door and Iva hadn't reported it, it could have been disastrous.'

'Is that it? Or is there more?'

'There's much more,' replied Mila glumly. 'She's been sharing privileged information in return for tip-offs and leads. And she hasn't yet officially registered Thomas as a witness, because she's suspicious that some of the ministers are involved in Guy's plan, and she wants to catch them too.'

'And if she makes it official, the ministers will be briefed about it.'

'Exactly,' Mila said, nodding. 'She recently tried to follow Lulu Banks, with no legitimate reason, she never carries out appropriate due diligence on sources, and she's set up and perpetuates a culture of secrecy and intimidation within the department. She makes it clear that no one can question her without losing their job, so no one stands up to her when she crosses the line.'

'And then she fired you,' said Albert, raising his eyebrows, 'so now you want revenge?'

'No,' said Mila strongly. 'I was collecting this information long before Iva fired me. I've been concerned about her attitude and approach for as long as I've worked for her. To begin with, I thought maybe I considered her methods to be discriminatory towards those from privileged backgrounds because I came from one, but over time I realised this wasn't the case.

She systematically picked out and targeted anyone that started life wealthy, and routinely turned a blind eye to the suspect activities of those from backgrounds like hers. And every time she heard the name Strathclyde or mention of Cybax in any context, she showed an unhealthy interest. I've been building a case against her for the best part of two years. She's biased and discriminatory, and I don't think she represents the ethos and values that are at the core of this department.'

'And you have evidence to back this all up?' asked Albert.

'Yes, of course,' replied Mila. 'As a result, I would press you to suspend her, or even better, just go ahead and fire her, as a matter of utmost urgency.'

'Okay,' said Albert heavily. 'Please transfer your entire case file to me. On what you've shown me so far, most notably the breach of security protocols, I have no choice but to suspend her, effective immediately. I take it you're happy to stand in as interim senior investigator while we sort this mess out?'

Mila was shocked. She'd thought she stood a good chance of getting her job back, and maybe had an outside chance of getting Iva's role once they interviewed for it, but she hadn't considered that he'd give the interim role to her straight off the bat. 'Of course,' she said, without hesitation. 'I would like that very much.'

'Great. Then you can go and deal with the mural mess over at Pixbot's HQ in Oxford.'

'Mural mess?' asked Mila, not a clue what he was talking about.

'Switch on the news,' he smiled. 'I think you'll be interested in what you see.'

* * * * *

Mila went back to her desk in the open-plan office, which, unusually, was filled with humans. She pulled out her smart glasses and put them on, silently instructing them to show her the latest news. The screen switched to show a male anchor behind a news desk.

'A bizarre mural has appeared on the side of the Pixbot building in Oxford,' he started, 'depicting their newly appointed CEO, Thomas Watson, devouring Eastern Europe. Other less technically developed countries are represented by emaciated people, whose natural resources are being stolen by the West, Russia, and China. The developing countries are shown as a junkyard for outdated tech, and the people are reaching longingly upwards towards the satellites above them, which are just out of their desperate reach.

'Pixbot is one of the biggest technology companies in the world. They were recently investigated by the Enforcement Office and were made to replace their whole executive management team, with only the former CEO, Richard Murphy, being allowed to remain in place. The mural also implies that Pixbot have been doing dirty deals, which the company is yet to refute. We contacted Pixbot for comment, however, they have so far refused to release a statement.'

Mila pulled off her glasses and couldn't help but smirk. Lulu had told her she had something to do before she went to find Guy, but Mila had never imagined anything like this. Then she remembered that she was in charge of the department now, and she had to go and investigate. Or was she in charge? Had Albert told Iva?

She didn't have to wait long for the answer. She looked up to find her former boss storming towards her. 'I always knew you couldn't be trusted,' spat Iva, leaning over Mila's desk. 'You're going to have to watch your back from now on.'

'Would you like me to put that on the record?' asked Mila, calmly meeting her furious gaze. 'I'm pretty sure every robot in here will have recorded it, but just in case, we could take an official statement if you'd like.'

'Fuck off, you bitch,' she said, spinning aggressively away and making her exit.

Everyone in the office had stopped what they'd been doing and watched, open-mouthed at the exchange between Iva and Mila. 'In case you hadn't gathered from Iva's parting speech,' said Mila confidently, 'she's been suspended, pending a full investigation into her conduct. I'm sure, for those of you who have worked with Iva over a prolonged period, this won't come as too much of a surprise. I've been appointed as interim senior investigator in the meantime.'

She paused, unable to suppress the smile creeping to her lips as she took in the sea of open mouths that hadn't yet closed. 'Jeffries and Smith, you're with me. We're going to Oxford to find out more about this mural. Everyone else, keep going with whatever you're working on. We'll have a full review of current projects when I get back, so please be ready.'

Mila waited for a few moments, and when nobody moved, said, 'I meant today, please.' The office snapped back to life. Jeffries and Smith rushed to get their coats.

If you enjoyed *In the Gleaming Light*, please please please leave a rating or review on Amazon or Goodreads. Reviews are a great way for readers to check out new books and authors really appreciate your feedback.

ACKNOWLEDGEMENTS

The genesis of *In the Gleaming Light* can be traced back to one specific conversation, whilst on a post lunch stroll across a stubble field with my friend Abbie. She introduced me to the concept of Universal Basic Income, and I couldn't shake the need to explore the topic further. If it hadn't been for that walk, I'm not sure this book would exist, so thank you!

There are, of course, a number of people I'd like to thank, who have helped bring this book to life:

My sister, Alice, for being my constant cheerleader, helping run my Instagram account, reading early drafts, and drumming up support for my books everywhere she goes. My other sister, Georgina, for providing more measured critique, and helping with knowledge of the east coast of Africa. My long-suffering husband, Chris, for dealing with my endless list of technical requirements, helping with everything from website development, to providing practical feedback on futuristic tech. My editor, Jeff Deck, for not pulling any punches - this book is better because of it.

Charlotte and Stephanie, who share my taste in books, and who (aside from providing the BEST book recommendations) read early drafts and provided encouragement.

Charles Radclyffe for reading an early version and for the honest feedback and discussion. The numerous other friends, family, colleagues, and ex-teachers, who have supported my books, shared on social media, and generally been in my corner - I am eternally grateful.

My wonderful, supportive, surprisingly sassy Instagram followers, who love books as much as I do, and all the bloggers, vloggers, and book reviewers who have helped promote my work.

And lastly, and most importantly, anyone who's ever picked up one of my books - thank you. There's an unbelievable amount of competition out there and I have to pinch myself every time someone chooses one of mine.

A NOTE ABOUT INFLATION

Some of you may be wondering about the worth of financial amounts mentioned in *In the Gleaming Light*, given the effect of inflation. For ease of reading, I've ignored inflation and the time value of money, so readers can assume that a two hundred and fifty thousand pound salary in 2048 would be equivalent to a two hundred and fifty thousand pound salary in 2019.

ABOUT THE AUTHOR

Harriet was born in Germany in 1987, the family returning to the UK, to Dorset shortly afterwards. She lived there until she was 5, her grandfather teaching her the basics of cheating at cards and swindling chocolate, her mother starting to instil a (some would argue) unhealthy relationship with cake, and the neighbours demonstrating that some people don't understand cherry blossom is there to be picked, mixed with mint and water and sold as perfume.

Then there was Scotland; stealthy guinea pig breeding, riding horses, advanced cards, more cake, then to Devon and school in Exeter. She loved maths in the early years, but by the time she got to A Level, Sociology was her favourite subject, opening her eyes to things she'd never before considered, namely, nobody is really right, nobody is really normal and primary socialisation has a lot to answer for.

At the age of about 12, Harriet started rowing for Exeter Rowing Club. This quickly took over her life and before too long she was clad in lycra, training 6 days a week and competing at events around the country.

After finishing her A Levels, Harriet went to university in St Andrews, studying Philosophy for two years, then switching to Management. She was particularly interested in the change elements of her course and especially the areas concerning how people create and react to change. After four very civilised years by the sea, she ventured to London, to foray into the strange world of insurance (surprisingly, more interesting than you might think). She worked as a Project Manager on large change programmes before founding her own consultancy in 2015.

Harriet has since worked on a number of insurance related projects that helped influence and inspire *In the Gleaming Light*, specifically around the use of connected devices in the home, data collection and utilisation within financial services, and how automation can both reduce costs, and significantly improve vast swathes of tiresome, long-winded processes.

Harriet now lives in New Hampshire with her husband Chris and two young daughters. When she isn't writing, editing, eating, running around after her kids, or imagining how much better life would be with the addition of a springer spaniel, she occasionally finds the time to make hats.

CONNECT WITH HR MOORE

For more information about HR Moore, check out her
website and blog:
http://www.hrmoore.com/

Follow her on Instagram:
@hr_moore

Find her on Facebook:
https://www.facebook.com/harrietrmoore

Follow her on Goodreads:
https://www.goodreads.com/author/show/7228761.H
_R_Moore

DISCOVER OTHER TITLES BY HR MOORE

The Relic Trilogy, available on Amazon:

Legacy of the Mind

Origin of the Body

Design of the Spirit

Printed in Great Britain
by Amazon